Praise for *Based on a T...*

'If Simone de Beauvoir had wri... to Marguerite Duras, the result m... Briscoe, *Guardian*

'A wonderful literary trompe l'œil ... ...t, strange, compelling – and tremendously French' Harriet Lane, bestselling author of *Her*

'A sophisticated modern take on an old trope … An unlikely mash-up of thriller and conte philosophique, *Based on a True Story* insists on the author's right to blur the lines' *Evening Standard*

'Keeps the reader guessing until the end … Combining the allure of *Gone Girl* with the sophistication of literary fiction, *Based on a True Story* is a creepy but unapologetically clever psychological thriller that also aces the Bechdel test ★★★★★' *Independent*

'An incredible true story of obsessive female friendship that grips until the very last mark on the very last page' Denise Mina, bestselling author of *The Long Drop*

'A suspenseful look inside the mind of a writer' *Grazia*

'A superior identity-theft thriller on the same spectrum as *The Talented Mr Ripley*, or *Single White Female* … De Vigan has produced a concept thriller with a lavish dash of theorising about the status of fiction and reality' *Sunday Times*

'This unique novel opens a window into the writer's mind and mental health in a way I have never experienced before … It's worth it to unravel De Vigan's subtle but clever clues and for the unique plotline' *Sun*

'A cracking page-turner and a journey into what the essence of fiction, and indeed autobiography, might be. Excellent' Nicholas Searle, author of *The Good Liar*

'This is an addictive read. Clever, compulsive and deft … I even began to question the reality of the pages in my hand. Fantastic' Ann Morgan, author of *Beside Myself*

## BOOKS BY THE SAME AUTHOR

*No and Me*
*Underground Time*
*Nothing Holds Back the Night*

## A NOTE ON THE AUTHOR

**DELPHINE DE VIGAN** is the author of the bestseller *No and Me,* which was awarded the Prix des Libraires in France and which was a Richard & Judy selection in Britain. Her other novels include *Nothing Holds Back the Night,* which won the Prix FNAC and the Grand Prix des Lectrices de *ELLE,* and *Underground Time,* which was shortlisted for the Prix Goncourt in 2009. *D'après une histoire vraie* is a French bestseller and has won both the Prix Renaudot and the Prix Goncourt des Lycéens. It was adapted for a screenplay by Roman Polanski and Olivier Assayas. Delphine de Vigan lives in Paris.

## A NOTE ON THE TRANSLATOR

**GEORGE MILLER** is the translator of *Nothing Holds Back the Night*, *No and Me* and *Underground Time*. He is also a regular translator for *Le Monde diplomatique*'s English-language edition, and the translator of *Conversations with my Gardener* by Henri Cueco and *Disordered World* by Amin Maalouf.

# BASED ON
# A TRUE STORY

DELPHINE DE VIGAN

*Translated from the French by George Miller*

BLOOMSBURY

LONDON · OXFORD · NEW YORK · NEW DELHI · SYDNEY

Bloomsbury Paperbacks
An imprint of Bloomsbury Publishing Plc

50 Bedford Square          1385 Broadway
London                     New York
WC1B 3DP                   NY 10018
UK                         USA

www.bloomsbury.com

BLOOMSBURY and the Diana logo are trademarks of Bloomsbury Publishing Plc

First published in 2015 in France as *D'après une histoire vraie* by JC Lattès, Paris
First published in Great Britain 2017
This paperback edition first published in 2018

This book is supported by
the Institut français
(Royaume-Uni) as part of the
Burgess programme.

British Library Cataloguing-in-Publication Data
A catalogue record for this book is available from the British Library.

ISBN:     HB:      978-1-4088-7880-4
          TPB:     978-1-4088-7881-1
          PB:      978-1-4088-7884-2
          EPUB:    978-1-4088-7883-5

Typeset by Integra Software Services Pvt. Ltd.
Printed and bound in Great Britain by CPI Group (UK) Ltd, Croydon CR0 4YY

2 4 6 8 10 9 7 5 3 1

To find out more about our authors and books visit www.bloomsbury.com.
Here you will find extracts, author interviews, details of forthcoming events
and the option to sign up for our newsletters.

A few months after my last novel came out, I stopped writing. For almost three years, I didn't write a single line. Hackneyed phrases sometimes have to be taken literally: I didn't write a formal letter, a thank-you note, a holiday postcard or a shopping list. Nothing that required any sort of effort or necessitated any concern about form. Not one line, not one word. The sight of a pad, notebook or index card made me feel nauseous.

Over time, the act of writing itself became rare, hesitant and no longer occurred without apprehension. The simple act of holding a pen felt increasingly difficult.

Later, I experienced panic as soon as I opened a Word document.

I would search for the right position, the optimal screen angle. I'd stretch my legs out under the table. And there I'd stay, motionless for hours, staring at the screen.

Later still, my hands would start shaking as soon as I brought them near the keyboard.

I turned down every invitation I received without exception: articles, short stories, prefaces and contributions to edited collections. The mere mention of *writing* in a letter or message was enough to tie my stomach in knots.

I couldn't write any more.

Writing was out.

I now know that various rumours went round my friends, the book world and the social networks. I know people said I'd never write again, that I'd reached the end of something, that bonfires of straw – or paper – always burn out eventually. The man I love imagined it was my relationship with him that had made me lose my drive, or the flaw I needed to feed my work, and consequently thought I'd soon leave him.

When friends, relations and sometimes even journalists ventured questions about my silence, I cited various reasons or obstacles, including tiredness, foreign travel, the pressure that comes with success, or even the completion of a phase of my work. I gave the excuse of too little time, too little focus or too much to do, and got myself out of it with a smile whose fake air of calm didn't fool anyone.

Today I know that all this was just a pretext. None of it counted for anything.

To people who are close to me, I probably sometimes mentioned fear. I don't recall speaking of *terror*, but that's what it was. I can admit it now: writing, which had been my main activity for so long, which had so profoundly transformed my existence and was so precious to me, terrified me.

The truth is that just when I should have got back down to writing, according to the cycle that alternated fallow periods, incubation and actual writing – virtually a biorhythmic cycle, which I'd experienced for over a decade – just when I was preparing to embark on the book for which I had taken lots of notes and collected a mass of material, I met L.

Today I know that L. is the sole reason for my powerlessness. And that the two years that we were friends almost made me stop writing for ever.

# PART ONE

# Seduction

It was as if he was a character in a story or a play, a character whose history is not recounted like history, but created like fiction.

Stephen King, *Misery*

I'd like to describe how L. came into my life, and in what circumstances. I'd like to describe precisely the context that enabled L. to invade my private sphere and patiently take possession of it. But it's not that simple. And as I write the phrase, 'how L. came into my life', I'm aware of how pompous the expression sounds: a bit overblown; the way it emphasises a narrative arc that does not yet exist; a desire to announce a turning point or plot twists. Yes, L. 'came into my life' and turned it upside down: profoundly, slowly, surely, insidiously. L. came into my life as though she were stepping onto a stage right in the middle of the play, as though a direc- tor had ensured that everything around her dimmed to make way for her; as if L.'s entrance had been prepared for so as to communicate its importance, so that at this precise moment the spectator and the other actors on stage (me, in this case) would look only at her; so that everything around us froze, and her voice carried right

9

to the back of the auditorium; in short, so that she would make an impact.

But I'm rushing ahead.

I met L. at the end of March. By the autumn, L. was part of my life, like an old friend, on familiar ground. By the autumn, we already had our private jokes, a shared language of hints and double meanings, of glances that sufficed for us to understand each other. Our complicity was fuelled by shared confidences but also by what remained unsaid, by unspoken observations. In hindsight, and in view of the violence that later marked our relationship, it's tempting to say that L. *broke in* to my life, with the sole aim of annexation, but that would be untrue.

L. entered gently, with boundless delicacy, and I experienced amazing moments of complicity with her.

On the afternoon of the day we met, I'd been invited to do a signing at the Paris Book Fair. I'd met my friend Olivier there. He was a guest on a live broadcast from the Radio France stand. I mingled with the public as I listened to him. We then had a sandwich in a corner with his elder daughter, Rose, all of us sitting on the shabby Book Fair carpet. My signing had been advertised for two thirty, so we didn't have a lot of time. It wasn't long before Olivier told me I looked exhausted, truly; he was worried about how I'd get through 'all this', by which he meant having written such a personal, intimate book, and the reverberations that the book had caused – reverberations he knew I hadn't anticipated, and for which I was consequently unprepared.

Later, Olivier offered to walk with me to my publisher's stand. As we passed a dense, tightly packed queue, I looked to see which author was at the other end of it. I remember looking for the poster that would reveal their name, and then Olivier whispered: 'I think they're for you.' The queue stretched into the distance, then turned the corner, all the way to the stand where I was expected.

At another time, even a few months earlier, this would have filled me with joy and maybe even pride. I'd spent hours waiting around for readers at book fairs, sitting patiently behind piles of my books without anyone coming. I was familiar with that feeling of helplessness, that rather shameful solitude. I was now overwhelmed by an entirely different sensation: a kind of dizziness. For a moment it felt too much; too much for one person, too much for me. Olivier said he had to head off.

My book had come out at the end of August and for several months I'd been going from city to city, from events to signings, readings to discussions, in bookshops, libraries and media centres, where increasing numbers of readers awaited me.

It sometimes overwhelmed me, the feeling of having hit the bull's eye, of having carried thousands of readers along in my wake, the probably mistaken feeling of having been understood.

I'd written a book whose impact I hadn't foreseen.

I'd written a book whose effect on my family and those around me spread in a series of waves, causing collateral damage I hadn't anticipated; a book that quickly separated my unwavering supporters from my false allies, and whose delayed effects were to prove long-lasting.

I hadn't imagined the book's proliferation and its consequences. I hadn't imagined the image of my mother, reproduced hundreds, then thousands of times, the cover photo that contributed significantly to the spread of the text, the photo that very quickly became dissociated from her and now was no longer my mother but a character in the novel, blurred and diffracted.

I hadn't imagined readers feeling moved or fearful; I hadn't imagined that some would cry in front of me, nor how hard it would be for me not to cry with them.

There was that very first time, in Lille, when a frail young woman, who was visibly exhausted by repeated hospitalisation, told me the novel had given her the crazy, insane hope that in spite of her illness, in spite of what had happened and was irreparable, in spite of what she had *inflicted* upon her children, that they might, just maybe, be able to love her . . .

And there was another time, one Sunday morning in Paris, when a troubled man had talked to me about mental-health issues – of how others looked at him (at *them*, all the people who cause such fear that they're all lumped together: the bipolar, schizophrenics, depressives, labelled like shrink-wrapped chickens according to the current trends and the magazine cover stories) – and talked to me about Lucile, my invulnerable heroine who redeemed them all.

And on other occasions, in Strasbourg, Nantes, Montpellier, there were sometimes people I wanted to hug.

Gradually, I established a sort of imperceptible rampart, a cordon sanitaire that enabled me to go on, to be present, but at a safe distance. I developed a movement of the diaphragm that blocked the air at my breastbone to make a tiny cushion, an invisible airbag so that I could then gradually breathe out through my mouth once the danger had passed. That way I could listen, speak, understand what was being created around the book, the to and fro between reader and text, as the book almost always sent the reader back – why, I cannot explain – to his or her own story. The book was a sort of mirror, whose depth of field and contours no longer belonged to me.

But I knew that some day it would all catch up with me – the number, the sheer *number* of readers, of comments, invitations, the number of bookshops visited and hours spent on intercity trains – and that then something would give under the weight of my doubts and contradictions. I knew there would come a day when I would not be able to extricate myself, and there would have to be a thorough stocktaking, if not a settling of the score.

That Saturday at the Book Fair, I had signed without a break. People had come to talk to me and I was having trouble finding the words to thank them, answer their questions, meet their expectations. I could hear my voice trembling. I was having trouble breathing. The airbag was no longer working; I couldn't face up to things. I'd become permeable. Vulnerable.

Around 6 p.m. the queue was closed off with a stretch barrier between two posts to deter latecomers, obliging them to turn around. Nearby, I could hear the staff on the stand explaining that I was about to stop: 'She has to go. She's stopping. We're sorry, she's leaving.'

When I'd finished signing for the people who'd been designated as last in the queue, I hung around for a few minutes talking to my editor and the sales director. I thought about my route to the station. I felt exhausted. I could have lain down on the carpet and stayed there. We were on the stand and I'd turned my back on the Book Fair aisles and the little table where I'd been sitting until a few minutes earlier. A woman came up behind us and asked me if I could sign her copy. I heard myself say no, just like that, without hesitation. I think I told her that if I signed her book, more people would get in line, expecting me to start again and a new queue would inevitably begin to form.

I could tell from her eyes that she didn't get it, that she couldn't understand. There was no one else around;

the unlucky latecomers had drifted off; everything seemed calm and peaceful. I could tell from her eyes that she was thinking: Who does this bitch think she is? What difference do a couple of extra books make? And isn't that exactly why you're here? To sell books and sign them? So what have you got to complain about . . .

I couldn't say: Madam, I'm sorry, I can't do any more. I'm tired, I'm not up to it. Simple as that. I know that others can last for hours without eating or drinking until they've made sure everybody is satisfied. They're real troupers, genuine athletes, but I can't; not today. I can't even write my name any more. My name's a fake, a hoax. Believe me, my name on this book has no more value than if pigeon shit had happened to land on the title page.

I couldn't say: If I write a dedication on your book, madam, I'll split in two, that's exactly what will happen. I warn you, back off, keep a safe distance. The tiny thread that's keeping the two halves of my self together will break and I'll start to cry and maybe even scream, and that could get very embarrassing for all of us.

I left the Book Fair, ignoring the remorse that was already flooding through me.

I caught the metro at Porte de Versailles. The carriage was packed, but I managed to find a seat even so. With my nose against the window, I began rerunning the scene; it played out in my head once and then again. I'd refused to sign the woman's book even though I was standing there talking. I couldn't get over it. I felt guilty, ridiculous, ashamed.

I'm writing about this scene now, and all its exhaustion and excess, because I'm almost certain that if it hadn't happened, I wouldn't have met L.

L. wouldn't have found in me something that was so fragile, so shifting, so liable to crumble.

When I was a child, I used to cry on my birthday. When the assembled guests launched into the familiar song with words that are more or less the same in every family I know, I would burst into tears as the cake with its candles was brought towards me.

I couldn't bear being the centre of attention, the bright eyes all focusing on me, the collective emotion.

This had nothing to do with the genuine pleasure I experienced at a celebration in my honour. It didn't in any way spoil my delight at receiving presents, but there occurred at that precise moment a sort of feedback loop, as though in response to the collective noise produced on my account I could only make another, even shriller noise, at an inaudible and disastrous frequency. I don't know until what age this went on (the anticipation, tension, joy, and then me, in front of everyone, suddenly sniffly and distraught), but I have a precise memory of the feeling that used to overwhelm me at 'our sincerest wishes, and may these candles bring you happiness', and the desire to immediately disappear. Once – I must have been eight – I did run away.

At the time when birthdays were celebrated in class (at nursery school), I remember my mother having to write a note to the teacher to ask her to ignore mine. She read the note aloud for my information, then slipped it into the envelope. The word 'emotional', which I didn't understand, appeared in it. I didn't dare ask her, aware that writing to the teacher was already something exceptional, an effort, which had the aim of obtaining from her something equally unusual, a privilege, a special dispensation. In fact, for a long time I believed that the word 'emotional' had something to do with the size of an individual's vocabulary. I was emotional, and lacked the words to express myself, which appeared to explain my incompetence at celebrating my birthday in company. So it seemed to me that in order to live in society you had to arm yourself with words, not be reticent about accumulating them, diversifying, grasping their tiniest nuances. The vocabulary thus acquired would through time form a breastplate, thick and fibrous, which would enable you to operate in the world, alert and confident. But there were still so many words I didn't know.

Later, at primary school, when I had to fill in the registration card at the start of the year, I continued to cheat when it came to my date of birth, shifting it by a few months to the middle of the summer holidays, just to be on the safe side.

Similarly, in the school canteen or at friends' houses (until quite an advanced age), I several times swallowed or hid the lucky charm that I was alarmed to find in my slice of Epiphany cake. I found it impossible to declare my victory and be the general focus of attention even for a few seconds, let alone several minutes. I'd pass up lottery wins, crumpling my ticket or ripping it up when it was time to claim the prize, even going so far as to pass up a voucher for Galeries Lafayette worth a hundred francs at the end of my last year in primary school. I remember gauging how far I was from the podium – I would have had to get there without stumbling, looking natural and relaxed, then climb a few steps and probably thank the headmistress – and concluded it wasn't worth it.

Being the centre of attention, even for a moment, tolerating being looked at by several people at once, was quite simply unthinkable.

I was very shy as a child and young girl but, for as long as I can remember, this handicap revealed itself especially when faced with a group (that is, when I had to deal with more than three or four people at once). The classroom in particular was the first manifestation of a collective phenomenon that has never ceased to terrify me. Until the end of my schooldays, I was incapable of sleeping the night before I had to do a recitation or make a presentation, and I shall pass over in silence the avoidance strategies I've developed over the years in an effort to avoid all public speaking.

By contrast, from a very young age, I seem to have been at ease in face-to-face situations, one-to-ones, and to possess a genuine ability to meet the Other, as soon as that Other takes the form of an individual rather than a group, to link myself to him or her. Wherever I have visited or settled, I've always found individuals with whom I can play, talk, laugh, dream; wherever I've been, I've made friends and formed lasting bonds, as though I grasped early on that that was where my emotional protection was to be found. Until I met L.

That Saturday when I left the Book Fair, I'd intended to rush to the station to go to the country to meet the man I love and spend that evening and the next day with him. François had travelled to Courseilles the previous day, as he did most weekends. Over the years, the house, which he'd just bought when I met him, has become his refuge, his redoubt, and seeing him cross the threshold on a Friday night with a loud sigh of pleasure or relief makes me think of the little beep of satisfaction that cordless telephones make when you put them back on their stands to recharge. Our friends know how much of his equilibrium this house provides and how rarely he turns his back on it.

François was expecting me. We'd agreed I'd call him when I caught the local stopping train, which halts in the middle of nowhere a few kilometres from Courseilles.

---

When the metro stopped at Montparnasse station, I hesitated. I think I stood up, but I didn't get off. I felt too troubled to set off again. Unavailable. The incident at the Book Fair had suddenly revealed how exhausted I was, how tense and fragile I'd become. François was already worried about this, but I had trouble acknowledging it. I travelled on to the 11th arrondissement. I sent him a text to let him know I was going back to my place and that I'd call him later.

When I got to my neighbourhood, I called in at the Super U. The children were at their father's for the weekend. François was in the country. During the journey, I'd formulated a plan for a quiet evening, an evening of silence and solitude, which was exactly what I needed.

I was wandering the aisles of the Super U with a red plastic basket over my arm when I heard someone call me. Nathalie was behind me, looking delighted, but not entirely surprised; we ran into each other several times a year in the local supermarket. Inevitably, these chance encounters had become a sort of running gag in which we both played a role: we burst out laughing, we kissed, 'Isn't this funny?', 'What are the chances?', 'I never come in at this time', 'Neither do I' . . .

We chatted for a few minutes in the yoghurt aisle. Nathalie had also spent the afternoon signing at the Book Fair and had done an interview about her latest book, *We Were Living Beings*. She'd thought about coming to see me at my publisher's stand, but hadn't had time and decided to go home early, as she'd been invited to a party that evening, which was why she'd come to the Super U for a bottle of champagne. How I agreed to go to this party with her within a matter of seconds, when a moment earlier I'd been looking forward to being alone, I don't remember.

A few years ago, before I met François, I spent a number of evenings with Nathalie and another friend, Judith. All of us were more or less single and keen to have fun. We called our evenings 'JDNs' (Judith, Delphine, Nathalie). JDNs entailed one of us securing an invitation, along with the other two, to a wide range of celebrations (birthdays, housewarmings, New Year's Eve parties), or even getting ourselves into the most bizarre places without any of us having been invited. In this way we managed to gatecrash local association inaugurations, dances, office leaving parties, and even a wedding where none of us knew the bride or groom.

I like parties, but almost always avoid so-called 'dinners in town' (I don't mean dinners with friends, but the kind of dinners that are deemed fashionable to some degree). My reluctance stems from the fact that I'm unable to fit in with the codes they require. It's as if my shyness suddenly returns; I revert to being a blushing little girl or teenager, unable to take part in the conversation in a natural, fluid way. I have the terrible feeling of not being up to it, of being in the wrong place, and worst of all, when there are more than four guests, I generally become mute.

With time, I've finally realised – or perhaps it's an excuse to make it bearable – that relations with other people only interest me when there's a certain degree of intimacy.

JDNs became less frequent and then ceased, I don't really know why. Perhaps simply because all our lives changed. That evening in the Super U, I said yes to Nathalie, thinking that a party would give me the opportunity to dance, which had become very rare. (Because although I remain terrified of the thought of having to make a good impression at a dinner, I am nonetheless capable of dancing alone in the living room at a party where I know no one.)

I realise that these details may give the impression that I am digressing, losing my thread on the pretext of filling in context or background. But that's not the case. The sequence of events seems important to me to understand how I met L., and in the course of this story I'll probably have to go back again, further back, to try to grasp what was really at stake in this encounter.

Given the disorder that she created in my life, it's important for me to identify what made L.'s hold on me possible, and probably mine on L.

Anyway, I was dancing when I first saw L. and, as I recollect, our hands brushed against each other.

L. and I were sitting on the sofa. I'd left the dance floor first, when some music I didn't care for came on.

It was not long before L., who'd been dancing near me for over an hour, sat down beside me. With a smile, she had acquired the narrow space between me and my neighbour, who moved up towards the arm of the sofa, leaving her room to sit down. She made a knowing face at me as a sign of victory.

'You're very beautiful when you're dancing,' she said, almost as soon as she sat down. 'You're beautiful because you dance as though you think no one's looking at you, as though you're alone. I bet you dance like that when you're alone in your bedroom or living room.'

(My daughter told me once when she was in her teens that she'd always have a memory of me as a mother who danced in the living room to express her joy.)

I thanked L. for the compliment but didn't know how to respond, and in any case she didn't seem to expect a response; she kept her eyes on the dance floor, and was still smiling. I looked at her surreptitiously. L. was wearing loose black trousers and a cream-coloured blouse with a collar decorated with a fine satin ribbon or dark leather; I couldn't identify the material with any certainty. L. was perfect. She made me think of Gérard Darel ads. I remember it clearly: precisely that – the simple, modern sophistication, the skilful mix of classic, conservative materials and bold details.

'I know who you are and I'm pleased to meet you,' she added a moment later. I should probably have asked her name, who invited her, even what she did for a living, but I felt intimidated by such a calmly assured woman. L. was exactly the sort of woman who fascinates me. L. was impeccable, with her smooth hair and perfectly filed vermilion nails that seemed to gleam in the dark.

I've always admired women who wear nail varnish. To me, varnished nails represent a certain ideal of feminine sophistication that I have ended up acknowledging, in this respect at any rate, will remain beyond me. My hands are too broad, too big, too strong in a way, and when I try to paint my nails, they seem even bigger, as though this vain attempt at dressing up emphasised their masculine character (the operation in itself has always struck me in any case as laborious, requiring a meticulousness and patience I lack).

How much time does it take to be a woman like that? I wondered as I looked at L., as I had observed dozens of women before, on the metro, in cinema queues and at restaurant tables. Coiffed, made up and neatly pressed. Without a crease. How much time to reach that state of perfection every morning and how much time for touch-ups before going out in the evening? What kind of life do you have to lead to have the time to tame your hair by blow-drying, to change your jewellery every day, to coord-inate and vary your outfits, to leave nothing to chance?

By now I know that it's not simply a matter of having time, but rather of your type, what type of woman you choose to be, if indeed you have the choice.

I remember the first time I met my editor, in her little office on rue Jacob, I was first of all fascinated by her sophistication; the nails, of course, but also all the rest, which was simple and impeccably tasteful. She emanated a femininity that was classical but perfectly judged and controlled, and it impressed me. When I met François, I thought that he liked women of a differ-ent type from me, more prepared, more refined, under control. I recall telling one of my friends in a café the reasons why we were bound to fail; it simply wasn't possible, but yes, because of that, François liked women with smooth, well-behaved hair (I mimed ideal hair as I said it), whereas I was dishevelled. I felt this disparity in itself encapsulated more profound differences, funda-mental ones; in a general way, our meeting was just a banal error of direction. It took me some time to admit that was not the case.

A bit later, L. got up and started dancing again among the dozen or so people, slipping among them to face me. Today, and in the light of what happened, I do not doubt that this scene could be read as a seduction display and indeed that's how it strikes me. But at the time it seemed more a sort of game between the two of us, a silent complicity. Something about it intrigued me, amused me. L. sometimes shut her eyes. The movements of her body were discreetly sensual, unostentatious. L. was beautiful and men were looking at her; I tried to catch the look in the men's eyes, to capture the moment when their gaze became engaged. I am sensitive to women's beauty and always have been. I like watching them, trying to imagine which curve, which hollow, which dimple, which slight mistake in pronunciation, which imperfection in them arouses desire.

L. was dancing, scarcely moving, her body gently swaying in rhythm, matching each note, each nuance. Her feet were now stuck to the floor and no longer moved. L. was a stem, a liana, yielding to the breeze, to the cadence. It was beautiful to watch.

Later, though I cannot now link these two moments, L. and I found ourselves sitting at the kitchen table in front of a bottle of vodka. In between, I think I remember people I didn't know coming to talk to me. I spent some time with them and then L. held out her hand to invite me to come and dance. I lost sight of Nathalie;

perhaps she'd gone home. There were lots of people and the atmosphere of the party was happy.

I don't know how I came to tell L. about the woman at the Book Fair, about my remorse, a bitter aftertaste that lingered. I couldn't stop thinking about that moment and my reaction; there was something in that scene that revolted me, that wasn't me. I had no way of contacting the woman, of apologising to her, signing her book. It had happened; the scene had been played; there was no possibility of going back.

'Deep down, what's worrying you isn't just that the woman may have been hurt and maybe travelled miles to see you, left her children with her sister, that she may have had a row with her husband because he'd planned to go shopping and didn't understand why she was so keen on meeting you. The thing that's actually haunting you is that that woman may no longer like you.'

She said this gently and without irony.

'Maybe,' I admitted.

'I don't imagine the place you're in is easy. The comments, the reactions, this sudden attention. I imagine there must be a risk of collapse.'

I tried to play this down, keep it in proportion.

She went on: 'All the same, you must sometimes feel very alone, as though you were standing completely naked in the road, caught in the headlights.'

I looked at L., astonished. That was exactly how I felt, *naked in the road*, and I'd expressed it in those exact

29

terms a few days earlier. Who had I confessed that to? My editor? A journalist? How could L. have used exactly the same words as me? Had I even uttered them aloud?

Even today, I don't know if that evening L. was reproducing words she'd read or heard, or if she'd really intuited them. I realised quite quickly that L. had an incredible sense of the Other, a gift for saying the right thing, telling people exactly what they needed to hear. She was never slow to ask the most pertinent question or come out with the remark that showed the person she was speaking to that she alone could understand and comfort them. L. not only knew how to identify at first glance the source of the problem, but especially how to pinpoint the flaw, however deeply buried, that each of us has.

I remember explaining my concept of success to L. without any pretence, certain that my words would not be misinterpreted. To me, the success of a book was an accident. In the strict sense. An abrupt, unexpected event caused by the chance conjunction of different, irreproducible factors. So that she didn't take this as false modesty, I made clear that the book itself did of course have something to do with it, but it was merely one of the variables. Other books could potentially have had a similar, or even greater, success, but in their case the conjunction was less favourable, one or other of the variables was missing.

L. didn't take her eyes off me.

'But an *accident*,' she said, emphasising the word to show that it was not hers, 'causes damage – sometimes irreversible damage – doesn't it?'

I finished the glass of vodka in front of me that she'd refilled several times. I wasn't drunk, in fact I felt as if I'd reached a degree of consciousness I had rarely attained before. It was very late. The party had suddenly wound down and we were alone in the kitchen, which had been thronged with people just a few minutes before. I smiled before replying.

'It's true that the success of a book is an accident from which you don't emerge intact, but it would be wrong to complain. I'm sure about that.'

We took a taxi together. L. insisted. It was very easy to drop me off, my place was on her route; it wasn't even out of her way.

In the car we were silent. I felt tiredness take over my limbs, pressing my neck, gradually numbing me.

The driver stopped in front of my apartment.

L. stroked my cheek.

I have often thought back on that gesture, its gentleness, its tenderness, perhaps its desire. Or maybe nothing of the sort. Because, ultimately, I know nothing about L. and never have.

I got out the car, went up the stairs and collapsed on the bed fully dressed.

I don't have a precise recollection of the days that followed, I probably had some commitments to fulfil: events in bookshops and media centres, talks in schools. I had tried to limit my trips outside Paris to one a week so that I could be with the children and had planned to stop all events at the end of May. There comes a point when you have to re-establish silence around you, get back to work, recover your path. I desired this moment as much as I feared it, but I'd arranged things so as to bring it about and turned down all invitations after this deadline.

When I got home one Friday evening after two days away (I'd been invited to Geneva by a reading group), I found a letter in my mailbox among the bills. My name and address were printed on a label on the lower half of the envelope. I concluded from this that it was junk mail and very nearly threw it away without checking what was inside. But a detail caught my attention.

On the label in large characters was the number of my apartment, a number that doesn't appear on any official correspondence. I didn't know it existed for a long time. In the real world, it appears on a little bronze plaque to the left of each door, beside the old post-office plaques. It took me several years to notice it. My apartment is no. 8 and my neighbours' no. 5, and this lack of logic deepened my sense of the numbers' mystery.

Intrigued, I opened the envelope and unfolded the letter inside, which was typed on a sheet of A4. What sort of person nowadays still has a typewriter? I wondered before I began reading.

I shall reproduce the text in its entirety here. Its syntax and vocabulary were presumably chosen so that I'd be unable to determine the sex of its author.

```
Delphine,
You probably think you've got away
with it. Perhaps you think you've
got away with it scot free, because
your book is a so-called novel and
you changed some names. You may even
think you can just pick up your
miserable little life again. But
it's too late. You've sown hatred
and you'll reap your reward. The
arse-lickers all around you pretend
they've forgiven you, but they've
```

no intention of doing so, take it
from me. They're furious and they're
waiting for their moment. They won't
let you get away with it when the
time comes. I'm well placed to know.
You've planted a bomb and you'll
have to pick up the pieces. No one
will do it for you.

Don't misunderstand my intentions.
I don't wish you harm. In fact I wish
you the best. I wish you a brilliant
success, up there in the supertax
bracket, as I imagine you're on the
left like all you Bobos, and that you
plan to vote for François Hollande.

You sold your mother and hit pay
dirt. You're doing all right, aren't
you? Family sagas pay well, don't
they? They rake it in.

So stick the cheque in the post,
pls.

Back then, I used to get a lot of mail via my publisher,
dozens of letters from readers, sent on every week in little
bundles in a manila envelope. Emails too, forwarded to
my mailbox from my publisher's site.

But this was the first time I'd received an anonymous letter at my home address. And the first time I'd
received such an angry letter about one of my books.

---

I'd only just finished reading it when my mobile rang. I didn't know the number that came up and I hesitated before answering. For an instant, I thought it might be the person who had written the letter, even though that made no sense. I was so disturbed (and relieved) that it didn't strike me as strange to hear L.'s low, slightly muffled voice, though I hadn't given her my number.

L. had thought about me often since we met, she said, and suggested we went for a cup of tea or coffee, or a glass of wine, or any drink I liked, some day that suited me. She realised her suggestion might strike me as strange, a little forward. She laughed, then added, 'But the future belongs to the sentimental.'

I didn't know what to say. The image of the *Sentimental Wolf* came to mind, a picture book that I'd read dozens of times to the children when they were little, in which the hero, Lucas, a smart young wolf, leaves his family to make his own life. When it's time to say goodbye, his emotional father lists the things he can eat: Little Red Riding Hood, three little pigs, goats and kids, etc. Dressed in Bermuda shorts and a roll-neck sweater (I mention these details as they add to the character's undeniable charm), Lucas sets off on his adventures, eager and confident. But every time he comes across one of the prey on his list, he lets himself be sweet-talked and instead of eating them all up, he goes on his way. Having let go several four-legged feasts – with whom he strikes up friendly relations – a famished

Lucas meets the terrible ogre (in my memory he's the ogre from Tom Thumb) and swallows him whole, or almost, thereby delivering all the vulnerable creatures of the neighbourhood from this threat.

In truth, apart from this tale, no example of the good fortune of the sentimental came to mind. It seemed to me, on the contrary, that most of the time the sentimental were the favourite prey of the wicked and the despotic.

Be that as it may, I heard myself say, Yes, why not, that would be nice, or something of the sort. We agreed to meet the following Friday in a café L. knew. In the course of the conversation, she asked me several times if everything was OK, as though, from where she was, she could tell I was upset.

Later, when I asked how she got my phone number, L. told me that she had enough *contacts* to get anyone's mobile number.

I found a note of this first appointment in my diary. Beside L.'s name I'd marked her phone number and the address of the café. At that time, and for a while longer, I could still hold a pen, and my life was contained in that black diary, the same Quo Vadis brand I had purchased new every autumn for the last fifteen years. With the help of its pages, I'm trying to imagine the state of mind I was in when I saw L. again, to reconstruct the context. In that same week, I apparently took part in an event in a Paris bookshop, and met Lutetia, a researcher at the National Centre for Scientific Research, who was working on a study of how writers are portrayed in the media. I went to 12 rue Édouard-Lockroy (the address is highlighted in green marker, though there's no clue as to why). I ate at Pachyderme with Serge, whom I see a couple of times a year to catch up on life and work (that day we talked about the hunt for the ideal chair and Serge gave a hilarious account of his passing infatuation with one seat after another, and the rejected chairs piling up on his landing). In addition to these meetings, there were about ten others that I only vaguely recollect. From this I conclude that it was a busy time. I was probably a bit tense, as I am when life runs away from me, gallops ahead. I note, too, that I had begun my English lessons with Simon. I had just had one of these when I met L. at the Express Bar.

I didn't know much about her, as we'd mainly talked about me the first time we met. When I got home, that realisation had left me uneasy. That's why, as soon as I sat down, I launched in to several questions without giving her time to change the direction of the conversation. It hadn't escaped my attention that she was used to leading the dance.

L. smiled, like a good sport.

First she explained that her profession was writing for other people. She wrote their confessions, their states of mind, their exceptional lives, which only needed setting down, or, more rarely, their untroubled progress, which needed to be transformed into an epic. A few years ago, having previously been a journalist, she'd made this kind of writing her career. L. was much in demand from publishers and even had the luxury of turning down commissions. Over time, she'd become a bit of a specialist in women's autobiography; actresses, singers and female politicians fought over her. L. explained how the market worked: most of the big jobs were shared among three or four writers. Most of the time she'd be competing with a couple of well-known authors who, in addition to their own writing, also worked as ghosts. 'Star ghosts', to be precise, an invisible literary species to which she reckoned she belonged. Neither their names nor hers appeared on the cover; at most it might feature on the title page as a 'collaboration'. But in truth most of the time nothing outside or inside the book gave any clue that the supposed author might not have written a single word. She reeled off the titles of her most recent works, among which were the memoirs of a top international model and the story of a young woman who'd been held captive for several years. Then L. told me about the hours she spent interviewing these people to gather the material, how long it took to tame them, the bond that gradually formed, cautiously at first, then increasingly intense and trusting. She considered them her 'patients'; clearly she didn't mean it absolutely literally, but neither was the word chosen at random, because what she listened to were their torments, their contradictions, their innermost thoughts. Some of them even felt the need for her not to look at them or had to talk to her lying down. Most of the time she went to their homes; she took out her dictaphone and her mobile (once she'd lost a whole session; the recorder stopped working during the interview without her realising, and since then she'd backed everything up with a second recording) and let the words and the memories start to flow. She'd spent the previous summer in Ibiza, living in the home of a famous TV presenter for several weeks. She'd adopted her rhythm, met her friends, blended into the background. Gradually, the confidences had started to come, over breakfast, or during a night-time stroll, or in an empty house the morning after a party. L. had recorded everything, hours of bland exchanges during which a revelation would sometimes crop up. She'd just finished the book, after spending a few months on it. L. liked mentioning this material she was given: living, raw material, which had something at its heart that contained the Real. She uttered that word several times, because ultimately only the Real mattered. And all this came from the encounter, from the particular relationship that gradually formed between her and them. She found it hard to finish one book and begin another. Every time she felt guilty: guilty of abandonment, like a fickle, indecisive lover, who breaks things off before she gets bored.

Later that evening, L. told me she lived alone; her husband had been dead a long time. I didn't ask how; I felt that this piece of information contained additional pain that L. wasn't ready to talk about yet. She told me she hadn't had children, but it wasn't a regret, or rather it was a regret she couldn't acknowledge, a regret that she'd distanced herself from, like a poison. Did there have to be reasons and justifications? It simply hadn't happened. I realised at that moment that I couldn't have said how old she was; L. could just as easily have been thirty-five as forty-five. She was one of those girls who looks like a woman before her contemporaries and one of those women who remains forever a girl. L. asked if I lived with François (I remember she used his first name) and I explained why we'd decided to keep our own places while we had children living with us. Yes, I probably was afraid of habit, erosion, irritation, compromises, all sorts of really banal things that happen to people who love each other after they've lived together for a few years, but above all I was scared of upsetting the balance we had. Also, at our age, when we all have our burden of defeats and disillusionments, it seemed to me that by living like this, we gave and received the best of ourselves.

I like the easy exchange you experience with some people, that way of getting to the heart of a subject immediately. I like talking about the essential, emotional things, even with friends I see only a couple of times a year. I like the ability in other people (often women) to talk intimately without going too far.

So there we sat opposite each other in the café, L. no longer in that attitude of seduction I'd seen at the party, or slightly on the offensive. Something about her seemed gentler. We were two women getting to know each other, who shared a certain number of preoccupations and immediately sensed affinities that linked them. That always strikes me as both banal and miraculous. The conversation switched to lighter things. I remember L. quite quickly got me talking about my female friends. Who were they? Where were they from? How often was I in touch with them? This is a subject I like and can talk about for hours. I have friends from nursery, primary and secondary school, my foundation course, everywhere I have been. I've made friends in the different companies I've worked for and have two from festivals or book fairs. It's undeniable that I'm someone who forms attachments, and attachments that last. Some of my friends left Paris long ago, others have returned. I've also made new ones. I admire them all for different reasons. I need to know what becomes of them, what they're experiencing, what moves them, even if our lives are very busy. I also like my friends to meet each other, and some of them have formed their own friendships, which are now quite independent of me.

I was trying to explain this to L. and how much each of them, unique and singular, meant to me, when she asked, 'But none of them call you every day? None of them share your daily life?'

No, none of them were so constantly present. It seemed to me that that's how things went. Over time, our relationships had evolved. We might see each other less often, but it was no less intense. We had our own lives. And we always met with the greatest ease; that was true of all of these friendships, the oldest as well as the most recent. The ability we had to be instantly intimate, despite not having seen each other for weeks or even months, never ceased to amaze me. My closest friendships had turned into a looser, less exclusive link, soluble in a life made up of other ties.

L. seemed surprised. She regarded it as impossible for an adult to have several friends. Several *true* friends. She wasn't talking about girlfriends, but *the* person with whom you could share everything. Uniquely. The person who could listen to everything, understand everything, without judging. I told her that I had several such friends. Each of these relationships had its own tonality, its rhythm and frequency, its favourite subjects and its taboos. My friends were all different from each other and I shared different things with them. Each of them was important to me in a unique way. L. wanted to know more about them. What were their names? What jobs did they do? Were they single or living with someone? Did they have children?

In trying to reconstruct this conversation today, I'm tempted to think that L. was testing the ground, assessing her chances of conquest. But in reality I'm not sure whether things were that clear. L. had a genuine curiosity, a deep and fresh interest that I had no reason to mistrust.

People who ask real questions, the ones that matter, are rare.


It had got dark and the waitress had lit candles on every table. I texted the children to let them know that I'd be a bit late and told them not to wait for me to eat.

It was all so simple.

———

Later, when I took a pen from my bag to jot something down on a piece of paper, probably an address or the name of a shop, L. smiled at me.

'I'm left-handed too. You know that left-handers can recognise one another?'

L. didn't talk about my book or my forthcoming work that day.

L. was advancing ever so softly. She had all the time in the world.

At the time I met L., I was thinking about writing a novel that would have as its setting, or starting point, a reality TV show. I'd been mulling the idea over for ages and in the past ten years had amassed a lot of material. In 2001, a few months before the popular *Loft Story* was broadcast, I'd watched a programme on TF6 whose premise fascinated me (it seems very staid compared to what exists now): three teams of young contestants were locked up in three different empty apartments. These participants had to complete a number of tasks that determined how long they could spend on the internet ordering furniture and food. For the first time in France, people were filmed twenty-four hours a day on multiple cameras. As far as I know, *Net Adventures* was France's first reality TV show. By some coincidence – I think he was the friend of a friend's son or something – I met one of the contestants. He described what he had gone through when he left the apartment. Back then, what interested me was how young people returned to real life after being shut away for several weeks. I sensed we were on the verge of a television revolution, but I had no idea of its scale. Then *Loft Story* burst on to the scene and for a few months it was all people talked about. I don't think I missed a single episode of the first prime-time season, and that devotion finally got the better of my desire to write.

A few years later, as reality TV further extended the boundaries of vacuousness and voyeurism, my fascination shifted. Beyond the participants and their psychological future, I was interested in how these programmes managed to shape characters, to make them experience largely scripted relationships or situations (or created them in the edit), while giving the viewer the illusion of reality. How did these alliances, tensions, conflicts – fabricated and orchestrated by invisible creators – corroborate the appearance of the Real?

Through a friend, I managed to contact a producer who had worked on several consecutive seasons of a major reality show. She'd left the production company and I was hoping she'd feel free to recount a few anecdotes. On the phone she seemed quite favourably disposed and admitted straight off, 'Of course we create characters! But the best thing is that we create them without the people who play them knowing.'

At the time when I met L., I'd been filling notebooks for a while for a novel that would deal with this issue or would be underpinned by it. I was looking for material. I almost always worked like this: first research, then writing (which is, of course, a form of research by other means). I would have an immersion, impregnation phase, during which I'd assemble my arsenal. In this documentation phase, I'd keep an especially close eye on my impulse: the impulse that gave me the desire to invent, to compose, that led me each morning to the Word file, which I soon became obsessive about saving.

It was all about the spark, the click. Then came the writing: months of solitude in front of the screen, hand-to-hand combat, during which persistence alone would pay off.

I wouldn't be able to find the time and mental space necessary to get down to work for a few weeks. Louise and Paul were both about to take their baccalaureate and I wanted to be there for them, to make myself completely available. I'd planned to begin the new book after the summer, when everyone went back to work and autumn was in the air.

Of course, I sensed it wouldn't be that simple. I had to recover my groove, the imperceptible markers of my path, the invisible thread spun from one text to another that you think you hold but which keeps slipping from your grasp. I would have to put everything I'd heard and absorbed aside, everything that had been said or written, my doubts and fears. I knew all that. And all that from now on was part of an equation with several unknowns to which I had to submit. At least I knew the first line of the solution: I had to recreate silence, withdraw, reconstruct the bubble.

I had a few weeks ahead of me. I was no longer so busy or tired. I spent time at home with the children. I went to see François when I could, or he came to me. Things followed their course. I felt I occupied an in-between zone: one of those transitional, vaguely expectant phases that mark the end of one period and make way for the next. One of those times when, to avoid a short circuit, you take care that events do not overlap or collide, and you complete what needs to be completed.

I couldn't wait to go into purdah.

Judging by my diary, I saw L. several times during this period. I don't remember exactly how we got in touch. I imagine that after the evening in the Express Bar, one of us called the other. I think L. may have sent me the addresses of a couple of places we'd talked about. She invited me to go and see a play that had been sold out for weeks that I hadn't managed to get tickets for. Another time, I remember we had coffee in a bar on rue Servan; she'd called me from the street straight after an appointment in my neighbourhood. By various means, L. had signalled her desire that our relations should extend beyond these first meetings.

In early May, L. suggested going to the cinema. Shortly before, I'd told her how much I loved going to see films in the middle of the afternoon – a student pleasure I'd been enjoying since leaving my former company – and the transgressive experience of sitting in the dark for two hours, away from my desk. I liked going to the cinema with other people and talking about the film afterwards, in that rather vague, sometimes emotional state just after seeing it. But I also liked going alone, so that nothing alters those first impressions, nothing disturbs the possibility of your whole body feeling like a sounding board. When the lights come up and the credits roll, being alone prolongs the moment, stretches it out, of staying seated in the atmosphere of the film, completely absorbed by its mood. We had this conversation one of the first times we went out together. L. told me she couldn't bear going to the cinema alone: she was convinced that everyone was looking at her. So that was why she asked me to go with her to see Delphine and Muriel Coulin's first feature film, *17 Girls*. The film had come out just before Christmas but she hadn't been able to go because of an urgent deadline. It was still showing for a few days in a cinema in the Latin Quarter. I knew Delphine Coulin's literary work and had read somewhere that she'd written and directed this film with her sister. The idea of creative siblings appeals to me, so I was definitely tempted by the film.

I can find no mention of this outing in my diary, probably because it was organised on the day we went, which explains why I didn't write it down. We met outside the cinema. L. had arrived early and bought the tickets.

The film tells the story of seventeen girls from the same school who decide to get pregnant at the same time. It was inspired by real events in 2008 in Gloucester in the US. The Coulin sisters relocated the story to a small town in Brittany. It's a beautiful film, suffused with a languorous sense of expectation, a kind of nameless ennui, the longing for an elsewhere that never seems to materialise. Shots of the young girls sitting motionless in their rooms are the melancholy tableaux that give the film its rhythm, like a countdown. In themselves, they speak of a time that no longer belongs to childhood, nor yet to adulthood, a hazy, uncertain in-between. For these girls, being pregnant is an act of liberation, the promise of a different life. Besides these recurring pregnancies, the film also tells the story of an influence: Camille, who is first to get pregnant, is the brightest star in the school. She's one of those girls whom others follow blindly and long to be like. One of those teen-age idols we all knew, who eventually disappear and no one knows what became of them. When the lights went up, I turned to L., who seemed rather tense. I immediately noticed the way her jaw had tightened, and a slow throbbing in her cheek, making first a hollow, then a slight bump just below her ear, while the rest of her face remained still. Outside, she offered to drive me home. She had her car for once. She didn't normally use it in Paris, but she'd been on her way back from a meeting in the suburbs and hadn't had time to take it to her garage. I said yes.

L. had found somewhere to park near the cinema and we walked there in silence side by side.

Once in the car with her seatbelt fastened, L. opened her window. At first she paused it halfway, then let it slide all the way down. Cold air rushed in. She remained like that for several seconds, looking straight ahead. I saw her blouse rise and fall in time with her breathing. After a while she eventually said: 'I'm sorry. I can't drive.'

She had her hands on the wheel and was trying to breathe deeply, but her breathing was short and effortful.

'Was it the film?'

'Yes, it was the film. But don't worry. It'll pass.'

We waited. L. stared at the road exactly as though the car were hurtling along an expressway at a hundred miles an hour.

I tried to defuse the situation. I was prone to this kind of reaction too, films that go off like a time bomb when the credits roll. I knew the feeling. It had happened to me several times, it had even forced me to sit down on the kerb (Jerry Schatzberg's *Scarecrow*) and rendered me speechless (Céline Sciamma's *Water Lilies*). I really understood. Sometimes a film causes a visceral reaction. To distract her, I told L. about the day I first saw *The Hours*, based on Michael Cunningham's novel. Though I hadn't shed a single tear during the whole film, I crumpled as soon as it was over. It just happened without warning; I began crying hot tears, unable to leave the cinema, or explain anything to the father of my children, in whose arms I had collapsed.

Something in my internal protection system had clearly given way.

I tried a dash of self-mockery, hoping to distract her a little. L. was listening carefully, but it was clear that she could neither laugh nor nod; her whole body seemed engaged in an attempt to regain control.

Several more minutes went by in silence before she turned the key in the ignition, and several more again before she put the car in gear.

We didn't speak on the drive home either. I thought over the scenes in the film that had affected me, looking for a clue as to what had so overwhelmed her. I didn't know enough about L. to identify the point of impact. But I remember I thought about the character of Florence, the rather unattractive red-haired girl, who appears at the start of the film and is kept at arm's length by the other girls. She's the one they mock; she's rather awkward and ridiculous, without it being possible to say quite what causes her rejection. Florence is also the first to admit to Camille that she's pregnant. Pregnancy opens the door to the group she'd been excluded from, and, without meaning to, Florence encourages the others to follow suit. More and more girls fall pregnant. Later, in a very cruel scene, the girls discover that Florence's pregnancy is a trick; it was just a lie so that she'd be accepted by the group, which now casts her out without any kind of hearing.

L. pulled up outside my building. She smiled and thanked me. Probably just 'Thanks for coming with me', but said as though I had accompanied her to a painful examination at the hospital or to hear news of a serious illness.

I felt a sort of impulse towards her, a desire to take her in my arms.

By some curious intuition, I remember thinking that L. hadn't always been the beautiful, sophisticated woman I saw before me. Something in her, something buried and barely perceptible, suggested that L. had come back from far away, a dark, treacherous place, and that she'd undergone a phenomenal transformation.

From then on, we saw each other more and more often.

L. lived very near me. She worked from home, set her own hours and decided how she used her time. L. would call me because she was passing, or had read a book she wanted to tell me about, or had found a quiet place to have tea. She integrated herself into my life because she was free to come and go, because she permitted herself the unexpected and the spur-of-the-moment, because it seemed normal to her to say, 'I'm downstairs,' as though we were fifteen: 'I'll wait for you at the corner, let's meet at the baker's, at Monoprix, at Réaumur-Sébastopol station, I need to buy a jacket this afternoon, come and help me choose a lamp for my desk.' L. liked deciding things at the last minute, changing her plans, cancelling a meeting to prolong the pleasure of an encounter, going out for dessert, or simply not interrupting a conversation that interested her. L. cultivated a kind of openness to the moment that made her unusual in my eyes, since I had so long tried to quell my anxiety through a more or less successful effort to anticipate things.

I admired L. for her ability to refuse constraints and only imagine the future in an immediate way. For her, there was the present moment and the one just after: nothing beyond that was more important or more urgent. L. didn't wear a watch and never looked at her mobile to check the time. She was totally present and behaved like that in all circumstances. It was a choice, a way of being in the world, a refusal of all forms of distraction or dispersal. I spent whole afternoons talking to her without her ever worrying about the time, and I don't think I ever heard her mobile ring during those two years.

L. never put off a meeting: things happened on the spur of the moment or they didn't happen. L. lived *now*, as though everything might come to an end that very day. L. never said, 'I'll call later to arrange when to meet,' or, 'Let's try to meet up before the end of the month.' L. was available immediately, without waiting. What's done was done.

I admired her determination and don't think I ever knew anyone with such presence in the moment. L. had long known what was important to her, what she needed and what she had to protect herself against. She had made a sort of pre-emptive choice that enabled her to assert her priorities categorically, and avoid the disturbing elements she had definitively excluded from her environment.

The way she lived – insofar as I could tell – seemed to me to express an internal strength that few people possess.

One morning, L. called me at seven because she'd just discovered her dictaphone wasn't working. She had an appointment at eight thirty with a female politician whom she'd started working with. She had no chance of finding a shop open and wanted to know if I could lend her mine. We met half an hour later at the counter in a café. I watched her cross the street. I observed how she walked, so stable and assured despite her heels; her blonde hair pinned up with a clasp accentuated the length of her neck and the elegance of her bearing. She seemed lost in thought. Putting one foot in front of the other evidently was the least of her worries. (For me it's sometimes a major concern.) Heads turned as she came in; she had a look that you couldn't ignore. I recall that moment perfectly because I thought: it's seven thirty in the morning and she has everything under control. Nothing was creased or crumpled; every element of her person was perfectly in place, and yet there was nothing frozen or manufactured about L. Her cheeks were only a little pink from the cold, or some flesh-coloured make-up; she had light mascara on her eyelashes. She smiled at me. She exuded a genuine sensuality, something to do with her ease and facility. To me, L. embodied a mysterious blend of movement and formality.

I'd long ago accepted that I was not one of those impeccable, irreproachable women I'd dreamed of being. I always had something that escaped or stuck out or collapsed. I had strange hair that was both straight and frizzy. I was unable to keep lipstick on for more than an hour, and there was always a point late in the evening when I would rub my eyes, forgetting I was wearing mascara. Unless I was extremely careful, I'd bump into furniture, trip over steps and uneven ground, and go to the wrong floor in my own building. I'd got used to this, and other things besides. It was best just to laugh it off.

And yet when I saw her arrive that morning, I thought that there was a lot I could learn from L. If I took the time to observe her, perhaps I could capture something that had always eluded me. By sticking close to her, I could understand how she managed to possess all those things at the same time: grace, assurance, femininity.

It had taken me ten years to learn to stand up straight, and almost as long to wear heels; maybe I could become that sort of woman one day after all.

That morning, L. sat on a stool close beside me. She was wearing a straight skirt, quite close-fitting, I could see the shape of her thigh muscle beneath the fabric. Her tights were dark and had a slight sheen. I admired her posture, which accentuated the roundness of her breasts, discernible under her blouse; she had a way of arching her back, just enough, so that it seemed natural, almost casual. I thought that I needed to learn to hold myself like that, and her legs too, one crossed over the other despite her tight skirt; L.'s body balanced on a bar stool was like static choreography that dispensed with music and attracted glances. In the absence of a favourable predisposition, was it possible to copy that posture?

It was seven thirty in the morning and I'd made do with having a shower and pulling on jeans, a sweater and ankle boots. I'd combed my hair by running my fingers through it. L. looked at me and smiled again.

'I know what you're thinking. And you're wrong. There's a big difference between what you feel, the way you see yourself, and the impression you create. We all bear the trace of how we were looked at when we were children or teenagers. We bear it, like a mark that some people can see. When I look at you, I see tattooed on your skin the imprint of mockery and sarcasm. I see how you were looked at. Hatred and mistrust. Sharp and without indulgence. A way of being looked at that makes it difficult to construct yourself. Yes, I can see it and I know where it comes from. But believe me, not many people can. Few people are able to discern it. Because you hide it really well, Delphine. Much better than you suppose.'

L. was spot on most of the time. Even if from her lips things seemed more dramatic than they really were, even if she had a tendency to mix things together, there was always a core of truth.

L. seemed to know everything about me, without me saying anything.

As I try to explain how I became close to L., to identify the stages of this attachment, another moment comes back to me, which dates from roughly the same time.

We'd gone to see an exhibition, a late-night opening, and afterwards we had a *croque-monsieur* in a café near the museum. It was raining heavily, so we waited for it to stop. It was quite late when we caught the metro. We were sitting side by side near the door on flip-up seats. The carriage was full, but not so full that we had to stand. A man and a woman got on. The woman immediately gripped the central post right in front of us. 'Gripped' is the word that occurred to me when I saw her; she seemed to be having difficulty standing. The man was older than her. He quickly resumed the monologue he'd evidently begun on the platform. He was talking loudly; most of the carriage could hear. The woman's head was lowered, her shoulders slightly stooped. I couldn't really make out her face, but it looked to me as though her body was starting to give under his verbal assault. The man was criticising how she'd behaved at the dinner they'd just been to. Exasperated and with a look of disgust on his lips, he was spouting phrases as though he were making a political speech: 'You sit like a stupid bitch, you eat like a stupid bitch, you talk like a stupid bitch, you make me fucking ashamed.' (I'm transcribing virtually verbatim; I don't think I've forgotten anything, such was my shock at this man's brutality and the public humiliation he inflicted on this woman.) People drew away from them; some moved seats. The man, far from easing off, kept going: 'You're the only one who doesn't realise, Magali. Everybody was upset, oh yes, and everyone was thinking: what's he doing with a bitch like that? You exude awkwardness – what can I say, it really pisses me off. And let me tell you, even when you started talking about your work, what do you think? That that's of interest to people, the life of a poor nursery teacher? They don't give a fuck. No one gives a fuck. You think people are interested?'

L. was looking at the man, not discreetly, furtively, like the rest of us. L. was staring at him, ostentatiously, with her head raised towards him, like at the theatre. Her jaw was set, the throbbing had returned, intermittently creating a little hollow in her cheek.

'Just look at the way you're standing, it's unbelievable. You're like a hunchback. Oh yes, I forget, you're the one who has to carry the world's woes, Magali. Silly me. Ha, ha, ha, yes. It's true. Madam carries the whole world's misfortunes and God knows, there are plenty: kids whose parents are illegal immigrants, kids whose parents have lost their job, kids whose parents are crazy and all the rest of it, but hey! Madam is laid back about it every day come half-four, once she's had a good tea! Have you taken a look at yourself, Magali? All you need is a blouse from the Trois Suisses catalogue and you'd look like a cleaning lady.'

We had just stopped at Arts et Métiers station. L. stood up. She was very calm. Each of her movements seemed to have been calculated in advance to the nearest millimetre. She positioned herself in front of the man, directly in front, and looked straight at him without saying a word. The man stopped talking and the murmuring around us ceased. A strange silence descended on the carriage. L. faced the man without taking her eyes off him, while people got on and off. The man said: 'What's this stupid bitch's problem?' The signal that the doors were about to close sounded.

Then firmly and with astonishing speed, L. pushed the man onto the platform. He fell backwards, put out his hands to save himself, and the doors closed before he had time to grasp what had happened. Through the window, we could see his stunned, incredulous face. He shouted, 'You filthy whore!' and then he was gone.

L. turned to the young woman and uttered a sentence that I have never forgotten: 'You don't have to put up with that. No one should put up with that.'

It wasn't a hope, or words of consolation. It was an order. The woman went and sat down. She looked relieved. A few minutes later, I saw her smile, lost in thought, then she gave a little laugh, short, dry and almost guilty. I thought she looked as though she had straightened up a bit.

Even now I find it hard to explain how our relationship developed so quickly and how, within a few months, L. came to occupy such a place in my life.

L. exerted a real fascination over me.

L. surprised me, amused me, intrigued me. She scared me.

L. had her own way of laughing, speaking, walking. L. didn't seem to be trying to please me, didn't seem to be playing a game. She impressed me, in fact, with her ability to be herself (as I write these lines, I realise how naive they are; how could I know who L. was after so short a time?). Everything about her seemed simple, as though all she had to do was clap her hands to appear like this: natural and perfectly adapted. When I left L. after spending time with her or after a long phone call, I'd often remain under her influence. L. exerted a gentle hold over me, intimate and troubling, the cause and extent of which I was unaware of.

Within weeks of meeting, L. established a frequency of contact that I no longer had with any of my friends. She was in touch in one way or another at least once a day. A little note in the morning, a message in the evening, a tiny story written specially for me (L. had a knack for recounting an anecdote about something that had happened to her in just a few words or painting the portrait of someone she had just met). L. sent me pictures she had taken out and about; strange, incongruous allusions to our conversations or things we'd experienced together: a man on a train immersed in the Chinese edition of my latest novel, a concert poster for La Grande Sophie, whose songs I'd told her I liked, an ad for a new dark chocolate bar from my favourite brand. Unerringly, L. expressed her desire to be in touch with me. To become my friend.

Without realising, I began to expect these signs. And the calls. I rang her more often to tell her inconsequential things. We began emailing each other.

I didn't see at once how much L. was reviving my nostalgia for my post-adolescent years, the time when I entered adulthood, when I took stock of my vital energy. L. reactivated my seventeen-year-old self's feeling of omnipotence, the incredible energy that bore me along for a few months before feelings of fear, anxiety and guilt caught up with me. L. reactivated that precise time in my life: my return to Paris after four years with my father, my first student conversations in cafés on the rue de Rome, cinema outings in the Latin Quarter, meeting my friend Coline, pranks on the metro, the Slavic-sounding language we invented, our silent conversations during classes, written from right to left in homage to Abel Tiffauges, which you could read if you held it up to the light or a mirror. A continuous thread, inextinguishable, which maintained contact. A way of sharing everything: fear and desire.

L. reactivated that: the exclusive and imperious way of being linked with each other that you can experience when you're seventeen.

And yet the regular, intense relationship that was established between L. and me fitted quite well within the parameters of my adult existence. For example, although she hadn't asked me many questions about François, she had completely absorbed how we lived and the rhythm of our time together. She knew my timetable and knew that certain days were reserved for him. L. also very quickly became interested in my children. She'd probably realised that that would give her privileged access to my private life, indeed that it was a necessary condition of our relationship becoming closer. L. often asked me about Louise and Paul, asked me to describe their personalities or to tell her about memories of their childhood. I sometimes thought that L. wanted to make up for lost time, the time that she hadn't known. But L. showed equal interest in the period they were currently going through: were they feeling confident as the baccalaureate approached? Had they chosen their courses?

L. showed me some prospectuses about the career that interested Paul and sent me a file about the national civil aviation school, whose entrance exam my daughter wanted to sit. Later, she emailed me very detailed information about the Guild of Arts and Crafts as well as a list of preparatory classes in science.

I have to confess that the curiosity that L. showed so quickly about the children surprised me at first. Then it struck me that my perplexity stemmed from a stupid prejudice: why shouldn't a woman who doesn't have children take an interest in someone else's? The truth was that L.'s ability to listen was unequalled when it came to the things I worried about as a mother: the fact that Louise and Paul are twins, the fear they were feeling at the prospect of being apart, the inevitability they probably felt about having to go through this, their respective choices, the application process, the files to prepare, their personal statements, inputting their choices in the mysterious computerised application form after the baccalaureate, and then the wait . . . lots of stages that L. shared with me as though she were intimately involved.

L. asked questions, requested news, sometimes gave advice.

Today, it's tempting to claim that L. was not interested in Louise and Paul but in the place they occupied in my life: their manifest influence on my mood, my sleep, my availability. Today it would be easy for me to write that L. was interested in me as a mother solely because she was interested in me as a writer. It didn't take L. long to grasp that these two aspects of my personality are not separate. L. probably wanted to gauge the extent to which Louise and Paul were likely to interfere with, disturb, prevent or, conversely, stimulate my writing. In addition, the courses both of them had chosen would mean they would be leaving Paris, one for the provinces and the other to go abroad. It would be easy now to think that L. was delighted that they were planning to leave after the summer. But I know that would be unfair; it wasn't that simple. In truth, nothing with L. was ever simple. In hindsight, it seems to me that the interest that she showed in the children was deeper and more complex than that. L. experienced genuine fascination for mothers in general and for me as a mother in particular. I'm certain L. loved to listen to me talking about my children: the memories of their early years, how they grew up, their teenage anxieties. L. asked for details, was amused by our little family mythology. In retrospect, I have to say that L. understood my children to an astonishing degree. Several times I spoke to her about a worry, an argument, a lack of understanding between them, or between them and me, and she immediately grasped the issue and helped me respond. Yet L. never felt the need to meet them. I would go as far as to say that she avoided any circumstance that might have led to such a meeting. She never came to the cinema when I went with them, and when I suggested meeting somewhere, she'd ask if I'd be alone. Likewise, she never came to the apartment when she knew the children would be there and when in doubt, avoided the risk.

It took me a while to realise this.

In the end, I thought it was a matter of reserve, or a way of shielding herself from an emotion she was afraid of confronting. In the end, I thought that the issue of motherhood was more painful for her than she cared to admit.

In the space of a few months, I think L. managed to get a fairly accurate overview of the way I lived: my priorities, the time I gave to people, the fragility of my sleep.

When I think about it, L. very quickly positioned herself as a resource: someone trustworthy, unusually available, on whom I could rely. Someone who worried about me, who gave of her time like no other adult I knew.

L. was a generous, funny, singular woman I met at a party. That was how I first described her to François.

François knew how hard I found it to let people go, to make do with just bumping into them. He knew I needed to know what became of them, that I refused to lose them completely. So he said with gentle irony: 'As if you didn't have enough friends . . .'

One evening in June, L. sent me a photo of a huge piece of graffiti in black and red, which she'd noticed on a grubby wall in the 13th arrondissement. Someone had daubed at eye level: WRITE YOURSELF, YOU WILL SURVIVE.

I've always liked observing women. In the metro, in shops, on the street. I like watching them in the cinema, on TV. I like watching them play, dance, hearing them laugh or sing.

I think this interest relates to childhood, is intimately connected with it. It's the extension of the role-playing games I played with some of my friends when I was a little girl, when all you needed to do was invent a new name to be transformed. You be Sabrina and I'll be Johanna. Or vice versa. I'd be a beautiful princess with curls like Candy and an irresistible dimple. I'd be a young, talented actress like Jodie Foster in *Bugsy Malone*. I'd have blue eyes and porcelain skin. I'd be Christine Rosenthal, who danced to 'Belinda' in the end-of-year show at the primary school in Yerres. I'd be Christelle Portal or Isabelle François, the stars of L'Aigle school, magnetic brunettes. I'd be the sole girl in a boy band, whose members would only have eyes for me. I'd be a magnificent creature with long, smooth hair and breasts as soft as velvet.

I'd be someone else.

L. revived the unfulfilled hope of being more beautiful, wittier, more confident, of being someone else, in short, like in the Catherine Lara song I used to listen to over and over when I was a teenager: 'Irresistible, I wish I'd been one of those women the whole world falls in love with, madly in love, thunderstruck . . .'

Even now, even if I've gradually got used to myself on the whole, even if I feel as though I'm at peace, even in harmony, with the person I am, even if I no longer experience the commanding need to swap all or part of myself for a more attractive model, I think I've retained that way of looking at women: a recollection of the desire to be someone else that I had within me for so long. A way of looking that seeks in every woman I encounter what is most beautiful about her, most ambiguous, most luminous. Nevertheless, at least thus far, my sexual desire has been expressed only towards men. The wave, the frisson, the warmth in the pit of my stomach, in my thighs, difficulty breathing, my body in a state of alert, skin prickling with electricity, all of that only in contact with men.

Still, one day a few years ago, I felt as though I experienced feelings for a woman that circulated in the blood, got under my skin. I'd been invited to a festival abroad to coincide with the publication of one of my books in translation. I answered readers' questions in a dark, air-conditioned room (it was oppressively hot outside). After my contribution, I listened to this woman talk about her latest novel. I'd read several of her books but had never met her before. She was brilliant, funny, witty. Her speech was a succession of pirouettes, counterpoints and digressions. The audience was in the palm of her hand, as was I. She played with words and their multiple meanings; she was having fun. The audience, the laughter, the attention on her, it all seemed to be a joke, as though ultimately none of this pantomime (the writer meeting her public) should be taken seriously. She was beautiful in a masculine way; it had nothing to do with her features but rather her posture, though I cannot identify exactly what gave this strange attraction she exerted on me substance. There was something extremely feminine in the way she took on the masculine, adopted its codes and subverted them.

That same evening, the two of us went for a drink together near the port.

Earlier in the evening, when we were still with the group (a dozen or so writers and festival organisers), she talked about herself, about her passion for cars and speed, her taste for wine, the teaching she did at the university. I felt a sudden desire that she should take an interest in me, that she should suggest we make our escape, that she single me out from the others. That she choose me. And that's exactly what happened.

I was sitting opposite her in the warm night and although we were roughly the same age, I felt as though I was a clumsy young girl, that she was in every way superior. Her mind, her language, her voice, all of those things fascinated me. I remember we spoke about the city she lived in, the beauty of airports, the way books lived on in our memory, despite forgetting. I remember I told her about my mother's suicide, which had happened a few months before, and the questions that still haunted me.

For the first time I wanted to lie down beside a woman, to be in contact with her skin. To fall asleep in her arms. For the first time I imagined it possible, that I could desire a woman's body.

We walked back to the hotel late that night. In the corridor, we separated without lingering; it was clear, limpid, each to her room. I have often thought about her, but haven't seen her since.

Was L. an object of desire for me? Given the way we met and the speed with which she assumed such an important place in my life, I have of course asked myself this question. And the answer is yes. Yes, even today, I would be able to give an accurate description of L.'s body, the length of her hands, the strand of hair she used to sweep behind her ear, the texture of her skin. The softness of her hair, her smile. I wanted to be

L., to become her. I wanted to be like her. Sometimes I wanted to stroke her cheek, to take her in my arms. I loved her perfume.

I don't know what part sexual desire plays in all this; maybe it never entered my consciousness.

The day of the baccalaureate results, L. was the first person who called to find out if Louise and Paul had passed. We'd decided to celebrate the children's success at home that evening with friends, a small party that I imagined as intimate and joyful before they went out in the neighbourhood, probably until the next morning. I invited L. along; that way she could meet them at last, and also François, whom she still had never met. After a brief hesitation, L. became enthusiastic; yes, it was a very good idea, what could she bring? Some wine, snacks to have with the aperitif, a dessert?

During the course of the evening, L. left a voicemail to say she wasn't coming; she was sorry, but her back was very painful and she was worried that it was a symptom of the onset of a bout of renal colic, which unfortunately she got quite often, and she'd prefer to stay at home and rest.

I called her the next day to see how she was. She thought she'd avoided an attack but was feeling tired. As usual, it didn't take her long to regain the upper hand in matters of interrogation: how had the party gone? Were Louise and Paul happy, proud, relieved? Did they go out with their friends afterwards? And what about me – how did I feel about it all? She imagined that it must be a funny stage for a mother, celebrating her children's baccalaureate, and their eighteenth birthdays coming up soon, preparing to let them go, being happy for their success and the fact they'd got in to the colleges they wanted, but at the same time didn't all that mean I'd soon be on my own? How was I feeling about this moment? Wasn't it going too fast, didn't it seem to have come suddenly, without warning, even though eighteen years had gone by since the children were born? Wasn't it quite simply stunning?

Once again, L. was formulating things exactly as I would have put them myself: the feeling of wanting to hold back time, the futile struggle to stop the clock for a moment, or that the hours should stretch a little, and my incredulity at having reached this point.

L. was right. It was painful *and* wonderful. It had come round suddenly. It made me feel dizzy. I had hundreds of images and sensations that I didn't want to lose, fragile memories, already altered, which I now needed to preserve.

———

And then there was the question that sometimes came into my mind when I tried to bring together these two images: Louise and Paul at birth (two tiny beings born by Caesarean three minutes apart, who weighed barely 5 kg together) and Louise and Paul today (two young people with solid constitutions, measuring 1.78 m and 1.95 m respectively), a question I sometimes voiced aloud when I saw them in the kitchen in the morning, a question that expressed my astonishment – yes, that was the right word – as though the time that separated these two images had never existed: 'What just happened?'

The first time L. asked me what I was planning on writing, it seemed as though we were at last getting to the heart of the matter. I don't remember why I immediately thought this: everything between us that had gone before had simply served to lead us here, to this precise point, and L. had just laid down her cards to show me her hand.

I was sitting at the kitchen counter and she was standing in front of me. The kitchen opened onto the living room and a smell of stewing meat was gradually permeating the room. L. was chopping vegetables; we were trying a red wine as an aperitif.

She asked the question abruptly, unexpectedly, with nothing in what had gone before to justify its sudden appearance. We were talking about something else entirely and suddenly she said: 'What are you going to write now?'

For months, readers, friends and people I encountered had been asking me about 'after'. The question was generally framed like this: 'What are you going to write after this?' Sometimes the questions were broader still: 'What *can* you write after this?' In such cases, it seemed to contain its own response: *after this* there is nothing. It's a given. I had opened the black box, squandered the stock; the store was empty. In any eventuality, the question was not neutral. It seemed to me to conceal a confused threat, a warning.

Perhaps I was the only person unaware of what everyone else knew. That book had been a terminus, an end in itself. Or rather a threshold that couldn't be crossed, a point beyond which it was impossible to go, at least for me. After, there would be nothing. The familiar story of the glass ceiling, the incompetence threshold. That's what the question meant. Maybe this was a false interpretation on my part, a paranoid night-thought. The question may have been as simple as it seemed, concealing no ulterior motive or insinuation. Yet gradually, through repetition, the terrifying idea that I had written my last book gained substance. A book beyond which there was nothing, beyond which nothing *could* be written. The book had completed the circle, broken the alchemy, brought the impulse to an end.

During my encounters with readers, which she sometimes attended, my editor saw how destabilising it was for me to be continually faced with this question. Several times in her presence, I had to hold myself back from panicking and replying: Nothing. Nothing at all, madam, after this, one cannot write anything else, not a single line, not a single word, you zip it once and for all. You're right. And yes, sir, I've shattered like a bulb, I've blown all my fuses – look at the little pile of ashes at your feet. I'm dead because I've burned everything.

L.'s question was not exactly the same. She hadn't said *after*, she'd said *now*.

What was I going to write *now*.

The great leap, the angel's leap, the leap into the void, the hour of truth (these expressions flashed through my mind as L. chopped her vegetables with troubling determination) was *now*.

François had just left for the US to make a documentary series on American writers and Louise and Paul were spending the weekend with their father. L. had invited me over for dinner. It was the first time that either of us had proffered such an invitation, slightly formal and arranged in advance. It was the first time I'd been to her apartment and I had the strange impression when I went in that I'd stepped onto a film set. Everything seemed new, delivered that morning. That thought occurred to me, and then L. gave me a glass of wine and the impression vanished.

I finished my wine and began telling L. about my reality TV show project. It was getting clearer; I'd had a female character in mind for several weeks and had been making notes on her (I'd sketched her out on the first page of the notebook that was always in my bag). My future heroine was the star of a programme with high ratings, a young woman of twenty-five, entirely fabricated, adulated and overexposed. A character half-way between Loana in *Loft Story* and Truman Burbank in *The Truman Show*.

As I talked and tried to explain my project, I quickly registered her disappointment or, more accurately, her irritation. I felt it in the way her chopping speeded up; after the leeks she now attacked the carrots, her face over the chopping board. Her movements were rapid and precise. She was listening carefully but not looking at me.

When I'd finished explaining the broad outline of my idea, she paused for a moment before speaking.

I shall reproduce the exchange I had with L. here. I noted it down that evening almost as soon as I got home. It was impossible to go to bed. In an exercise book, which I found in the box of school materials, I tried to reconstruct the conversation down to its smallest detail, probably to distance myself from it, to keep it outside me. I may have sensed that that exchange contained its own delayed reaction and that it would spread slowly. I remember feeling afraid I'd forget it and that it might work on me unawares.

In the early months of our relationship, I continued to note our exchanges and L.'s monologues in this exercise book. Until the day when I could no longer write anything, but I shall come back to that.

L. looked up at me. It seemed as though she was trying to control the timbre of her voice, and even more, her delivery. 'I didn't imagine for a second that you were thinking of writing something like that. I read an article in *Le Monde des Livres* where you talked about a "phantom book", an even more personal one that you'd probably eventually get to. A secret book, hidden within that one.'

I knew exactly which interview she meant. I pretended I had only a vague recollection of it. 'Really? Did I say that?'

'Yes, you talked about a trajectory that passed through different points and said it would be hard to go back to fiction now. I read your last book with that in mind, the idea it had within it another, more important, more dangerous one.'

I was starting to feel hot.

I explained to L. that I'd been wrong. I'd done that interview in early August, several weeks before the book came out. I'd had no idea what would happen, what the book would stir up. I thought I'd foreseen its consequences, but I was wide of the mark. I didn't have broad enough shoulders for it. I wasn't up to it – it was as simple as that. That was why I now wanted to go back to fiction, to tell a story, invent characters, owe no debt to reality.

'So it's all about comfort?'

She wasn't hiding her irritation. I was taken aback.

'In a way, it *is* about comfort, yes. Mine and other people's. A tenable, bearable position that enables . . .'

'People couldn't care less. They get plenty of fables and characters, they've got adventures and plot twists coming out their ears. People have had enough of well-constructed intrigue, clever plot hooks and denouements. They've had enough of stories that are cranked out to sell books or cars or yoghurt. Stories produced in bulk and endlessly interchangeable. Take it from me, readers expect something different from literature and they're right: they expect the Real, the authentic. They want to be told about life, don't you see? Literature mustn't mistake its territory.'

I thought for a moment before responding: 'Is it so important whether the way life's described in books is true or invented?'

'Yes, it's important. It's important that it's true.'

'But who claims to know? People, as you say, maybe only need it to ring true. Like a musical note. Anyway, maybe that's the mystery of writing: it's true or it isn't. I think people know that nothing of what we write is entirely alien to us. They know there's always a thread, a theme, a fault line that links us to the text. But they accept that we transpose things, condense them and move them around. Dress them up. And that we invent.'

That was what I believed. Or wanted to believe. I was well placed to know to what extent 'people', or at least some readers, loved the Real, tried to disentangle it from the story, pursuing it from book to book. How many of them had wanted to know how much of my previous books was autobiographical? The real-life part. How many of them had asked if I'd really lived on the street, if I'd experienced a passion for an egocentric, duplicitous TV presenter, if I'd suffered workplace bullying? How many of them had asked after reading my last novel: 'Is it *all* true?'

But I wanted to believe something different: that the encounter with a book – the intimate, visceral, emotional, aesthetic encounter with a book – takes place somewhere else.

I could feel a silent, brutal anger taking hold of L.

'So your last novel was just a story like any other, then? It had no special importance? You imagine you've done enough for the truth to be told? And now that you've taken a little step sideways and almost sprained your ankle, you feel entitled to return to your comfort zone?'

I could feel her look of indignation trained on me like a weapon. I was starting to feel guilty about something that didn't exist, the first line of which I had not written, which was crazy.

'But there's no such thing as truth. Truth doesn't exist. My last book was just a clumsy, incomplete attempt to get closer to something ungraspable. A way of telling the story through a distorting lens, a prism of pain and regrets and denial. And love. You know all that anyway. As soon as you elide, or prolong, or tighten up, or fill the gaps, you're writing fiction. You're right, I was looking for the truth. I brought together sources, viewpoints, versions. But any writing about the self is a novel. The story is an illusion. It doesn't exist. No book should be authorised to have that printed on its cover.'

L. didn't respond.

I thought for a second about quoting Jules Renard's famous remark ('as soon as the truth goes beyond five lines, it's a novel') but stopped myself. L. was not the sort of person who would be impressed by a quotation out of context. She refilled our glasses and then came over to me.

'I'm not talking about the result. I'm talking about the intention. The impulse. Writing must be a search for the truth, or else it's nothing. If you don't seek to know yourself through writing, to explore what's inside you, your make-up, to re-open your wounds, to scratch and dig with your hands, if you don't question who you are, where you came from, what's around you, it's meaningless. The *only* sort of writing is writing about the self. Nothing else counts. That's why your book got such a reaction. You left the territory of the novel, you left behind artifice and lies and pretence. You went back to the Truth, and your readers were not mistaken. They're expecting you to persevere, to go further. They want what has been hidden, concealed. They want you to get to the point where you say what you've always avoided. They want to know what you're made of, where you come from. What violence engendered the writer you've turned into. They're not stupid. You only lifted part of the veil and they're fully aware of it. If you're going to write more little stories about the homeless or depressed middle managers, you should just have stayed in your marketing office.'

I was stunned.

In confrontations I lose my composure, I get breathless, the blood stops going to my brain, I become unable to express a sequence of coherent arguments. I defended myself in a ridiculous way, correcting the detail as though it were the essential: 'I worked in social observation, not in marketing. That's got nothing to do with it.'

I would happily have explained to L. what it was about, as a diversion, but L. put down her knife and disappeared. She was gone for a few minutes. I heard water running in the bathroom.

When she came back, I thought she'd been crying.

But that made no sense. Why would L. be so concerned about my next book? She had put some blusher on her cheeks and tied her hair back. And she'd put a cardigan on over her blouse. I spoke softly to try to calm things down: 'You know, fiction, autofiction and autobiography are never fixed positions for me; they're not a claim or even an intention. They're possibly a result. In fact, I don't think I see the borders in such a clear fashion. My works of fiction are just as personal and intimate as the others. You sometimes need dressing up in order to explore the material. The important thing is the authenticity of the act. I mean its inevitability, its absence of calculation.'

I couldn't find the right words. I was aware of showing regrettable naiveté in front of L. I was upset. I wanted to go further, defend myself. But in this confrontation, there was something at work that deprived me of the means.

After a short silence, she said, 'That's not what I'm talking about. You're the one who's talking about that. I couldn't care less about codes or pacts or labels. I'm talking about the act. What keeps you at your desk. I'm talking about the reason why you're tied to your chair, like a dog, for days on end, when no one's forcing you to be there.'

'So?'

'Well, that's something you can't keep ignoring.'


I didn't know what to say.

I didn't know what we were talking about any more, or how all this had started.

L. went back to making dinner. I watched her dry the vegetables she had just rinsed. I sensed that she was making an effort to slow her movements down, recover the rhythm that would show she was calm and that none of this mattered. I watched L., the speed of her movements in a relatively small space, her way of moving around the counter, opening cupboards, brushing against objects, corners, surfaces, a form of haste without reason, of impatience. L. tossed the vegetables into the hot oil in the wok.

She took the knife she'd used to cut them, rinsed it carefully under the water, wiped the blade with a soapy sponge, then dried it gently with a dishtowel. She put it in a drawer and took out a packet of cashew nuts, which she emptied into a little bowl. Without looking at me, she said: 'I know what your hidden book is. I've known from the start. I realised the first time I met you. You have it within you. We have it within us. You and I. If you don't write it, it's going to catch up with you.'

I didn't hear from L. the day after this dinner.

For several days, L. disappeared from my life, creating a sort of break or gap I was unprepared for.

I missed L. I remember thinking she might be punishing me, though that made no sense. I tried to call her several times, left a couple of messages, but got no answer.

The following weekend, Louise and Paul went off on holiday with their friends. Paul went camping in Brittany and Louise had been invited to go down south. That same evening, a courier delivered a wonderful bouquet of flowers with a little note from L.; I forget the exact wording. In essence, she apologised for losing her temper and was sorry about how heated our discussion had become. I sent a text to reassure her.

I was alone in Paris and eagerly waiting for François to come back to France for two weeks before he set off again on another long trip to the US. I knew how important the documentary series was to him, how long he'd dreamed about it. We'd talked to each other about these long periods apart. I'd encouraged him to go. François never questioned the time I devoted to writing or my way of life.

When he got back, we immediately set off for the country.

In the preceding years, as the number of invitations he received increased, François had – in an inversely proportional movement of retraction – gradually retreated to his domain, so to speak, to this place which he'd chosen as a point of anchorage on the smooth, slippery surface of the world.

On the day I first met François, as we drank margaritas at the bar in a provincial nightclub, he told me about this house not far from Paris that he was having a lot of work done on. He told me the opportunity to be somewhere silent, to get away, had become necessary to him, vital even. I told him straight out that I hated the countryside. It had nothing to do with nature, which I had nothing against – it was something else. The countryside for me was synonymous with isolation and contained an inherent notion of danger. The countryside was associated with fear and a certain idea of imprisonment.

I have no recollection of this conversation; it was François who told me much later how much what I said had unsettled him. We'd clearly embarked on a process of seduction and he had never known someone shoot themselves in the foot like that, right at the start, flouting the codes, not looking for coincidences or things in common, but instead emphasising disagreements and incompatibilities. Nonetheless, we eventually found common ground when we talked about the songs we used to listen to on Hit FM (we listed a few and this shared culture of summer music videos made us laugh).

I could describe the first time I went to Courseilles, nearly three years after that first conversation, and the strange route that finally led me to this man (and him to me), as I described it to L., at her request, shortly after we met. L. never hid the fact that she found our 'association' strange; I think that was the word she used (she didn't say 'couple' or 'the relationship you're in' or 'your love'); from her lips, it was explicitly a case of chalk and cheese. L. always seemed intrigued by the relationship François and I had and displayed a degree of perplexity about it. She wasn't alone. It took me some time to understand and probably to admit that beyond my own prejudices, we had a lot in common. At first I insisted on taking stock of ways in which we were opposites, or different from each other, deriving comfort from the idea that our worlds had no points of intersection – or if there were any, they were contingent and provisional. Later, when I had access to his inner self, when I finally understood who this man was, what animated him, where his energy and his flaws came from, when I was able to see what was behind the mask – sometimes open, sometimes guarded, sometimes arrogant and distant – he presented to the world, I understood the love that could be born from our meeting and I stopped feeling afraid.

When I was at Courseilles, L. finally called me. I was glad to hear from her. She acted as though no shadow had fallen between us. She wanted to hear my news, be sure that I was resting properly; the past few months had been so full of emotions, it was normal and even desirable that I should allow myself some time, that I had a break. I was on the phone with her quite a long time; I remember because the wind wasn't in the right direction and I had to go to the end of the garden and perch on a little mound of earth, the only place where network access is more or less constant when the wind's in the north. I remember that I felt touched and reassured by this call. L. was thinking about me. Once again, L. seemed to understand better than anyone what the past year had meant to me, the energy it had demanded, the doubts that had formed, the ambivalence of my feelings, the intimate mingling of feelings of plenitude and emptiness. Once again, it seemed to me that L. alone knew where I was at, even from a distance. Because L. had noticed the strange coincidence of these two events: the last book – which had gone beyond me, literally and metaphorically, and was now somewhere outside myself – and the children getting ready to leave.

L. told me she'd be in Paris all summer finishing a manuscript that she had to deliver in early autumn, an account of a recent news story; she couldn't reveal more for the moment, but it was a big project with a lot riding on it. But staying on in Paris alone didn't scare her, she liked the city when it slowed down and was given over to the tourists; she'd go on holiday a bit later. She asked me what plans I had for August and I remember telling her about our famous 'holiday house', as the children called it when they were small, a term that didn't designate a place so much as a time, the inevitable meeting repeated down the years. Every summer with the same friends that I met when I was about twenty, we rented a house for two or three weeks, a big one, never the same one twice and never twice in the same place. The first summers we went away together we didn't have children. Now they were the same age as us when we spent the night bar-hopping in a seaside resort on Spain's Atlantic coast. Now the holiday house accommodates anything from eighteen to twenty-five people depending on the year, children included, the shape of the group always varying around the same core, onto which some related characters have been grafted over the years, with the approval of the others.

Friends we can claim have changed our lives are rare, with the peculiar certainty that, without them, our life quite simply would not have been the same; with the intimate conviction that the impact of this link, its influence, is not just limited to a few dinner parties or holidays, but that it has radiated out, spread far beyond, that it has affected our most important choices, profoundly altered our way of being and contributed to affirming our way of life. My holiday-house friends are that sort: fundamental. Unfortunately for me (but fortunately for them, it seems), they long ago left Paris.

To be honest, most of my friends have left Paris. They now live in Nantes, Angers, Valence, Rocbaron, Caen, Évecquemont, Montpellier.

Perched on a little mound of earth at the bottom of the garden in Courseilles, as the air began to grow cool (going in for a pullover would have meant losing the signal and so interrupting the conversation), I don't know how I came to tell L. about the wave of departures that had left me like an orphan a few years previously, before I felt able to make ties with new people. I told L. how one after another my friends packed up and took their children, as though plague had struck the city, and the absurd feeling of loss, or even abandonment, that I felt when, within five years, they'd all gone.

L. said she understood. She knew the feeling; she'd even experienced it herself. Her friends hadn't gone off to the provinces; they'd simply disappeared after the death of her husband. She promised she'd tell me about it one day. She wished me a good holiday, and said she'd be thinking about me.

———

In August, François flew off to Wyoming and I took the train to the holiday house with Louise and Paul.

For the first time in ages, I felt as though things were regaining their normal shape and dimensions, as though all of this – the novel that had come out a few months before and the ripples of reaction to it, the succession of concentric circles that had spread incalculably far and profoundly altered my relationship with some of my family – as though all of this had never existed.

There, among the people who didn't regard me differently, whose looks had not darkened or become veiled, who had remained far from that vain agitation but very close to me, it seemed as though my body relaxed.

We laughed, slept, drank, danced; we talked and walked for hours. I told myself that one day I'd write about them, my friends who were dispersed all over, those from childhood and adulthood, and about those twenty-five or forty years that had seen us grow up and become parents, change lives, careers, homes and sometimes partners.

During this time, I didn't hear from L. I don't think I talked about her with my friends.

Three weeks later, Louise, Paul and I took the train back. We were happy, we occupied a family table in the TGV, we looked relaxed. Suddenly I felt really alive, incredibly alive; I was with my children in a train that was taking us back from the Landes. I'd made the sandwiches they loved – with and without butter and lettuce. We'd had a wonderful holiday. I watched the countryside rush by through the window. My children were going to leave and begin their own lives. I was proud of them, proud of the people they'd become, proud of both of them. I thought that beyond the anxieties and family wounds, I'd passed something on to them, which, in spite of everything, resembled joy.

On the bus, when all three of us were squashed in the rush-hour crush, I suddenly felt moved to tears. Something was ending and something else was about to begin. I'd been incredibly lucky from the start. Through all this time, luck fundamentally had stayed with me. The new academic year was looking wonderful and intense; I'd get back to my writing and I'd go and see the children, often, in their new places. I'd explore a new life in a new set-up and I'd adapt. I had to keep nostalgia at arm's length and get in step with the present. There was nothing to be scared of.

Delphine,
It's a drag. Being part of your
family, having the same name as you
is a drag. You have appropriated
that name, sullied it, shat on it.
That's what you've inflicted on all
of us, that and the irritating
question we constantly hear: 'Do
you belong to the same family as
the author?' Yes, I'm from the
same family as the author and that
pisses me off. Me and the rest of us,
believe me, it really pisses us off.
Is it possible now to exist beyond
that question, to have any other
identity apart from being in the
author's family? It's not a gift.
    You seem to be forgetting that
you're sick. Yes, sick. You're

really sick. And what's worse, it's
catching. You think you've got away
with it, but you've forgotten the
consequences. And any doctor will
tell you: these things can relocate,
but they never disappear. It's
hereditary. It's in you.

I heard you're getting shot of
your kids. The perfect mother
reveals her true colours at last!
Well played. The coast is clear,
isn't it? You can live it up, splash
your cash, be a cougar at all your
fancy parties. I know you're a
bad mother who's grabbed the first
opportunity to send her kids as far
away as possible on the pretext that
they've chosen to study.

Your children's mother is an
overexposed storyteller.

I pity them.

I stood there with the letter in my hand.

At first I felt a sort of scarcely identifiable discomfort breathing, and then a ball began to swell in my
chest, an uncontrollable sensation that I'd experienced
before. My fingers were shaking a little. I hadn't taken
time to unpack my case or put things away; I'd laid the
bundle of letters I'd collected from the mailbox on the
table. I'd made myself some tea and begun to separate
the junk mail from the correspondence, then open the

envelopes one by one, when I'd come across this one, postmarked the day before. Louise and Paul had gone to their rooms. They could emerge at any point and it was out of the question that I should start crying. I thought of calling François, but with the time difference, I had no hope of reaching him.

I folded the letter up. I took a deep breath and moved on to the next envelope. At that very moment, my mobile rang. It was L. She'd remembered that I'd be back from holiday around now and wanted to hear my news. For a split second I wondered if L. had seen me come into the apartment and, out of some strange reflex, I looked out the window. There was no movement: most curtains were drawn, blinds lowered, a little further down an open window revealed a couple sitting at a low table, smoking.

It only took L. a few seconds to realise that something was wrong. My voice above all betrays my mood, though not for want of trying to learn to modulate and control it, but to no avail: my voice betrays who I am, emotional, despite the constant increase of my vocabulary. L. immediately suggested we should have a drink. She'd finished the manuscript she'd been working on that morning; she needed to relax too. I agreed to meet her a bit later, to give me time to compose myself and go to the supermarket to restock the fridge. I put the letter in my bag with the intention of showing it to her.

In the café, L. unfolded the piece of paper in front of me. I watched as her eyes scanned the lines. Her hair was down; on her eyes she wore a metallic silver, which brought out the pallor of her skin; her lips were pale pink. She looked very beautiful. She took her time reading it; I saw her face transform with indignation.

'Do you know who it's from?'

'No.'

'Do you think it's someone in your family?'

'I don't know.'

As L. reread the letter, visibly shaken, I told her about the one I'd received a few weeks earlier. I remembered it as less virulent. L. seemed thoughtful for a moment, then looked at me again.

'Have you never thought about writing a book about *after*? A book that would describe the publication of your last novel, its consequences, what it provoked, precipitated, what it revealed? The way it works, as a delayed reaction?'

Yes, I'd thought about it. The idea had crossed my mind. Describing the book's reception, the unexpected support, the overwhelming letters. Describing the effort that some people had made to accept the text, their resolve to process it, which they never abandoned. The respect for literature. Describing late confessions, whispered after the book had been printed, the memories that resurfaced. The defensive strategies, the silent trials. Yes, it was tempting to write about that: the disturbance had not just affected the zones identified as *at risk*. The *at-risk* zones had circumscribed the point of impact, assimilated it, accommodated themselves to it. A more devastating earthquake erupted in other areas, those I had merely touched on or avoided, those I had voluntarily excluded from the scope of the narrative.

Every author who writes about him- or herself (or family) has probably been tempted at some point to write about *after*. Recount the wounds, the bitterness, imputed motives, ruptures. Some have done so. Probably because of the delayed effects. Because a book is nothing other than a sort of slow-release, radioactive substance with a very long half-life. And we always end up being thought of as what we are, human bombs, whose power is terrifying, as no one knows what use we will put it to. That is exactly what I was thinking, though I remained silent.

As I didn't reply, L. rephrased her question:

'Maybe it would be a way of responding to this person? Publish their letters, as they are, without changing a comma. Make them understand that you couldn't care less if it's complicated for him, or her, to share a name you didn't choose, and show there are a thousand ways to share the name that he, or she, has; all they have to do is invent another . . .'

'But it's not true that I couldn't care less.'

'It is! You *mustn't* care! You should write about all this, all you've told me since we've known each other, how relations with some people change, get ruined in spite of what you do; about the people who no longer care how you are, the ones who now like to think of you as a *celebrity* – as if that made any sense for any writer in the world we live in – the ones who are more interested in how many zeros there are on your cheque than the turning point it represents in your literary progress; those who would die rather than ask you the question direct; those who convince themselves that you've changed, that you're more distant, more remote, less accessible, less available; those who no longer invite you because they have decreed once and for all that you've gone too far; those who suddenly want to ask you round every Sunday; those who imagine you spend your evenings at cocktail parties or smart dinners, who imagine you're not bringing up your children, who wonder if you're not secretly drinking or have had an eyelid lift. Isn't that what you told me the other day, Delphine, when you made a joke of it? Now read this letter. Read it again carefully. It's no joke. It's about hatred. It's meant to hurt you.'

I felt L.'s growing anger and indignation as she spoke, and it did me a power of good to know that someone was taking my side like this, entirely, unconditionally.

Yes, of course all that could be written about, but there would be no point. I was responsible for what was happening; I may not have meant to, but I caused it. I had to take ownership of it, or at least get used to it in turn. And then there was nothing that could stop what other people fantasised about us. I knew that. Writing a book about *after* would deepen the divide or the lack of understanding. It seemed to me that I had better things to do. I reminded L. that I'd been thinking about another idea for months, a real work of fiction. I'd kept taking notes during the holidays, my project was taking shape, the plot was getting clearer.

L. interrupted: 'Plot? Are you saying that seriously? You don't need plot, Delphine, or developments. You're above all that now. Eventually you're going to have to acknowledge that.'

Now she was speaking very softly. There was no aggression in her voice. L. was keen that I should see her incredulity at what she'd just heard. Had I really devised, imagined a plot? She went on: 'You've no need to invent anything. Your life and character, the way you look at the world should be your only material. Plot is a trap, a snare. You probably think it gives you shelter or support, but you're wrong. Plot doesn't protect you from anything. It will suddenly give way beneath your feet or crash down on your head. Make no mistake, plot is a vulgar illusion. It doesn't give you a spring-board or support. You don't need it any more. You're somewhere else now, don't you see? You underestimate your readers. Your readers don't expect you to tell them stories that send them peacefully to sleep or reassure them. They don't care about interchangeable characters that could be swapped from one book to another. They don't care about more or less plausible situations deftly stitched together, which they've already read dozens of times. They couldn't give a fuck. You've proved to them that you know how to do something different, that you could take hold of reality, have it out with it. They've understood that you were looking for a different reality and that you were no longer afraid.'

We were no longer in the tense situation I'd felt in her kitchen a few weeks previously. We were two friends talking about my work and its consequences, and I was touched that L. felt so concerned about it.

L. wasn't asking if I was capable of writing something *after that*. L. was certain that I *was* capable and she had a very precise idea of the direction it should take.

Amused, I replied that she was playing with words and caricaturing what I'd said. I'd said 'plot', but that was just shorthand; none of my books had ever offered the reader a plot and resolution in the way she was using those terms. She should at least give me time to explain what I'd imagined, since she was so interested in the use to which reality could be put, and she might well find what she was after.

L. motioned to the waiter to bring us two more mojitos, a way of showing me that she had all the time in the world, all night if necessary. She leaned back in her chair. Her posture said, 'Go on, I'm listening. Let's drink to the book you refuse to write and the one you claim to be fixated on.' I finished my drink and began.

'The heroine . . . I mean . . . the main character . . . is a young woman who . . . who has just left a reality show that she's won. The viewers fell in love with her from the very first episodes. Social networks were alight. She was on the front page of the gossip and TV magazines.

In a few weeks, while she was still on the show – it's one of those ones where they're shut away – this girl became a star.'

I was waiting for a sign of encouragement from L., but her face only expressed extreme vigilance. I went on: 'Anyway, it's not really the show that interests me, or even being shut away, it's what happens after, when she comes out. I mean the moment when she has to confront this image of herself that's got nothing to do with who she is.'

L. was completely still, but had her eyes fixed on me. She was giving nothing away. She was listening intently. Once again, it felt as though words were failing me and I couldn't express my idea as I wished. Once again, I felt I had symbolically become the little girl blushing in front of her class, whose only thought was not to burst into tears. But I continued: 'For several weeks, her slightest gesture, her least significant words have been the subject of comment. An omniscient, all-powerful voice has continually decoded her reactions. Over time, this voice has delineated what now seems to everyone to be her personality. In other words, a fiction that no longer has much to do with her. When she leaves the show, she embodies a character whose contours she doesn't know, a sort of traced shape with copied dimensions, which is still feeding off her, devouring her like an invisible, insatiable leech. The press has been sniffing around the place she grew up. Her life has been reinvented to move viewers and for the most part relies on the accounts of people she doesn't know. In fact, the young woman discovers this image of herself as a warrior, though she has probably never felt so vulnerable.'

L. didn't hide a little pout, but encouraged me to go on. Through some unidentifiable sort of pride that means you don't consider yourself beaten if you're not actually on the ground, I went on: 'OK, and then there's another character, a guy who's a film editor who worked on the show throughout the whole series. In fact, through his choice of images and sequences, he played a big part in creating the self she's discovering. This guy's trying to get in touch with her because he wants to see her again.'

Bizarrely, I was starting to have trouble feigning any enthusiasm for what I was saying. Suddenly it was all grotesque.

'In fact' – (and why was I repeating 'in fact' every few sentences?) – 'even *he* doesn't really know who she is any more. He's hooked on a fictional woman, a woman he contributed to creating, but who doesn't exist.'

L. hadn't moved. My idea now appeared to me in a harsh light: it was all so predictable, so . . . artificial. It all seemed to me, at the very moment I was saying it, so pointless.

The waiter slipped between us and put the glasses on the table.

L. took a packet of hankies from her bag. She was playing for time.

She drank a large mouthful of her cocktail through a straw, mechanically swirled the mint leaves in her glass, and paused again before launching in.

'People thought about all that ages ago, Delphine, long before you wrote your books. We read Roland Barthes and Gérard Genette, René Girard and Georges Poulet. We made notes on index cards and underlined key ideas with multicoloured pens. We learned new concepts and words as though we were discovering America. We changed our idols and spent hours trying to define autobiography, confusion, fiction, the genuine lie and "true lying".'

I was well aware of what she was talking about, but I didn't know what she meant by 'we'. Maybe L. had studied literature at the same time as me. So she'd probably studied structuralism, the *nouveau roman* and the new criticism, and by 'we' she meant a generation, our generation, nourished on the same thinkers.

She continued: 'We worked on the evolution of narrative forms, on the desire of some writers to attain the essential, the driver of true life.'

I nodded.

L. went on; the tone of her voice had suddenly become more intimate: 'Mental and emotional turmoil, the changing colour of Emma Bovary's eyes, the ravishing of Lol Stein, Nadja – all of them defined a sort of trajectory, showed us a path, let us understand the quest of which you writers are now the guardians.'

This time L.'s allusions were very clear. Books by Crébillon, Flaubert, Duras and Breton had all been on the syllabus in the second year of my preparatory course for the École normale supérieure. And this syllabus changed every year.

What L. was saying was that *she* had been in that preparatory class the same year as me. L. was indicating a sort of common reference point. She pursued her thought, but I was no longer listening. My mind was trying to form an image of the young woman she had been at eighteen. Starting from the woman who was in front of me – so assured and self-possessed – I tried to draw a line, a solid line that went back through time, but ultimately there was nothing, no face.

In the end I interrupted: 'What high school were you at?'

She smiled.

She let the silence last for a few seconds.

'Don't you remember me?'

No, I didn't. I was now trying to summon the more or less buried faces of the girls in my class, flicking through those distant images as quickly as I could, but I had retained few of them and none looked like L.

'No, I'm sorry. But why didn't you say something?'

'Because I could tell that you didn't recognise me. That you had no recollection of me. That made me sad. You know, there's something I've learned. Something unfair divides the world in two: in life there are people you remember and people you forget. Those who leave an impression wherever they go, and those who go unnoticed, who leave no trace. They leave no print on the film. It's erased behind them. I bet you receive letters from people you were with in nursery school, secondary school, on ski trips, people who registered your name and face indelibly in a corner of their brain. People who remember you. You belong to the first category and I belong to the second. That's how it is. Nothing can be done about it. You see, I have a very clear memory of you. Your long skirts, your weird hair and that black leather jacket you wore all year.'

I protested: 'No, it's not that simple. We all belong to both categories.'

By way of justification, I told L. about my encounter with Agnès Desarthe. Did she remember that Agnès Desarthe was in the same preparatory class as us? Of course, L. remembered perfectly.

I must have been around thirty when Agnès published her second novel. She was doing a signing at her publisher's stand at the Paris Book Fair one evening. Back then I had no intention of publishing anything; I was a company employee and never imagined that my life might one day take another direction than the one I was trying to follow and stabilise, a life whose foundations I was always trying to consolidate, so as to protect me from myself and everything excessive in my character. But I was writing, though within the limits of what seemed acceptable, liveable, to me, a sort of private journal just for me. The idea of writing differently, of writing to be read, represented too great a danger back then. I wasn't stable enough and I knew it. I didn't have the psychic structure capable of supporting that sort of scaffolding.

I had come to see Agnès as I would probably have done if she'd become a singer or dancer, with the kind of additional admiration you have for someone who has accomplished something that seems unattainable to you. Agnès didn't recognise me. She didn't remember me, or my name, or my face. I remembered her and her maiden name and what people knew about her and her family. I remembered the kind of girl she was; I could have reminded her of the names of the students she was friends with, Nathalie Azoulai and Hadrien Laroche (both of whom have also published novels since). I can picture them as though I was there, as well as Nathalie Mesuret, whose clear complexion and scarlet lips used to fascinate me. They were the class elite (the *cool kids*, as my children would say today); they were beautiful and smiling; they were perfectly at home there, in the right place; they had every objective and statistical reason to be there. There was something in their demeanour that seemed to leave no room for doubt. Their parents were proud of them, supported them in their efforts; they belonged to the cultivated, enlightened Parisian world that I was beginning to discover – as I write this, I am well aware that it is pure projection on my part – but that's how they seemed to me in their ease: entitled.

I remembered Agnès Desarthe, but she struggled to recognise me. That's what I wanted to tell L.: we were all someone's castaway, the one who disappeared; it meant nothing, it had no significance.

I told L. that I'd kept the class photo (the one that Agnès, that evening at the Book Fair, had asked me to copy for her and that I mailed to her a few weeks later). L. couldn't get over it: 'You still have that photo?'

'Of course! I keep all the photos that come my way. I'm crazy about photos. I lose nothing, throw nothing away. I can show you if you like. You can see that you did leave an impression on the film after all!'

L. thought for a moment and then said: 'I don't think I'm in it. In fact, I'm almost certain. I was sick that day.'

L. looked sad and I felt guilty. We'd been in the same class for a year and I hadn't recognised her. Nothing familiar about her had struck or intrigued me, and even now I couldn't recall a figure that could have been her. It's true she had changed her name and now had her husband's (though he'd been dead for years), but at no point had her face awakened in me any reminiscence or feeling of déjà-vu.

We sipped our mojitos in silence for a few minutes. Other, distant images from that fragile year came back to me. It was strange summoning those memories, which I hadn't thought about for years.

L. leaned closer, suddenly more serious:

'Your idea isn't bad, Delphine. But your characters have no soul. You can't write that sort of thing today. Not in that form. The reader doesn't care. You have to find something more involving, more personal, something that comes from you and your history. Your characters need some link with life. They have to exist beyond the page, that's what the reader demands: that it exists, that it breathes. "In real life", as children say. At this point you cannot be involved in fabrication, artifice, deception. Otherwise your characters will be like paper tissues that get chucked in the first litter bin after they've been used. They'll be forgotten. Because nothing remains of fictional characters who have no link with reality.'

I was disturbed, but I couldn't agree with what she said. Didn't a character have the right to come from nowhere, have no anchorage, and be a pure invention? Did a character have to provide an explanation? I didn't think so. Because the reader knew what to expect. The reader was always up for yielding to illusion and treating fiction like reality. The reader was capable of that: believing and simultaneously realising that it didn't exist. Believing *as if* it were true, while remaining conscious that it was made up. The reader was capable of weeping over the death or the downfall of a character who didn't exist. It was the opposite of deception.

Every reader could attest to it. L. was wrong. She only wanted to hear one side of the story. Sometimes fiction was so powerful that it even had reverberations in the real world. When I went to London with Louise and Paul, we visited Sherlock Holmes' house. Tourists from all over the world were there to see this house.

But Sherlock Holmes never existed. Yet people come to see his typewriter, his magnifying glass, his deerstalker, his furniture, his interior, in a reconstruction based on Conan Doyle's novels. People know this, yet they queue up and pay to visit a house that is just a meticulous recreation of a fiction.

L. acknowledged this was true. And charming.

But what she was passionate about, what prevented her sleeping when she was reading a book was not just that it rang true. It was knowing that it had happened. Something had happened and the author had then spent weeks, months or years transforming this material into literature.

I finished the last of my mojito.

L. smiled.

She looked like someone who was not worried, who knew her time would come – someone who didn't doubt that time would work in her favour, would prove her right.

When Louise and Paul were born, I stopped writing the private journal I'd kept for years.

A few months later, writing, which had been chased out through the door, returned through the window, and I began a novel. I'm not sure how this desire made itself known and I can't say today what incident or encounter allowed me to put it into action. For years, intimate, unfiltered and almost daily writing had helped me know myself, construct myself. It had nothing to do with literature. And now that I was learning to live without it, it seemed to me that I could write other things without really knowing what, or what form they might take.

So as soon as I had two clear hours, I would work on this story.

One day I sent off the manuscript inspired by the months I'd spent in hospital as I entered adulthood. An autobiographical novel in the third person, in which I claimed a role for fiction.

A Parisian publisher received me in his office, visibly flustered. The text, he maintained, lacked *reality effects*.

Did I even know what a 'reality effect' was?

Before I had time to reply, he allowed himself to remind me: Roland Barthes had defined it – it was a literary device that clearly indicated to the reader that the text was trying to describe the real world, an element the function of which was to affirm the close relationship between text and reality.

And, he went on, those were lacking. Why veil your face? The autobiographical aspect of the book was clear, so why pretend to hide? Since the book was testimony, it needed some details that wouldn't deceive, to reassure the reader about the goods, take full responsibility for the story in the first person, and go on Jean-Luc Delarue's TV show to talk about it. What's more, anorexia was becoming fashionable. With a quiver in my voice and a Kleenex in my hand, I told him that if that was all he thought the text was, if it held no other interest, then he shouldn't publish it. I added (my voice rising in spite of myself) that one of my best friends had worked with Jean-Luc Delarue for ten years. And if telling my story on TV was all that this was about, I needn't have written a book. I managed to hold back my tears, but only just. I had never set foot in a publisher's office. I'd taken an afternoon off work to attend this meeting. I'd spent two or three days thinking about the kind of outfit that would be appropriate to wear in this sort of situation. I may even have bought a skirt or a blouse specially. It flashed into my mind that I could just run, but I didn't. I was too well brought up.

At the top of the stairs, we said an awkward goodbye.

I had nothing against reality effects; I adored them, was passionate about them, but the publisher was talking about something different. He wanted me to inscribe the text in the Real. He wanted me to say to the reader, Please note, sir or madam, that everything I tell you is authentic; here is a book that smells of Lived Experience, 100 per cent autobiographical, here is Real Truth, here is Life in the raw, guaranteed additive-free, reality that has not undergone any transformation, especially of the literary variety.

That's what I was thinking about as I walked home, slightly drunk, having parted from L. outside the bar where we'd had a third cocktail. The two of us had had a good laugh, sitting at the back, because in the end the conversation had switched to our adolescent crushes, from the time before Barthes and all that lot, when we'd pinned up posters in our bedrooms.

I'd told L. about the two years around the age of sixteen when I had contracted and then developed a spectacular fixation on Ivan Lendl, a Czech tennis player of unattractive physique whose obscure and striking beauty I perceived, to the extent that I subscribed to *Tennis* magazine (though I'd never picked up a racket in my life) and spent hours in front of the TV broadcasts from the Roland-Garros tournament and then

Wimbledon, instead of revising for my baccalaureate. L. was stunned. She'd adored him too! It was definitely the first time I'd met someone who loved Ivan Lendl, one of the most hated players in tennis history, probably because of his austere features, which nothing could crease, and his methodical, ponderous baseline game. In all likelihood, it was because he was so tall, thin and misunderstood that I loved him so much. At exactly the same time, L. was following all Ivan Lendl's matches too. She remembered it all perfectly, especially the famous Roland-Garros final he played against John McEnroe, which Lendl won after an unusually dramatic and intense battle. The photographs showed him victorious, his face distorted with exhaustion, and for the first time the whole world saw him smile. L. knew everything about him, remembered all the little details about Lendl's life and career that I'd forgotten. It was amazing, more than twenty years on, to imagine us both mesmerised in front of our television sets, her in the suburbs of Paris and me in a village in Normandy, both ardently wishing for the victory of the man from the east. L. also knew what Ivan Lendl had become since; she'd followed it all closely, his career and his private life. Lendl was married and the father of four children; he lived in the US, trained young tennis players and had had his teeth fixed. L. disapproved of this last point, the disappearance of the Czech smile (teeth unevenly spaced and, you imagined, overlapping) for an American smile (dazzlingly white, perfectly aligned false teeth); in her view, he'd lost all his charm. I could check on the internet if I didn't believe her.

It was a funny coincidence. One of several things we had in common that brought us closer.

But something else had come back into my mind.

When I returned to Paris to begin my studies, I signed up with an agency that recruited hostesses for various trade fairs and events. But very quickly it became apparent that I didn't match the profile. I lacked something, wasn't quite right, and every week, while the other girls were sent off to the exhibition centre at the Palais des congrès or to the motor show, the agency offered me, and some of the others, missions in hypermarkets in distant suburbs, vaguely accessible by RER. Standing in front of the shelves or at the head of a gondola, I demonstrated perfume brands, or mince, or washing powder; I did tastings of dehydrated crêpes, snacks and soft cheese I cut by hand. I gave out leaflets on roller skates, wore vaguely peasant-style lace aprons, headscarves or promotional T-shirts; I repeated happy slogans in the run-up to Mother's Day or Easter week-end to the point that I dreamt about them at night. After several months of working hard, if we got a good grade on our spot checks, we might hope to be sent to a shop in an inner suburb or even central Paris.

And so, in the second year of my preparatory course, I was sent on a two-day placement to the Bon Marché department store. It was an undreamt of sign of recognition, an amazing promotion. No need to catch the train at dawn, no cafeteria with orange walls and flickering neon lights. I had to stand at the top of an escalator and spend the day handing out discount vouchers for a new range of haircare products that a cosmetics company was launching in the department stores. I wore an outfit supplied by the agency, but its crumpled material didn't hide its poor fit. The most ridiculous thing, though, was the viscose scarf we had to tie round our necks, a pathetic imitation of a Hermès square on which the brand's name appeared as a pattern. It was almost 5 p.m. and I could feel my feet swelling up (a friend had lent me a pair of shoes that were a little too small) when I saw them coming up, standing in the middle of the escalator in a group. I hadn't foreseen this: the strong probability of meeting students from my school in the 7th arrondissement on a Saturday. I can no longer really visualise their faces, and I don't know their names. Nor do I know whether they were students from my class or the other preparatory group. They nudged each other as they passed me. There were quite a lot of them. Some of them stopped, looked back. I heard laughter. The girls snorted and the boys made jokes. One of them had taken one of my vouchers without looking at me. He began making fun of what it said and the girls laughed even harder. I remember that they were pretty and I felt like something the cat had dragged in, in a second-rate suit reminiscent of an air hostess. I pretended not to notice they had stopped just behind me, sniggering at me, repeating the same phrases over and over: Hello, madam, here you are, do please take one, here's a money-off voucher for our shampoos, conditioners, face masks, an exceptional range of haircare products, don't hesitate, go and have a look at our launch offers, over there, yes, the first department on the right. A woman asked me if she could have two, and I gave her another voucher. She wanted to know if the products were anti-dandruff and it seemed to me that the laughter behind me increased, and then suddenly I heard a girl's voice coming from the group, full of indignation and contempt: 'God, you're complete idiots. Are you really the nation's elite, little dickheads who've never made anything apart from your beds, taking the piss out of a girl who spends her Saturdays working? Have you looked at yourselves?'

I kept handing out my coupons at the top of the escalator, like an automaton whose movements couldn't be stopped by anything. I was having trouble breathing. My whole body was tensed towards them. I was waiting for them to go, without looking at them. I wanted them all to leave, to disappear. I heard their voices drift off and waited a bit longer before turning round. I saw their backs. They were elbowing each other. I didn't manage to identify the girl who had put an end to my ordeal.

But that evening, when I left the café and walked down the street alone, reliving a scene I hadn't thought about for years, the voice I heard was L.'s.

In these superimposed impressions, and their obviousness, I was certain that L. was the girl I hadn't seen, who had moved the group on.

During September, I was away again, helping the children settle in. Paul had got a room in the halls of residence at his school and Louise had found a flatshare with two friends who'd gone to do the same course as her. The trips to IKEA and Castorama, a few days in Tournai and then Lyons, took up the first weeks of the new term and kept the question of writing at bay. I was happy to be able to make the most of these times with the children. To delay the moment of separation.

I didn't have the mental space to get down to it; that's how I explained it to L. one night when she asked me on the phone how my project was going. In a gentle tone, without pressing, she asked if all this (the trips, the children moving out, documents to fill in, purchases to make) didn't give me a convenient alibi for not recognising my inability to sit down and write, an inability linked to the project itself and not the circumstances.

At other times, hadn't I been able to find the necessary time and space when I was working four days a week in a distant suburb? In her view, I was refusing to acknowledge that my idea was no good and that I'd been working for months on territory that wasn't right for me, which even ran counter to the way my work had developed. Wasn't it this mismatch, to which I was vainly clinging on, that was stopping me writing? She'd leave me to think this over. The question seemed fundamental to her, and she could allow herself to share it with me now that we were friends. She wasn't certain; it was just an intuition.

I didn't come up with arguments to contradict her.

It was true that in busier periods I'd found time to write.

But I was no longer so young and I no longer had the energy, it was as simple as that.

I showed L., who was so interested in my working methods (like no one before), my current notebooks, three or four of the same size, with smooth, soft covers that François had bought me at an Edward Hopper exhibition. Each cover had a reproduction of one of the artist's pictures.

I take notes in small notebooks. I like fine, light ones with soft covers and lined pages. I keep them at the bottom of my bag wherever I go, when I travel and on holiday, and I always put one on my bedside table at night. I jot down ideas or phrases for my work in progress, but also other words, the titles of future books, the openings of stories. Sometimes I decide to get organised: for a few weeks, one notebook is for ideas related to the work in progress and another is reserved for later work. It has happened that in periods of ferment, I've had five or six notebooks on the go, each of which corresponded to a different project. I always end up mixing everything up.

I gave my editor the impression that everything was going fine. I used rather vague language to distance myself from the lie: I was doing some extra research, I was preparing the ground, I was consolidating the foundations . . .

There was no cause for concern. I was *just about to get down to it*.

In reality, I was procrastinating, getting distracted, deferring from day to day and week to week the moment when I would have to admit that something was broken, lost, no longer working.

In reality, when I turned the computer on, as soon as I began to think, the critical voice kicked in. A sort of sarcastic, pitiless superego had taken possession of my mind. It chuckled, mocked, grimaced. It tracked down, even before it had taken shape, the poor sentence which, taken out of context, would provoke hilarity. On my forehead a third eye had been grafted above the two others. Whatever I prepared to write, it saw me coming in my clumsy clogs. The third eye was waiting for me at the corner, demolishing every attempt to begin, unmasking the deception.

I had just discovered something terrifying and dizzying: I'd become my own worst enemy. My own tyrant.

Sometimes a dark, unbearable thought overcame me: L. was right. L. was warning me because she could see the impending disaster I was heading for.

I was on the wrong path.

L. was trying to warn me and I was refusing to listen.

Louise and Paul had begun their new term and I was now alone at home. I hadn't imagined this and in a way was unprepared for it. I mean it had been impossible to foresee the silence, and the suspect stillness in which the apartment had suddenly been frozen.

Yet I'd tried before they left to anticipate my solitude in this deserted space. I'd tried to imagine how the emptiness might feel, and the new life that went with it. But I was wide of the mark. Now it was no longer an idea to be imagined, but a reality to be got used to. I wandered from room to room looking for something that had disappeared. One period of my life had ended and it had happened in a way that was natural and joyous, without jolts. It was in the nature of things and yet I felt an aching emptiness. In their empty rooms the beds were made, the books neatly aligned, the cupboards closed. A couple of objects were out of place, an item of clothing on the back of a chair.

I observed this fake untidiness, the kind of thing you see in furniture catalogues or interior decor magazines which doesn't look like what it is: a ridiculous simulation, a factitious representation of life. I wanted to cry.

L. rang me regularly, concerned about my morale.

L. seemed to really be taking it all to heart, empathising, and seemed to me more and more the only person able to understand what I was feeling: this apartment full of memories that I now had to inhabit alone, the time at home that I didn't know what to do with.

Yet I had a book to write and the moment had come to get down to it.

Each day I turned on my computer and adjusted my chair. With the screen at the right height, I opened the Word file that contained an opening I had started over and over for weeks, but which never got beyond two pages. I was looking for a title. Sometimes a title stimulated my appetite. But it never created more than a brief enthusiasm, followed by a general sense of numbness, an overwhelming feeling of fatigue that always, in the end, forced me to leave my desk for fear of toppling from my chair or suddenly falling asleep there, with my head on the keyboard (the image of Paul at eight or ten months came back to me: one day we'd got back from the square late and had gone beyond his nap time, so he crashed nose-first into his plate of baby food in his high chair).

Or else in the distance the mocking laughter would return.

Yet every day I would ritualistically recreate the conditions, as though nothing stood in my way, nothing frightened me.

There comes a moment when there is no further obstacle, when the necessary space has been cleared, where everything has been put in its place, ordered, classified, recopied. Silence has well and truly returned, the cushion has been positioned in the right place on the chair, the computer keyboard is simply waiting for the fingers to start tapping.

There comes a moment when you have to plunge in, recover the rhythm, the impulse, the determination. But nothing happened.

There comes a moment when you tell yourself that it's a matter of discipline, that all you need do is give yourself a good kick up the backside, then you play the game, turn on the creature at the appointed time first thing in the morning, sit at your desk: there you are, you're ready, stick at it. But nothing happens.

There comes a moment when you tell yourself that it shouldn't be like this, that it's not so painful, or that if it is, the pain is part of the pleasure, yet still nothing – it's simply a defeat. My blank stare before the screen.

A bit later came the time when there were no more excuses, no pretexts. Everything was ready, but nothing got written.

I was scared. I'd lost it.

The characters I'd described to L. had been emptied of their substance; they had drifted off without me realising and ended up out of sight. The idea of the novel as a whole had been deflated, had collapsed like a punctured balloon.

It rang hollow.

The story, the situation, the very idea of the book, the very idea of the *idea*.

Nothing made sense any more.

One evening in October I told my editor that I was giving up on the project I'd talked to her about. It wasn't working; it was running on idle. She asked me to send her what I'd written, even in draft, in its raw state; she could read between the lines, even the very beginning, even a few pages. I told her I hadn't written anything, not a single line, and hung up.

I was unable to explain the feeling of the dead end I found myself in, the disgust it all caused me, the feeling of having lost everything.

At no point did I imagine that the exchanges I'd had with L. could be linked with my giving up. Until then, no opinion, no words, no exhortation had had any influence on my work. Books imposed themselves on me: there was no discussion or negotiation. It wasn't a choice, it was a path and there was no other.

How could I have imagined that a couple of conversations could have been all it took to take my breath away?

At night I lay with my eyes open. I couldn't see anything: not a glimmer, not a spark.

Very early one morning, when I was on my way home after a night at François's place, I came across L. at the corner of my street. Not outside my door, but a few hundred yards away. There was no reason for her to be there. My street is narrow and has no shops on it. It was around daybreak and all the local cafés were still shut. I was walking with my head down and quite quickly because of the cold. Yet my eye was drawn to a long, white shape on the other side of the street, probably because of the immobility in which she appeared to be frozen. L. was wrapped in a long coat with the collar up. She wasn't moving. She seemed to have come from nowhere and not even be waiting for someone. After a few seconds I got the impression she was occasionally checking the entrance to my building. When she saw me, her face lit up. There was no embarrassment or surprise in her eyes, as though it were completely normal for her to be there at seven o'clock on a midwinter morning. She'd wanted to see me and had found my door closed. That's what she told me. She didn't try to make anything up and her straightforwardness touched me, because, as she made this admission, L. had a child-like expression that I hadn't seen before.

She fell into step with me and followed me into the apartment. I'd turned the heating down before I left and the temperature had dropped in the night. I offered her a shawl, which she refused. She took off her coat. She wasn't wearing a pullover but a sort of satin blouse in a flowing material that moulded the contours of her stomach, shoulders and arms. It was more the sort of thing you'd wear to party or a dressy dinner. I wondered where she'd come from and if she'd slept. I put the Italian coffee pot on the stove and we sat on the sofa. I was frozen. Beside me, L. seemed heated by some internal combustion that protected her from the cold. Her body seemed strangely sensual. Relaxed.

We remained silent for a few minutes and then she leaned closer. Her voice sounded a bit broken, as though she'd spent the night singing or smoking cigarettes.

'Have you ever been unable to go home?'

'Yes, of course. But not in ages.'

'Last night I made love with a man in a hotel room. At around five or six, I got dressed and took a taxi that dropped me outside my building. Once I was there, I couldn't go in. I didn't want to sleep or even lie down. As though some part of me was refusing to give in. Do you know that feeling? So I just wandered. And ended up here.'

The percolator had begun to whistle, so I got up to turn it off. With any of my friends, I would have poured the coffee and gone straight back to the sofa. I wouldn't have waited a second longer to laugh and begin a close interrogation: Who was this man? How long had she been seeing him? Where? And would she see him again?

But I put the coffee and sugar down in front of her and remained standing.

I was unable to ask her any questions at all.

I looked at L. I could see the fever that pulsed beneath her skin. From where I stood, I saw it very clearly, the acceleration of blood in her veins.

I remained there, apart from her, leaning back on my dishwasher. For the first time I thought that there was something within L. that eluded me, that I didn't understand. For the first time, I believe I was afraid without knowing why, without being able to represent that fear by a form or an image.

L. drank her coffee and got up. She thanked me.

It was daylight now and she felt ready to go home. She was exhausted.

I'd like to be able to give an account of L.'s personality in all its aspects, however contradictory.

L. showed herself in different lights, sometimes serious and under control, sometimes mischievous and unpredictable. That's probably what makes representing her character so complex: these sudden breaks in her self-control, this mixture of authority and seriousness that would often suddenly check an access of humour or fantasy, whose intensity made me think of those unexpected gusts of air that make windows fly open from the pressure of the wind.

L. continued to impress me with her ability to instantly pick up on others' moods and adapt herself to them. She knew how to get round the irritation of a waiter in a café or the tiredness of an assistant in a bakery, as though she'd perceived how they were feeling the moment she crossed the threshold. She was always one step ahead. In public, she could strike up a conversation with anyone, and in less than three minutes would have heard about their desires and been entrusted with their confidences. L. came across as indulgent and tolerant, and gave the impression of being able to listen to anything without judging.

L. knew how to say the right thing to console and placate.

L. was one of those people who others turn to instinctively in the street for directions or information.

But sometimes the smooth surface would suddenly rupture and L. reveal a surprising facet of herself. From time to time, evidently out of a desire to contradict her usual equanimity, L. would get into an appalling, disproportionate rage, for example because someone who passed her on the pavement didn't change his course (she maintained that two people coming towards each other should *both* move one pace to the side, or at any rate make to do so, as a sign of respect or good will). Among incidents on the metro, I remember the time when L. imperturbably made comments out loud for over five minutes while a woman yelled into her mobile without the woman realising, causing hilarity among the other passengers.

Another time, when I met her in the place Martin-Nadaud, I found her purple with rage, shouting insults at a man who was yelling even louder, but whose vocabulary seemed very limited compared to hers. In her low, firm, authoritative voice, L. had gained the upper hand. When she eventually consented to leave, she told me that the man had behaved rudely and aggressively to two young girls who had walked past in shorts.

L. had very diverse topics of conversation. Among her subjects of choice were Parisian rudeness, petty bosses, inquisitors and torturers of all kinds, the different forms of somatization and their link with our times, and human teleportation. If you started from the principle that we are simply a collection of atoms joined together, there was no fundamental law of physics preventing us from living together respecting our respective boundaries. Nor would any fundamental law of physics prevent us, hundreds or thousands of years in the future, from teleporting ourselves from point A to point B in the same way that we could already send a photo or a piece of music almost instantaneously to the other side of the world.

Among other crazy notions, L. thought that left-handed people were different beings, who could instantly recognise one another, that they had a connection with each other and formed an invisible, long-rejected caste, whose discreet superiority was beyond the need for proof.

I soon discovered that L. also suffered from phobias: one day when we were having lunch in a local brasserie, I saw a mouse run along the corner of the bar, just behind her. It's not unknown to see mice in Parisian restaurants, even the fanciest ones, but I have to say that it's not common right in the middle of lunch. Especially as the creature trotted along so casually. It was a sight worth interrupting our conversation for.

L. froze, unable to turn round.

'A real mouse? Are you serious?'

I nodded my head, smiling.

And then I realised that L. was not putting this on at all; she'd gone white and a fine sweat had broken out on her forehead. It was the first time I'd seen her look so pale.

I tried to reassure her: the mouse had vanished, there was no cause for concern, no reason why it would come back. L. wouldn't hear of it. She didn't take another bite of the salad that she'd just started. She asked for the bill and we left.

Later I discovered that L. couldn't bear any kind of rodent and she told me she hadn't been able to get to the end of a short story I'd written because it featured white mice.

Gradually, over the course of various conversations, I learned that L. had read *everything* I'd written and published: my novels, short stories, contributions to edited collections, *everything*, except the story she'd been unable to finish.

In addition, L. acknowledged that she cultivated certain obsessions and took a keen interest in those of others. She had a theory about this. No one could survive in our society without developing a certain number of rituals that they weren't always conscious of. L. had noticed, for example, that we all went through phases when it came to food. Did I know what she meant? If I thought about it, didn't I see that over time what I ate had changed and gone through different phases, different periods, corresponding to different ages and influences, with some foods disappearing and, conversely, other previously neglected ones suddenly becoming things I couldn't do without? She asked me to consider my breakfast, for example. Was it always the same? I acknowledged that I had indeed changed what I ate several times. I'd had a bread + yoghurt phase, a cereal + bread phase, then cereal + yoghurt, then brioche on its own . . . When I was twenty, I drank tea; at thirty, coffee; and forty, hot water. That made her smile. L. confessed that she'd gone through so-called colour phases just after she became an adult: an orange period in which she ate only foods of that colour (oranges, apricots, carrots, Dutch cheese, pumpkin, melon, prawns), and a bit later a green period (spinach, beans, cucumber, broccoli), which she ended when she got married.

Likewise, L. had noticed that we perform a certain number of actions in our daily lives in an unvarying order without the involvement of decision or reflection. These sequences, she maintained, were survival strategies we put in place more or less consciously. Our linguistic tics, far from being random, revealed better than anything else we said the extent to which we were capable at a given moment of adapting to the major constraints of our environment (or resisting them). According to L., the current expressions we used collectively translated our most intense forms of distress better than any detailed analysis of our lives or how we spent our time. So, in an era in which nothing appeared to work any more and society as a whole seemed frozen, in suspense, people endlessly repeated: 'That works for me.' Similarly, parties, films and people were no longer 'very' this or that – very nice, very crap, very quick, very slow – they had become 'too' – too nice, too crap, too fast, too slow – perhaps because we found our way of life overwhelming.

When it came to strategy, L. had a very effective one to guarantee her personal space or the confidentiality of her conversations. When she arrived in a café at lunchtime, she always asked for a table for three, though there were only two of us. This ploy enabled her to enjoy a large table (or two small ones pushed together) when everyone else was elbow to elbow. After twenty minutes, with a weary look, she'd tell the waiter that we'd have to order without waiting for the third person, though we'd keep the extra place, just in case. Towards the end of the meal, when the place had emptied considerably, L. would apologise to the waiter: she was sorry; the person had stood us up.

I must say that with her I was never bored.

L. asked herself all sorts of questions aloud, or rather expressed aloud the questions that probably a lot of women ponder (I certainly do): Up until what age can you wear skinny jeans? A miniskirt? A low neckline? Would you yourself be able to see that it was too late, that it was getting ridiculous, or should you ask someone close to you (before it was too late) to warn you when the time came? Was it *already* too late? Had we crossed the red line without realising?

I couldn't get over it: L., who had seemed so sure of herself when I met her, so certain of her choices, so aware of her aura, expressed – with more humour – similar worries to me.

This quickly became one of our favourite subjects: the effort of adjustment required to see ourselves as we are – a focusing, in the photographic sense, to which we had to regularly submit in order to place ourselves on the age scale, to know where we stood.

The discovery of a new wrinkle, of another stage in the general slide, the irremovable dark circles, all that could be shared, and now be subjected to critical – and comical – analysis.

L. confided that she couldn't meet someone over thirty without immediately wondering how old they were. For several years, age had been the first question she asked herself about any person she bumped into or was introduced to, male or female, as though it were a primary, unignorable piece of data, to evaluate the power relationship, seduction, complicity. For my part, I'd noticed that as I got older, young people often struck me as younger than they actually were. That was, according to L., precisely a sign of age, no longer being able to distinguish between someone of twenty and someone of thirty, whereas they were perfectly able to tell and distinguish between each other.

What fascinated me about L. was that none of this inner questioning showed in her way of being. Nothing in her appearance or her behaviour betrayed any worry or self-doubt. It seemed to me, on the contrary, that the way she dressed, moved, laughed, was flamboyant proof that she was entirely at ease with the woman she was.

The power of attraction L. exerted on me was probably all of this: I admired her for her clear-sightedness about the world and about herself, but also for her ability to bluff, to play the game.

One evening, as we were walking side by side down the middle of the boulevard Richard-Lenoir, L. told me that in the early nineties she'd seen a film by Pascale Bailly called *How People Cope*. The title alone had seemed to her to sum up her state of mind, her permanent questioning about other people that she couldn't free herself from: How *did* they cope? According to what rhythm, with what energy, by virtue of what beliefs? Because at the time, when she observed them, other people seemed to her to be coping much better than her. Had I seen the film? As I didn't answer, L. pursued her train of thought, talking about another film from around the same time, directed by Laurence Ferreira Barbosa, with an equally good title: *Normal People Are Nothing Exceptional*. That film was mainly set in a psychiatric hospital, and she'd loved it.

I stopped dead.

I remained speechless for a few seconds, searching her face for a clue.

L. was looking at me, taken aback. It had just got dark, lights were coming on in windows, gusts of wind were whipping up the dead leaves, which sounded like crumpled paper.

I think I felt at that moment a sort of dizziness, which I couldn't identify as being related to pleasure or fear.

Not for the first time.

Yes, I'd seen both films, and for quite private reasons they were part of my personal pantheon. That L. should be talking to me about precisely those two, both of which had remained somewhat private, was a troubling, even stunning coincidence, to the point that it crossed my mind to wonder whether she had read or heard somewhere my precise memory of them. But we had no mutual acquaintances and I didn't ever recall talking about them in the press.

Yes, I'd also often wondered how people cope. And in truth, if these questions had changed, they had never gone away: how do people manage to write, love, sleep through the night, vary their children's diet, allow them to grow up, let them go without clinging on, visit the dentist once a year, play sport, remain faithful, not take up smoking again, read books *and* comics *and* magazines *and* a daily paper, not be completely out of touch with music, learn to breathe, not expose themselves to the sun without protection, do their shopping once a week and not forget anything?

This time, I needed to be sure. I looked straight into her eyes and asked L. why she had told me about these films. Had I already mentioned them? She looked surprised. She'd brought them up because they were films that had affected her. And also because, to tell the truth, she was still asking herself that sort of question. That was all. That was why she thought of them.

We walked on in silence.

Did she also experience permanent doubts about the way she behaved in the world, sometimes hesitant, sometimes over the top? That fear of not being able to find the right rhythm, strike the right tone? The feeling of taking things too much to heart, of not knowing how to keep yourself at a safe distance?

Or had L. adopted my worries as she might have adopted a disguise, in order to hold up a mirror in which I could recognise myself?

When I pondered these questions, I always eventually told myself that I had no reason to doubt the similarities between us or relinquish the reassurance that they gave me.

L. observed other people.

In the street, in parks, on the metro.

L. had no hesitation about taking herself as a subject of study, with a clear-sightedness that delighted me.

It wasn't enough for L. just to ask the questions; she also suggested answers.

L. was well able to laugh at herself.

L. had theories about everything: matching clothes to your age; the imminent renaissance of the press; the return of heritage vegetables; the best way to stop hiccoughs; telepathy; the use of concealers; the advent of domestic robots; the evolution of language and the use of dictionaries; the effect of dating sites on relationships.

One morning as I was getting ready to leave the apartment, I heard Gilles Deleuze's voice on the radio. I shall reproduce the sentences that I noted down from memory a few seconds after this short archive clip was broadcast:

*If you don't grasp the little grain of madness in someone, you cannot love them. If you don't grasp their point of craziness, you miss out. Someone's point of craziness is the source of their charm.*

I immediately thought of L.

I thought of L., who had perceived my point of craziness, and vice versa.

Perhaps that is what any encounter is, whether of lovers or friends: two forms of craziness that recognise and captivate each other.

On days when she was sure she wouldn't bump in to François, L. would come to my place for dinner or a cup of tea.

Autumn drew on and as I wasn't writing, I made do with living. I'd stopped chaining myself to the computer at a fixed time. I'd declared a kind of truce, to give myself time to find another book, to let it take hold of me. I often thought of words I'd read somewhere, though I couldn't recall where: stories lie buried in the ground, like fossils. They're relics from a pre-existing world. And the writer's task is to use the tools in her toolbox to carefully remove and extract them, as intact as possible.

That's why I looked down at my feet as I walked, probably on the lookout for a little shard beneath the paving stones that would give me the strength to dig.

When winter began, it became difficult for me to go near the keyboard.

Not just to open a Word file, but also – progressively, insidiously – to answer emails, to write letters. I cannot date the very first time I felt a horrible burning sensation in my throat as soon as I sat in front of the machine. I know that it recurred more and more strongly: an acid reflux that took my breath away.

I bought antacids at the chemist's.

To go on using the computer, I had to trick my body, tell it in the clearest possible way that I wasn't going to attempt anything, nothing that had anything at all to do with writing. I adopted a casual, temporary position. I didn't put the cursor near the Word icon at the foot of the screen. These were the only stratagems that enabled me to face the machine.

Fortunately there were notebooks. Notebooks in which I continued to jot down words and arrange them: tiny beginnings, scraps of sentences plucked from silence, shapes sketched in broad strokes. The notebooks were in my bag. This was the idea that I was clinging to: the fossil was caught in the pages, in the fibre of the paper; the fossil was waiting for its moment. A title, an association, some notes made from life that would make sense when the time came, and would carry me with their echo. A mine, a treasure, and all I would have to do was dig down when I was ready. I told L. about this one day when she expressed concern about what I was doing.

I was with her the day someone rifled my bag on the metro. I've forgotten what made us take Line 4 at rush hour and can find no clue. We were crushed together, swallowed up in a compact mass of bodies, both jostled around and thrown into one another by the rhythm of the carriage. So of course I didn't notice anything. We parted when we changed trains and I took Line 3, which was equally busy, to go home. It was only later that evening, when I was looking for a packet of tissues, that I realised my bag had been slit with a box-cutter from top to bottom, its full length. I immediately thought about my notebooks. Gone. The pocket that contained my credit card, my cash and my ID had also disappeared. Someone had taken it all (the texture of the notebooks would make them look like a long purse or card wallet), or else they'd only taken the money and the notebooks had then fallen out through the gaping hole. I rummaged in my bag. My hand explored each corner over and over, in a desperate, absurd repetition. I kept saying aloud: it can't be, it can't be. And then I started to cry.

Later, I rang L. to tell her what had happened and to check the same thing hadn't happened to her. Her bag was intact. But now that she thought about it, she *had* seen two men behind us whose behaviour had struck her as odd. The kind of men who take advantage of the crush to rub up against you.

L. gave me the number of the banks' card-cancellation service.

L. expressed concern about how I was.

L. asked if I wanted her to come round.

I went to bed right after I hung up. There was nothing else I could do. I'd heard myself tell her in a controlled voice that it wasn't the end of the world. It wasn't the end of the world. My notebooks had disappeared and I felt as though both my arms had been cut off. But that was ridiculous, excessive, disproportionate. That was the proof, if proof were needed, that something wasn't right.

# PART TWO

# Depression

Inside him a voice whispered for the first time: *Who* are *you when you write, Thad? Who are you* then?

Stephen King, *The Dark Half*

'I know you watch those series with your children and that you've seen the best ones. So please stop and think for a minute. Compare them. Look at what people write and what they film. Don't you think you've lost the battle? When it comes to fiction, literature was outdone long ago. I'm not talking about the cinema – that's something else again. I'm talking about the DVD box sets on your shelves. I find it hard to believe they've never kept you awake at night. Have you never thought that the novel – or at least a certain kind of novel – might be dead? Have you never thought that the screenwriters have pipped you to the post? Or nailed you to it, even. They're the new omniscient, omnipotent creators. They're able to create from scratch three generations of families, political parties, cities, tribes – whole worlds, in fact. They can create heroes that people relate to, that they think they know. You see what I'm talking about? The intimate bond between the character and the viewer, the feeling of loss or bereavement they feel when it's over. You don't get that with books any more; it happens elsewhere now. That's what screenwriters do best. You're the one who was talking to me about the power of fiction, how it can extend into reality. But that's no longer the stuff of literature. You're really going to have to face it. Fiction is over for you novelists. TV series provide a much more fertile terrain for fiction and an infinitely larger audience. But there's nothing sad about this, believe me. It's actually excellent news. You novelists should be delighted! Let the screenwriters do what they're much better able to do. Writers need to return to what makes them stand out, to what matters. And do you know what that is? No? You do, of course you do. Why do you think readers and critics wonder about the autobiographical element in literary works? Because today that's its sole raison d'être: to give an account of reality, to tell the truth. The rest doesn't matter. That's what readers expect of novelists: that they'll lay their guts out on the table. A writer needs ceaselessly to question his way of being in the world, his education, his values. He has perpetually to question the way he uses the language that was passed down to him from his parents, and the one that was taught to him at school, and the one his children speak. He must create a language that is his own, with distinctive inflections, a language that links him to his past, his history. A language of belonging and liberation. The writer has no need to manufacture puppets, no matter how flexible and fascinating they may be. He has enough to occupy him within himself. He must continually return to the damaged terrain that he's had to traverse to survive; he must return tirelessly to the scene of the accident that turned him into this obsessive, inconsolable individual. Don't fight the wrong battle, Delphine, that's all I want to say to you. Readers want to know what's gone into books and they're right. Readers want to know what sort of meat's in the stuffing, if there are colourings, preservatives, emulsifiers or thickeners. And it's literature's duty now to play it straight. Your books must never stop examining your memories, beliefs, suspicions, your fear, your relations with those around you. That's the only way they'll hit home and resonate.'

That's what L. said one evening in an empty café near the town hall in the 20th arrondissement.

It had got dark and we had stayed on, at the back of a room with walls covered in 1950s advertising posters, bathed in light. Somewhere a radio station I couldn't identify crackled away. I reflected that this café was probably the last remnant of a bygone age, the only one in the district that had resisted the assault of a trendy makeover, which was claiming the streets a little at a time. A tiny island of resistance that would soon fall.

I'd listened to L. without trying to interrupt. L. was exaggerating, schematising, systematising, but I didn't have the strength to respond.

No, I didn't want to abandon the territory of fiction to anyone. But I looked at my hands and my hands were empty.

No, I wasn't ruling out returning one day to a form of autobiographical writing, whatever it might be called. But it only had meaning if it was possible to express the world, to reach the universal.

In any case, I was exhausted.

So that's what L. said and I listened, half-amused, half-stunned.

Her speech forced me to reflect on what I'd always refused to theorise. Her convictions had collided with the modest edifice I'd built to give meaning to my work or at least to enable me to talk about it.

And her words insinuated themselves into the heart of the doubt that I'd become unable to formulate.

L. told me one day that I'd written only two books. The first and the last. The four others were, in her opinion, just a regrettable diversion.

In the course of the autumn, Louise and Paul came back for the weekend two or three times, together or separately. A new bond was forming among us, one that had been modified by distance and missing each other. An intense, chatty relationship that was a continuation of all the years we'd spent together, yet also different. My children had grown up. I remained a mother full of emotion and wonder.

François was juggling various projects and had just started work on a second season of his documentary series, a long-term project that would again mean many weeks abroad. I was familiar with his insatiable curiosity, the entire days he spent reading, his appetite for travel. And fundamentally that suited me very well; our joint commitment to what we were trying to make; the will – or the illusion – to be able to simultaneously handle what can and cannot be shared. François respected my need for solitude, my independence, my moments of absence. I respected his choices, his whims, his constantly renewed enthusiasm.

L. called several times a week to let me know she was in the area. In truth, she was never far away. And I always invited her up. Because amid the confusion that I refused to name, I found her presence reassuring.

L. brought flowers, pastries, bottles of wine. She knew where to find the cups, tea, coffee, the corkscrew and the stemmed glasses. She would wrap my shawl around her, light my lamps, select the music.

When I took a call in her presence, L. would stay. She didn't pretend to look at her own phone or flick through the paper as most people would do. Instead, she'd nod as I spoke or furrow her brow. She was silently taking part in the conversation.

L. gave me a selection of new notebooks in three different sizes made from recycled paper. In the largest she'd written a little message of encouragement that I've forgotten, expressing faith in me. I can't find it now, as I threw them all away.

Every week she asked me how I was getting on with my work and reminded me she was available if I wanted to discuss it. As I had little to say about mine, she told me about hers. She'd just begun the autobiography of a famous actress. Three months earlier, she'd had to compete with two other highly sought-after ghostwriters. Along with the others, she'd met the actress at a party organised by her agent. Then the actress had made her choice. L. had probably found the right words and demonstrated the intuition about other people that continued to fascinate me. L. loved talking about the pleasure she got from giving shape to the material that the actress provided. She talked about this woman with the tenderness of a creator, as though the actress didn't exist outside the work they'd begun together, as though it were up to her to reveal this woman to the world, and to herself. L. was happy, and felt that she was now at the peak of her profession. Of what mattered. Because L. was not satisfied with just being chosen. She wouldn't write for just anyone. She felt entitled to turn down some collaborations and chose the people she wanted to work with. People, she confided, who had a destiny. Who had fallen, gone under, who had suffered and bore the scars. That was what interested her. Writing about how they picked themselves up, repaired and rebuilt themselves. Her role was to stage, put into words, highlight the material they entrusted to her. It was their soul that she put on the page, and when they thanked her, she always came back to this: all she had done was make their soul visible to the naked eye.

One evening, L. told me she could identify at first glance the people who had been victims of violence. Not just physical violence. Also people whose personality, whose self, had been put in danger by someone else.

She knew how to detect in them a form of impediment, entanglement, imbalance in the literal sense. Hesitancy, uncertainty, a fault line that no one but her seemed to notice.

It was almost winter and L. was hard at work. I, meanwhile, was making the most of this time when I could still proffer more or less credible excuses. Defer. I claimed I was preparing something. I continued to invent research and drafts.

I didn't know that two years would go by before I would be able to create a new word-processing file and write a sentence of more than three words.

Between the birth of the children and the year when their father and I separated, I created ten or so photo albums, each of about fifty pages. Thereafter, I continued to take photos, and sometimes had them printed, but I stopped arranging them and sticking them in. In hindsight, I could provide various hypotheses both about our separation and stopping creating albums, but that's another story. If my home were to catch fire one day, I think I would pick up these albums before the books, the letters and everything else. They represent an infinitely precious time in my life, in our lives. They are the epicentre of my nostalgia, a fragile casket at the heart of my memory. Often when I open them, I think how I'd love to be able to convey in words this time now vanished, borne witness to by the image, which is simultaneously so precise and so impotent.

When winter came, and with it the threat of idleness, I got it into my head that I should start making these albums again. It had been several years since the last one. I spent the best part of two days finding a shop that sold albums like the ones I had at home, then two more selecting the photos, most of which were saved digitally. The files were spread across a variety of obsolescent storage devices.

Once I had the pictures printed out, I sat at the living-room table in front of the blank albums, which I now had to fill. Fundamentally, it wasn't that different from writing, I told myself: a reinvented story would emerge from these images once they had been chosen, arranged, ordered and put on the page.

One day, as I was starting to stick in the prints, L. pressed the entry buzzer.

The photos were all spread out in front of me, sorted by period. L. sat down beside me, and became interested in the bundle in front of her. A series of fairly recent photos showed Paul covered in mud after a motocross session, and there were several shots of Louise with all her friends in her last year of school, taken in the snow on a winter's day.

'She looks like you,' L. said with evident emotion, as she looked carefully at Louise. At that moment, it occurred to me that Louise was the same age as L. and I had been when we'd first met. Since L. had revealed that we'd been in the same class, we'd only spoken of it once or twice. I had no recollection of her and it seemed insensitive to bring the subject up again. I didn't want to turn the knife in the wound.

L. must have read my thoughts, because she asked if she could see the class photo. I rummaged in the box till I found the print, the colours of which had faded a bit. The photo was taken in the school courtyard. The students are in five rows around Mr E., the philosophy teacher. Nearly all the boys are kneeling or squatting in the bottom rows. The tallest girls are perched on a bench that you cannot see. Having immediately identified my face and pointed to it, L. spent a long time looking at the photo, scrutinising every student. Then, starting with the top row, she traced her finger from right to left and began reeling off everyone's full names. Some of the names I would have been unable to recollect unaided, but once she said them, they came back to the surface of my memory and were confirmed.

Having named the last of them, she turned to me with a look of triumph. Out of a class of fifty, only about ten names had eluded her.

Suddenly her mood darkened.

'It's such a pity I was absent that day. I would have so loved there to be some proof . . .'

'Proof of what?' I asked.

'Of the year we spent together.'

But we didn't spend it together. I didn't share that time with her. My connections were with others. And in fact the main memory I have of that year is of a slow descent. Now that period feels so distant it might as well belong to someone else. The physical state I was in probably contributed to the blurring of my memory.

'Yes, it's a shame,' I eventually acknowledged. 'But why would we need proof?'

'Because you don't remember me.'

She was looking at me severely, but also seemed beseeching. Maybe I should have claimed I remembered her, that it had all come back to me at last. I didn't know how to comfort her, or even extricate myself with a joke.

I was about to close the box (which contained dozens of jumbled prints from around the same time), when L. asked if she could have a souvenir of me. Before I could reply, she looked in the box and held up a set of three photo booth shots in black and white for my approval. The missing photo must have been used for my student card.

I saw her put them carefully in her wallet without waiting for my response.

I think it was that day that she uttered a sentence I noted down on a Post-it just after she left: 'We've got a lot of things in common. But only you can write about them.'

L. stayed for dinner. Later in the evening, she re-entered the fray: Where did things stand? Had I got back to work? L.'s persistence was getting on my nerves. But at the same time, I couldn't help registering that she was the only person still asking me that question. Who still believed in it.

As I confessed to her I was unable to write, L. admitted she thought I was adrift. I was surprised by the expression. Adrift?

She wasn't questioning my idea about the photo albums – in fact, she found that quite creative – but it was all the other stuff. In her opinion, I was still much too connected to the outside world.

I objected: 'Absolutely not! I see no one, call no one. I'm unable to go out to a dinner or a party. I turn everything down. Apart from François and the children, I can't talk to anyone any more.'

L. responded in the opinionated tone I was familiar with: 'That's normal, as you well know. Because it's in that healthy silence that you'll be able to get down to work.'

What did 'get down to work' mean? What was the point of spending hours sitting in front of the computer, since nothing was coming out? I had to keep busy.

L. disagreed.

As a result of confronting the obstacle, something would emerge. Enlightenment or renunciation. If I kept running away, nothing would happen.

One morning my friend Olivier called to tell me that something disturbing was happening on my Facebook page, or rather on the Facebook page my readers had created. I didn't understand what he was trying to explain at all: something about someone writing terrible messages about me on a wall. Someone claiming to be part of my family had published dozens of posts accusing me of the worst horrors. Olivier was afraid that a journalist would come across these messages and spread them further. Did I have a way of contacting the group administrator? Had the group been set up by my publisher?

Once I'd managed to grasp what he was on about (I'm not on Facebook, so this wall that was visible to all and messages posted by an invented profile wasn't easy to fathom), I started to get worried. I didn't know the group administrators, and as far as I was aware, my publisher had nothing to do with them.

I thanked Olivier for alerting me and hung up. I was pondering the situation when L. called me for the same reason. She divulged the tone of the messages, but refused to read them out, as she thought that would only be hurtful and pointless. They were about the harm I'd done by writing my last novel, and the harm I'd done in general since I was very young. I was sick and I had destroyed everything around me. I had a border-line, destructive personality. I'd falsified history, mixed up dates, I'd written a book that was far removed from reality, I'd lied by omission, embellished reality with the sole aim of concealing my own pathology. The messages had kept appearing throughout the night, contradict-ing each other, criticising me for saying too much or not enough, of having sugar-coated reality or exagger-ated it; in short, everything and its opposite. According to L., they had not left the members of the group indif-ferent. Eventually, some of them had advised the writer to go and seek treatment. Over the course of the night, their author had lost credibility through the confusion and the growing virulence of the posts.

At some point during the day, the messages dis-appeared. Either the group administrator deleted them all, judging them out of order, or their author himself took them down.

That evening, L. buzzed my entryphone. She wanted to check I was OK and to talk about what had happened.

In her opinion, the author of these messages and the anonymous letters were one and the same. And these attacks called for a riposte.

As I didn't rise to this, she plonked herself down on the sofa in a position that clearly indicated that this time she intended to see through a proper discussion of the subject. She quickly launched in: 'Someone in your family has been provoking you for months and you haven't responded. He or she has written several times and you haven't reacted. So he or she has gone to the next stage, which means using other people as witnesses, because he or she is waiting for a response. It's simple.'

'But there's nothing to say.'

'Yes, there is. Of course there is. He's waiting for you to react. Write a book. Prove to him that you're not afraid, that in literature anything is allowed. Write about your childhood, write about your family, write about yourself. Seek. Only writing will allow you to discover who you are. You've started something you've got to finish.'

No, I didn't want to start that again. I wanted to go back to fiction. I wanted to protect myself and rediscover the pleasure of invention, I didn't want to spend two years weighing every word and comma, to wake up in the middle of the night, my heart beating frantically after nightmares I couldn't interpret.

L. was getting heated, but I now knew this more emotional side. I tried to explain why this was no longer possible: 'Listen, if I hadn't written that book, I'd never have written anything again. Even today I'm sure of that. It was a sort of trial I had to go through. An initiation ritual. But writing about yourself and your family means risking hurting people, even the ones you think you've spared or idealised. I don't want to do that any more. I'm not saying I regret doing it, but I don't have the strength to do it again. Not like that. Yes, you're right, I have a weapon that others for the moment do not. Others, whoever they may be, don't have the right of reply. At best, they can send me anonymous letters or try to fling mud at a wall that doesn't belong to them. Whereas if I do it again, I can be sure I'll be read by thousands of people. And will leave a trace that won't be effaced for several years.'

'So? You're lucky to have within your grasp something that everyone envies. You can't act as though that didn't exist, as though it wasn't part of you. Yes, writing is a weapon and that's all to the good. Your family created the writer you've become. They created a monster – forgive me – and the monster has found a way to make her cries heard. What do you think writers are made of? Look at yourself! Look around! You writers are the product of shame, pain, secrets, collapse. You come from dark, nameless places, or you've been through those places. You're all survivors in your own way, each one of you as much as all the others. That doesn't give you unlimited rights. But it entitles you to write, believe me, even if that makes waves.'

L.'s state of excitement was starting to concern me.

A few years ago, when I was preparing to write something about the violence of workplace relationships – or something in that general area or taking that as a starting point – I met a psychiatrist who specialised in workplace suffering and psychosocial risks. Back then, I was thinking about a violent end to the novel I was working on. I wanted to know if such an end was possible, probable, from a psychological point of view: is a woman who has been harassed and the daily victim of insidious aggression for weeks, a woman who has suffered workplace bullying, capable of committing an act of violence or even murder? Was it possible for such a woman to carry out such a thing?

Having described the context, I framed my question like this: 'Is it plausible that this woman might commit a dangerous act, even involuntarily? If you say no, I can swap my rifle to the other shoulder.'

We were in a café and the psychiatrist looked hard at me with a certain amusement: 'Goodness, you are armed and dangerous!'

I laughed. The phrase I had used – swapping shoulders – haunted me for several days. How much anger had I brought to writing this book? What pain was it prolonging, in disguised form?

I was careful not to relate this anecdote to L.

She didn't need my approval to continue.

L. was angry because she thought I was allowing myself to be intimidated by threats that should actually have spurred me to fight. L. was expressing her outrage out loud and exhorting me to rebel.

'They're going to have to realise that this is just the beginning, you know. You've been wearing kid gloves and tiptoeing around, letting various things go. You've set aside the most violent, the darkest part, and that's what they resent! Do you want to know why? Because to them, that's a sign of weakness. You've been careful, you've wanted to be the good little girl who wouldn't hurt a fly. You've called the reader as a witness – you, who've never done that – to share your doubts and procrastination. You've endlessly reminded him of the measures you've put in place: "Please note, ladies and gentlemen, this is a novel, an attempt to approach the truth, but it's just my view of things. I make no claims, take no liberties. I definitely don't want to . . ." and so on. You're down on one knee. You've opened the breach through which they'll flood, the better to get at you. You're wrong, Delphine. You've shown them that you were worried about them and their feelings, and it's through that weakness that they're now trying to annihilate you.'

I didn't protest and didn't correct her. I refrained from all comment.

I wondered if L. had been drinking before she arrived. What she was saying was out of proportion, irrational.

And yet, I felt as though I were hearing some truth, under the grandiloquence of her indignation. In order to calm her, I said I'd think it over. But she hadn't finished.

'Yes, writing is a weapon, Delphine, a bloody weapon of mass destruction. Writing is even more powerful than anything you can imagine. Writing is a weapon for defence, shooting, alarm. Writing is a grenade, a missile, a flame-thrower, a weapon of war. It can lay things waste; it can also rebuild.'

'I don't want anything to do with that kind of writing.'

L. looked at me. Her expression instantly darkened. Her voice struck me as suddenly abnormally gentle: 'I'm not sure you have the choice.'

Yes, I should have been worried that L. felt so concerned about what was happening to me.

Yes, I should have been alerted by the appearance of 'they' in her words.

Yes, I should have backed off from her a bit, at least for a few days and finally got down to some work.

But did I have genuine cause for alarm? L. was a woman of my age who spent her life writing other people's life stories. She had a radical, extreme vision of literature, but it was a vision I found rich and which I sensed could be interesting to debate, unemotionally; in other words, disconnected from my own case.

Besides, L. was taking up my cause. And in such a moment as this – a moment of doubt and difficulty – L.'s compassion was an invaluable reassurance.

A few days later, I had gone down to the cellar to look for some old papers and came across my forgotten manuscript while I was rummaging through a trunk of archives. I'd written this text about a decade earlier, before I'd published anything. I don't remember in what circumstances exactly, but I'd written it. It was a rather confused period that was resistant to memory. The pages were ring-bound and the title page protected with a clear cover. The title made me smile. It was a good title. Under the flickering light in the cellar corridor, I leafed through the manuscript. I had patchy recollections of a conversation with a literary editor who'd encouraged me to persist but felt I hadn't pulled this project off. I gave up on it without difficulty and put the text aside, concluding it had been too ambitious for me.

I rummaged in the trunk, looking for other copies but, after a more thorough search, it seemed I had kept only one.

I spent the afternoon lying on the bed rereading the manuscript. I didn't take any calls, didn't take a break. I didn't feel the need to go four times round the block on various pretexts nor to polish all the shoes in the cupboard. For the first time in ages, I managed to stay focused. When I'd finished reading, it seemed to me that in a dark, distant corner of my brain, an emergency exit sign had just come on.

Later I looked for a backup of the relevant Word file. I didn't find one. Since then, I'd changed computer twice and lost most of my data one stormy night.

At the end of that day, I rang my editor to tell her the news: I was going back to an unfinished novel, having just found the sole copy to have survived my house moves. There was a huge amount of work to do – it all had to be rewritten; but for the first time in ages, I'd rediscovered the desire to do so. My editor asked me if I was sure. Was it really a good idea to exhume an old text? Wasn't it like putting on a dress that no longer suited me or shoes that had become too tight?

I told her I was confident: I had my hands on ample raw material, raw but precious, and I knew what to do with it.

I remember talking to her about the text, what it might turn into, now that I had the perspective to see its naiveté. My editor was glad to hear from me. It was good news; she was eager to have something to read.

When I hung up, I thought about going down to the copy shop to get the manuscript copied and sending it to her at once, but quickly thought better of it. I'd rather my editor read the revised version.

I had only just finished this conversation when the phone rang. Automatically, I looked out the window at the building opposite. (A few days earlier I'd become aware of this strange reflex, the first occurrence of which I cannot date: when I returned home, when I put on the light, at the slightest unusual noise, my eyes would turn to the stairwell of the building opposite to make sure no one was watching me.)

I saw L.'s name appear on screen and took the call. As she often did, L. asked how my day had been, what I'd done, whether I'd gone out. Had I dragged myself round Monoprix again? It only took a few minutes of bland exchanges for L. to notice a change in my mood.

'Is there something new? Have you started on something?'

At first I kicked it into touch. It was too soon to talk about it. I tried to divert her, to shift the conversation onto other things, but L. wasn't one to be fobbed off.

'Tell me, Delphine. Something's going on. I can tell from your voice.'

I was amazed. I'd never met anyone who had such intuition about other people, a sort of sixth sense. Precise. Sharp. Honed.

L. was right. Something uncertain and tiny had happened.

I'd rediscovered the manuscript. I was launching once more into the possibility of writing. I had regained a sense of hope.

Gently, L. coaxed me to talk about it. She was dying to hear more.

I sat down. I wanted to weigh my words. Not deceive her. Not offend her. I wanted to take time to explain and suddenly I felt like a teenager about to announce to her parents that she's leaving the path they've mapped out for her.

Choosing my words carefully, I explained to L. that I'd found a manuscript, a novel, and had reread it. It struck me as interesting. There was a lot of work to do, but it could be a good starting point. I wanted to give it a go.

Yes, it was fiction. 'Pure' fiction.

On the other end of the line, L. let the silence last a long time. And then she said: 'If you're so sure of yourself, that's good. You're probably right. You're the one who knows, anyway.'

It was only after I hung up that I said to myself: her voice had changed. An inflection of distress had made that sentence almost inaudible which, rather than reassuring me, reminded me how lost I was. No, I didn't know; I didn't know anything.

I didn't hear from L. for two days. I spent the time making notes on the manuscript, separating what seemed worth saving from what was best forgotten. Gradually I began to glimpse what this story could become once it was recast.

One evening, L. rang to invite me to her birthday, which she was organising for the following day. She mentioned that there were unlikely to be more than five or six people, because she preferred intimate gatherings. I was definitely not to bring a gift or flowers (which she couldn't bear); if I had to bring something, just a bottle of wine.

I said yes without hesitation. I hadn't seen anyone for two or three weeks. I was happy to get out for a bit and meet some of her friends. I suggested I arrived early to help her prepare and she readily accepted. We'd have time to talk a bit before the others got there.

That Saturday, I arrived at around seven. Everything was ready.

L. removed the apron from round her waist and offered me an aperitif. She was wearing a short, close-fitting leather skirt and opaque tights, a very simple black T-shirt made of slightly shimmery material. I realised that this was the first time I had seen her in such a sexy outfit.

There was a gentle aroma of cinnamon and spices in the apartment. L. had just put a tagine with apricots in the oven, a recipe she'd already successfully tried out and which she was sure I'd like, since I liked sweet and savoury combinations.

The counter that separated the kitchen from the living room was covered in various multicoloured foods, presented in a selection of little bowls. L. had made it all herself: aubergine dip, hummus, taramasalata, marinated peppers. Some desserts, apparently homemade, were arranged on the sideboard.

No, she said, there was nothing I could do to help. It was all ready. She was pleased I'd come early.

It occurred to me that L. must have spent two days in the kitchen making all this.

I sat down in the living room. She'd lit perfumed candles and put half-a-dozen plates and sets of cutlery on a side table. That way, she explained from the kitchen as she checked the oven temperature, everyone can help themselves and sit where they like. I looked around. The room was lit by a set of identical little lamps, tastefully positioned. The low, glass-topped table was impeccably polished. Like the first time, I had the sensation of being in an artificial environment, created from scratch. L.'s living room – its lighting, the selection of materials and colours, the precise positioning of every object and its distance from the others – all seemed straight out of one of those reality TV shows in which the expert, over the course of a weekend, transforms your interior into a double-page advert for IKEA.

For as long as I can remember, I've had trouble showing an interest in interior decor. As soon as there are people in my field of vision, the decor fades and disappears. If I go to a new place with François (such as a restaurant), afterwards I'm able to describe, with an accuracy that amazes him, the people who were around us, the type of relationships they had, their clothes and hair; the main thrust of their conversations rarely escapes me. François, on the other hand, can describe, without missing a single detail, the arrangement of the room, its atmosphere, the type of furniture and, when the situation arises, the ornaments and other little objects that were there. I will not have taken in any of this.

And yet in L.'s apartment there was something that disturbed me without me being able to put my finger on what it was.

L. poured me a glass of white wine while we waited for her friends. We talked about various things; L. had all sorts of anecdotes to relate about the more or less famous personalities she had worked for. That evening, L. was more forthcoming than usual about her work. She talked about the close bond that was forged over several months, meeting after meeting, but then lapsed into silence. She never saw any of the people she had ghosted for afterwards. That was just how it was, maybe because of the necessary, sudden intimacy, which later became awkward.

Time passed and we remained in her living room, waiting for her friends.

L. got up from time to time to check how her tagine was doing in the oven and I would take the opportunity to glance at my watch.

At around eight thirty, we opened a bottle of Meursault and began sampling the little appetisers that L. had made.

When, around nine, no one had arrived, L. went and turned off the oven, so that the meat wouldn't dry up. She didn't seem worried; in fact she seemed to be rather exaggerating her air of calm. She said that she hadn't specified a time in her invitation, and people were always busy with all sorts of chores on Saturdays.

A little later I asked L. if she'd checked her mobile was on, in case her friends had had some problem.

Around nine forty-five L. got up to look at the time on the oven and declared that they wouldn't be coming. Her voice was no longer so assured. I didn't dare question her further and suggested we waited a little longer.

At ten o'clock, as we opened a second bottle, I asked L. if her friends had said they'd all be coming together. She didn't know. I suggested she call them, or at least some of them, to see what was up.

L. replied that there was 'no point'. It struck me that she'd gone to a lot of trouble for nothing if no one came. I asked L. if she'd spoken to them on the phone when she invited them.

L. said no. She'd sent an email, as she did every year. And just like every year, they hadn't come.

At around ten fifteen I gave L. the cashmere scarf I'd bought her, in spite of her instructions. When she unwrapped the scarf and unfolded it, I saw she had a lump in her throat. Her cheeks flushed and she was holding back her tears. For a moment, I thought she might break down in front of me. So to comfort her, I put my arms around her. For a few seconds, I thought I could feel from her body the struggle that was going on between display and capitulation. When I freed her from my embrace, L. had regained her composure and smiled at me.

'I said no presents! But thank you, it's wonderful.'

At around ten thirty, by which time L. seemed to have forgotten about it, I took the tagine out of the oven and we had two scalding platefuls.

Later, perhaps because we'd almost finished the second bottle of wine, L. told me that since her husband's death, her friends (the ten or so people that they used to see regularly when Jean was still around) no longer responded. Every year on this day, which was not only her birthday but also the anniversary of Jean's death, she continued to invite them all the same. But they never came.

I tried to find out more, but as soon as I started asking questions, L. clammed up.

After a few minutes' silence, L. told me she didn't feel ready to talk about it. She could no longer face the risk of being judged.

She promised she'd tell me some day. I let it drop.

Later, L. spent a few minutes in the bathroom. While she was gone, I looked at the empty room, the pretty plates arranged in piles, the untouched food. I remember thinking about all that effort, and it seemed terribly sad.

When she came back, we tried the various desserts and put on some music.

I laughed, I can't remember why.

After midnight, when we were on to our third or fourth toast, L. got interested in the manuscript I'd rediscovered. Had I started work? Had I got anyone to read it? I told L. that it seemed too early; I wanted to make some progress first.

In the hall, as I was about to leave, she looked sadly at me as I put on my coat and took my hand to thank me.

'Good thing you came. You don't know what that means to me.'

And then, in the soft voice I was beginning to recognise, she asked me to let her read – her and only her – the rediscovered manuscript. Completely confidentially.

I promised.

When I got home, I closed the curtains before turning on the light.

The hypothesis that L. could have conceived and executed this whole masquerade with the sole aim of cajoling or moving me came into my mind much later.

I sat down on the sofa, looked around and experienced a strange sort of relief. And suddenly, by contrast, it struck me what disturbed me about L.'s apartment.

Nothing in it was worn or faded or damaged. No object, or piece of furniture, or fabric hinted at any previous life. Everything was new. Everything seemed to have been bought the day before or a few weeks ago. The rooms had no soul; there was no mess.

I hadn't seen a single photo or postcard or trinket that could evoke any memory.

As though yesterday had never existed. As though L. had reinvented herself.

'No, honestly, it won't work. I'd rather be straight with you, even if it seems a bit harsh. It's not a question of work; it's something else. It's a text without a pulse, written at some point in the past, in unknown circumstances. How could it possibly be linked today to your trajectory, your evolution, to what you need to write? Trust me. I'm not saying it's rubbish or that no one will be interested. I'm saying that it's no longer your thing. It no longer has anything to do with you, the author you've become. It would be an incomprehensible backward step. A disaster. I read it, of course, all the way through, obviously I did. You asked me to tell you what I thought and I'm allowing myself to tell you that it would be a mistake, a serious mistake, even completely revised and corrected; even improved, transformed and revisited. It's not a question of maturity. I don't want to discourage you. I don't want you to think for one second that I don't think you can do it. You know how much I believe in you. But not this. It's a non-starter. If I were you, I'd stick it back in the bottom of the drawer where you found it. You're scared. You're panicking. You're ready to pounce on the first bone you come across. But it always comes back to this, you see, it always comes back to the same point: you're blocked because you refuse to write what you need to write. This isn't a projection on my part. It's something I sense within you. I sensed it from when we first met. I sensed you were afraid. You're afraid to follow your nose. You're wrong because it's not up to you to choose the kind of writer you are. I'm sorry. It's just not up to you. And while we're on the subject, I sometimes wonder if you shouldn't be suspicious of the comfort you live in, your little life that's ultimately quite comfortable, with your children, your man, writing, all carefully gauged. I sometimes wonder – and this is just a thought – but I sometimes wonder if it's not just a bit . . . numbing. Maybe you need that, that balance. I get that. I know what I'm talking about. I know what character flaw deepens the violence and that it can't be repaired. You think you need it because you lack confidence, but be careful you don't fall asleep. I understand you're scared, but fear is no protection, fear doesn't prevent the danger. You know that. And I know where the danger comes from. What your Achilles heel is. I know the kind of attack they'll use to bring you down, so don't let them, that's all I want to say. They're well aware of how to get at you and have no idea of what literature is, forgive me. You have to admit it. Who do I mean? *You* know. I'm just saying that you don't have to give in on the pretext of preserving links that are long gone and no one but you believes in. Ask yourself who really loves you. Since that's what we're talking about. I'm not sure that you can do without solitude; I even think that it's in your interest to prepare for it, because that's the writer's lot, to dig a ditch around herself – I don't think there's any other way. Writing doesn't fix anything, at least that's something we agree on. It digs, it furrows, it marks out ever-wider, ever-deeper trenches, it creates the emptiness around you. A necessary space. But, to come back to this text, yes, of course, if you send it to your publisher, they're not going to say no. They'll encourage you, they'll tell you it's a good idea. They're not crazy – they need you to bring a bit of money into the coffers. But make no mistake, that's all that interests them. Even if your next book is bad, they'll manage to flog it to a few thousand readers. And since they are accountable to the people upstairs, they'll not make problems, believe me. But just think a bit about what you need to do, about the score you're playing from. You're afraid of emptiness, but you mustn't give in. Since we're on the subject.'

The next day I put the manuscript back in the bottom of the trunk where I'd found it.

I told my editor a few days later. She didn't ask to see it and didn't seem surprised. She advised me to take my time, as much time as I needed.

I hadn't talked to François about the manuscript and no longer had any reason to do so, as I'd given up on it so quickly. When he wasn't travelling, François spent entire days reading books; it was the core of his job. In some respects, his job brought us closer. We could converse for hours about other people's books; we liked sharing our discoveries, our enthusiasms, discussing our differences of opinion. But I wasn't just a reader. I wrote books. Books on which he was likely to express his judgement. That's probably why I refused to show him my prose and sometimes wouldn't even talk about it. I was afraid of disappointing him. I was afraid he'd stop loving me. Two years before, when I finished the first version of my previous book, I'd refused to show it to him. He only saw the text when the first proofs had been printed.

Writing was my most intimate, isolated and protected place. The least shared. A free zone, which I only talked about on the surface, sparingly. Most of the time I talked to my editor before embarking on a book, then long months would go by before I sent a first draft of the complete text.

That's the way I'd always done it.

What L. had very quickly grasped was: writing is a defended territory, off limits to visitors. But now that territory had been undermined, assailed by doubt and fear, and this solitude was becoming unbearable.

I wanted to fight alone, but I needed an ally.

A few days later I was trying to answer my mail when I realised it had become almost impossible for me to remain seated at the computer for more than five or ten minutes. In addition to the fear I felt when I turned on the machine (a violent tightening sensation in my chest), it was increasingly painful, physically, to face the screen, even for the short time it took to answer a few emails. Writing was becoming a battle. Not only writing a book (which to be honest was no longer an issue), but any writing at all: replying to friends, to requests passed on by my publisher, putting words together to construct sentences, however humdrum. I hesitated over expressions, doubted my grammar, tried unsuccessfully to find the right tone. Writing had become a trial of strength and I wasn't up to it.

And always in front of the screen there was this burning in my throat preventing me breathing.

I hadn't told L. that I'd refused to write a short story for a women's magazine and postponed, for the third time, an opinion piece a weekly had asked me to write.

I hadn't told L. that I was six weeks overdue with the preface to a new edition of Maupassant's last novel, which I'd agreed to write a year before.

I hadn't told L. that I couldn't string three words together.

My hands shook and a mute, confused panic throbbed in my veins.

One evening I agreed to go with François to the opening of an exhibition organised by one of his friends. I hadn't been out since L.'s birthday.

We were among the first to arrive. We greeted the host and looked at the prints on the wall, which included a series of black-and-white portraits from the sixties that I liked very much. A drinks reception had been arranged. I was glad I'd come. I took a glass of champagne and looked around. It was time to converse, exchange opinions over a drink, show sociability. While I hesitated over plunging in (it's true that you lose the power of speech if you stay at home), I saw some writers and journalists I knew arrive. People I should, at very least, greet. But instead of going up to say hello, I saw myself retreat, an absurd movement of withdrawal and panic, retreating as I might have done if I'd been overcome with dizziness on a ledge 60 feet above the ground, flattening myself against a solid surface. Back against the wall. Exactly like when I was at parties aged fifteen and an invisible force would push me to the edge, the periphery, the margin. Blending in to the background rather than risking being seen. That evening, the same force pushed me out of the circle, unable simply to say, Hello, how are you? An angry voice in my head said: Shit, Delphine, you've done it dozens of times, you know how to do it, be straightforward and natural, be yourself. But it was too late. It was off to a bad start, I was adrift. Across the room, François had turned round and was looking at me with concern.

In less than two minutes, I had travelled back thirty years and become once more the timid, aloof girl who couldn't play the game.

This was what I had come to as a result of not writing, of not being able to write; this was what awaited me if I didn't find a way out: unprecedented regression.

I'd lost count of the number of people I should have called back, to whom I'd promised a drink, lunch, dinner; people who, in normal times, I would have been delighted to see, but not now – what could I tell them? That I no longer had the slightest idea, the slightest inclination. I wonder if I haven't been on the wrong path from the start. I wonder what I'm doing here, in the middle of nowhere. I'm a broken-down writer. It's such a cliché I don't even dare express it. Broken-down, yes, I'm sorry. It's pathetic, but no, it's not a question of time or success or anything like that; it's so much deeper. I can't explain it; it has to do with the very essence of writing, its raison d'être. Perhaps I was wrong from the start, perhaps there's nothing for me to do here. I missed a turning in the road that it would have been wise to take, another life, yes, a different kind of life, less presumptuous, less vain, less exposed. I don't know why I'm saying this. Tiredness probably, but it sometimes seems to me that some strange particle has got into my brain and the trans-missions, the connections, the desires are scrambled, all the things that didn't work too badly are now prone to jolts and breakdowns. So I prefer to remain alone, you see, stay on the sidelines for a while. Don't hold it against me. I'd be happy to hear your news if I didn't need to give you mine in exchange, but I'm well aware that that's not how it works.

One morning I got a call from the editor for whom I'd agreed to write a preface for Maupassant's novel, *Notre Coeur*, which was going to be republished in a liter-ary classics series. I should have delivered my text a few weeks earlier, but I'd buried my head in the sand and not given any sign of life.

The young woman was getting worried. The book had been announced in the catalogue and couldn't be postponed again, especially since a lot of secondary school teachers had already planned to put it on their syllabuses.

When I hung up, I was seized with panic. Writing a preface was manifestly beyond me. I wasn't even capable of writing an email to ask for more time or to withdraw. Worse, dozens of unanswered messages had accumulated in my inbox, most of them unopened.

That afternoon, I experienced a sort of final jolt (a few days previously I'd read a scientific article on the final jolt of dying cells, which is probably why that expression came into my mind). I couldn't give in without having tried: going for broke, as they used to say on a game show my grandmother watched when I was a child.

I must at least write this preface. I'd agreed to do it. If I didn't keep my word, if I didn't stick to something, I'd lose control.

I was familiar with the novel. I'd read it several times. I could pull it off; I *had* to pull it off.

I turned on the computer, determined to honour the commitment I'd made.

I forced myself to keep breathing long enough for the machine to launch its main applications and bring up the Office icons. I tried to adopt a relaxed attitude, the attitude of someone who's not terrified by the idea of facing the blank page with a silent cursor blinking in the middle. I opened the file the publisher had emailed me, which contained the questionnaire I was supposed to fill in. But I'd scarcely had time to see the page come up before I was seized with an overwhelming nausea. I rushed to the waste-paper bin and threw up. I couldn't get my breath back. I had to get away, that's what I felt, as far away from the keyboard as possible so that this would stop. Between retches, doubled up, trying to drag the waste-paper basket with me, I crawled to the bathroom. Once I had closed the door, I threw up the last of the bile in the basin.

When I'd rinsed my face and brushed my teeth, I saw my pale face in the mirror. I looked like someone who had just glimpsed the worst. The image of the computer, the thought of the computer, gripped my skull like a vice.

Then I realised I was *at the bottom of the pit*, right at the bottom.

It wasn't just an image. I saw myself very clearly at the bottom of a pit whose smooth sides made any attempt to climb out in vain. I saw myself – for a few seconds I had this vision of myself in terrifying detail – at the bottom of a pit full of earth and mud.

Today it's tempting to think that this vision was nothing other than a premonition.

I came out of the bathroom and called L. for help.

I called her, and no one else, because at that moment she seemed the only person able to understand what I was going through.

L. arrived within half an hour.

She took off her coat, made tea, then made me sit in the armchair by the window. L. asked me for my computer password.

L. sat down in my place, at my desk.

L. said: 'We'll start by answering your mail and then we'll write the preface.'

L. read out the diplomatic expressions she used to explain a refusal or postpone a reply. From her lips, it all seemed so simple. So fluent.

L. told me she'd also get in touch with people I knew who'd contacted me in recent weeks and whom I'd apparently not answered either. Then she wrote a letter to the residents' association in my building, which I had let slide.

Lastly she came to the preface.

The text I had to write would be presented as an interview. That was the idea behind the series: a contemporary writer explains why he or she loves a reissued classic. L. read out the structure suggested by the publisher, fifteen or so questions I was supposed to respond to. She seemed happy with that. That was lucky; all I had to do was talk to her about the text and she would take care of knocking it into shape. After all, that was her job, and in two or three days we'd have it done.

L. replied to the editor to propose a delivery date.

L. came round again the next day, and the day after that.

I told L. why I liked the novel. I sat in the armchair by the window, quite close to her, while she wrote.

On the final day, just after she'd printed out the text so that I could look it over, L. picked up a pen to jot down some detail that had just occurred to her.

Leaning over the manuscript, and probably feeling relief at having finished, L., who had told me she was left-handed (and had been in my presence), held her pen in her right hand and wrote perfectly legibly.

Yes, I should have expressed surprise.

Yes, I should have asked L. why she was suddenly writing with her right hand.

Yes, I should have asked why she had suddenly started wearing ankle boots like mine.

I should have thanked her and made clear that there was no need for her to come back the next day, as we'd finished.

That evening, while L. was still at my apartment, the editor acknowledged receipt of the preface. It was just what she wanted; she was delighted.

Then I did something I often do with my friends: I gave L. a hug of gratitude. I felt her body stiffen in contact with mine. L. withdrew from the embrace and looked at me, moved: she was very happy she could help and free me up from a few things, if that would enable me to refocus on the essential.

She repeated that phrase: refocus on the essential.

Now that I'm setting out the facts, reconstructing them more or less in the order in which they occurred, I'm aware of a sort of pattern emerging, as though in invisible ink, the gaps that offer a glimpse of L.'s slow and confident progress, strengthening her hold by the day. And with reason: I'm writing this story in the light of what this relationship turned into and the damage it did. I know the fear it plunged me into and the violence with which it ended.

Now that I'm able once again to sit in front of the screen (in what state is another story) and even if that ability remains fragile, I'm trying to understand. I'm trying to establish links, connections, theories. I'm well aware that this commitment may encourage the reader to develop a certain mistrust towards L. A mistrust that I didn't feel. Surprise, amusement, perplexity, yes. But not mistrust. Mistrust came much later.

François went back abroad to complete his documentary and I entered a period of great isolation.

This period lasted several months and I find it hard today to delineate it.

I have to admit that reference points get mixed up, confused, all the more so since my diary reveals nothing: the pages I'm turning over now are blank. The only exceptions are Louise and Paul's visits, their initials marked in blue pen, and a few weekends when I left Paris to visit them, a breath of fresh air that got me out of my torpor.

Once the preface had been written and sent off, I agreed to L. coming round to impose a little order. She'd noticed that correspondence and bills were piling up on my desk, sometimes unopened, and was worried they would become overdue.

L. signed some cheques and bank payment orders on my behalf, and answered numerous letters (insurance, union, bank . . .), then dealt with the bills I'd let slip.

L. looked after answering the various requests that continued to come in, mostly via my press agency.

I watched L. turn the computer on, open a pad of writing paper, choose an envelope of the appropriate size, sort my emails; in short, act as though she were at home, and it all seemed simple. To tell the truth, she was using her left hand again, with an ease that would have been hard to fake, which was why I came to believe that I'd been mistaken the day I thought I saw her writing with her right.

'You've reached a point in your life where it's getting dangerous to give your trust,' she declared one morning after she'd spent nearly an hour on my computer.

'Why do you say that?'

'Because I'm well placed to see the traps that are laid for you. I'm well placed to know what your publisher, your friends, your family, your acquaintances expect of you now. And what they're doing to lead you there, all the while pretending to stay out of it.'

'But all those people have very little to do with each other and probably expect different, even contradictory, things of me.'

'I'm not so sure, Delphine. They're all encouraging you to lead a particular sort of life without taking the risk that you are. To go back to your old ways in a sense, to the nice, compassionate stock in trade that was your literary trademark.'

'I don't get what you're talking about.'

'I just want to draw your attention to it. It might be time to show a little discernment in the way you approach the outside world. None of the people you consider close have any idea what you're going through. None of the people you think you've chosen as friends knows what a struggle you're engaged in just now. Who's worried? I mean, who's *really* worried?'

I still didn't see what she was driving at, but I couldn't let her get away with saying whatever she liked. 'The people who love me are worried, or at least are interested because I'm worried. They're interested to the extent that's reasonable, the way people are interested in the life of someone they love and wish well.'

'OK . . . if you say so. That's not the impression I got, that's all. Few people put themselves forward if you don't call them up. Few people cross the barricades we've planted in the unstable, marshy ground of our trenches. Few people are able to come and look for us where we really are. You're like me, Delphine, you're not the sort who asks for help. At best, you may mention afterwards, ideally in passing, that you've been through a tough time. But as for asking for help in the present, at the time when you're sinking, or drowning, I bet you've never done that.'

'I have. I do. Now I do. For concrete things that I know this person or that can help me with. It's one of the things I've eventually learned to do.'

'But don't you think that real friends are ones that you don't have to call?'

'I don't know what "real friends" means. Either you're friends or you're not. And when you're friends, there are times when you can force the barriers and other times when that's harder.'

'But have your friends been able to break down the barriers, to impose at the right moment, without asking?'

'Yes, of course. That's happened several times.'

'For instance?'

'I've got lots of examples.'

'Tell me just one.'

'Well, for instance, when the father of my children and I separated a long time ago, I went through a strange time. It happened in stages without me realising, after I moved out. Gradually I stopped phoning my friends, asking after them, I let days and weeks go by. I was hunched over my pain. I hibernated. I hid myself away to shed my skin; I don't know, it was a form of detachment I'd never experienced, as though nothing counted any more apart from the children. I had no strength. It lasted a few months. Most of my friends continued to keep in touch, to call me, show they were there, even at a distance. One Friday night in March at about eight o'clock, after Louise and Paul had gone off to their father's for the weekend, the bell rang. I opened the door. Chloé and Julie were standing there with a birthday cake and the candles were lit. They started singing on the stairs. I could see them both smiling in the candlelight. Their smiles said: we came anyway, it doesn't really matter what state we find you in. I didn't cry, but I was very moved. What really got me, you see, what still gets me when I tell the story, is the cake. Because they could have got a tart from Picard or any baker's on my street. But they didn't. Hundreds of miles away, they'd made an almond pithivier with perfect sugar icing. They'd transported it in a box, taking all the necessary precautions. They'd thought of candles and a lighter (neither of them smoked), they'd arranged to meet in the same carriage on the TGV (one of them was coming from Nantes and the other from Angers) and then they'd taken the metro and come up the stairs with their overnight bags. Once they were outside my door, they put the candles in, lit them and rang the bell. I was so moved, seeing them at my door for my birthday, with a homemade cake. It was like a promise of a life where there would always be indulgence and kindness. It was a promise of great joy.

'A few years later, when my mother died, Tad and Sandra, the childhood friends I've told you about, who lived far apart, caught the train to Paris. They took time off work to pay their respects to my mother, to help me, to be with me.'

L. had been listening carefully, without saying a word. She smiled.

'Those are nice stories. But they're from before.'

'Before what?'

'Before all this.'

She cast her eyes around without indicating anything in particular. I didn't ask her to explain; she gave the impression she hadn't understood.

'What would be interesting now would be to see who might come to your door on a Friday night when you haven't asked for anything. In your opinion, which of your friends would show up unexpectedly?'

'Now it's different. Now I have François.'

'Where?'

I pretended not to have noted the irony.

'In my life. My friends know that. They know I can count on him.'

'That's good. OK, I imagine it's different. Let me say, between ourselves, I'm not sure anyone can protect you from yourself. But OK. And maybe that explains ultimately why no one's too worried by your silence.'

I had no desire to continue this conversation, which I considered unfair and cruel. Could I allow myself to remind L. that not only did her friends not phone on her birthday, they didn't even come round when she invited them? Could I allow myself to tell L. that she came across as someone very alone, someone who had created a huge void around her?

I reckoned that L.'s bitterness stemmed from her own loneliness and that made me sad. I couldn't hold it against her. L. had lost her husband. Something serious had happened in her life, cutting her off from most of her friends. L. was projecting onto me things that didn't apply. But in her way, she was trying to help.

It was almost noon and L. said she had a lunch appointment.

She left, having advised me to get some fresh air; I looked like death.

It was only a few days later that I came to the conclusion that L. was right. Apart from François and the children, it had been some time since anyone had written or phoned.

That was most likely how L. established herself in my life, with my consent, by a sort of gradual process of enchantment.

I've often tried to identify the flaw that made me so vulnerable. So permeable.

I was receiving increasingly aggressive anonymous letters.

The children had left home and had begun making their own lives elsewhere.

The man I loved was busy with his work, his trips and a thousand projects, which I encouraged him to accept. We'd chosen this lifestyle that left room for other obsessions, other passions. Out of naiveté or overconfidence, we'd believed ourselves safe from any attempt at conquest.

When you're an adult, friendship is built on a kind of recognition, of complicity: a shared territory. But it seems to me that in the other person we also look for something that we only possess in a minor, embryonic or frustrated form. So we tend to form links with those who have been able to develop a way of being that we incline towards but have not attained.

I know what I admire about each of my friends. In every case I could name what quality she possesses that I do not, or possess in too small a quantity.

L. probably embodied a sort of assurance, reflection, conviction in my eyes, which I felt I lacked.

L. returned almost every afternoon.

L. was better than anyone at divining my mood, my worries, and seemed to have a pre-existing awareness of the events that concerned me. She had the upper hand over me in a way that none of my friends ever had.

L. remembered everything. Since the very first time, she'd registered the most insignificant anecdote, the smallest detail, dates, places, names mentioned in passing in conversation. I did wonder if she might be taking notes after each time we met. Today, I know that it was second nature for her, a type of selective hyperthymesia.

L. seemed the only person to have appreciated the struggle I was engaged in, in which the stakes might well seem ridiculous – whether or not I wrote a book would not change the way the world turned – but L. had understood that it affected my centre of gravity.

L. had become necessary, indispensable to me. She was there. And perhaps I needed that: for someone to be interested in me exclusively. Don't we all have that crazy desire? A desire that comes from childhood and that we've had to abandon, sometimes too early. A desire that, by the time we're adults, we know to be egocentric, excessive and dangerous. But to which we succumb nevertheless.

L. probably filled a sort of emptiness I was unaware of, soothed a fear I couldn't have named.

L. caused the reappearance of something I believed to be buried, repaired.

L. seemed to fill that insatiable need for solace that exists in all of us.

I didn't need a new friend. But in the course of our conversations, and through the constant attention she showed me, I eventually came to believe that L. alone could understand me.

L. rang me very early one morning. Her voice was less controlled than usual, she seemed slightly breathless. As I began to get worried, she confessed that she had a few problems, nothing serious, but she had a favour to ask: could I put her up for two or three weeks until she found a new apartment?

L. moved in with me the following Monday. She arrived with a boy of about twenty. The boy's height, his exceptionally long eyelashes and the adolescent nonchalance of his movements encouraged your eyes to linger. He was handsome.

He'd called round to her place a little earlier and helped her to transport the four sizeable suitcases that she had chosen to bring. He was scarcely through the door before he went back downstairs to collect the ones he'd left there. He put them down on the landing, then went back again to collect some bags from L.'s car. I live on the sixth floor and there's no lift, but the boy didn't seem to be struggling. When I saw all the luggage, it occurred to me that L. had thought big. I couldn't imagine her moving without some of her wardrobe and she'd probably brought some of her work files.

When the boy returned for the third time, I offered him coffee. He turned to L., seeking her approval, but

L. appeared to ignore his questioning look. After a few seconds, the boy declined.

When he'd gone, I asked L. who he was. She laughed. What did it matter? It doesn't, I said, I was just curious. L. told me he was the son of a friend. She never said his name, didn't thank him and barely said goodbye.

I'd planned to put L. in Paul's room. I remembered she had really admired the colour of the walls the first time she visited. I gave L. time to unpack. I'd cleared several shelves and part of the cupboard so that she could put her things away. I'd made the bed and cleared the desk, on which she had soon installed her laptop. She had very little time left to finish the actress's biography to meet the publisher's deadline; that was why it was impossible for her to look for a new apartment at the moment. I never found out why she'd had to move out in such a rush.

It wasn't long before I realised that L. had moved in almost everything she owned, apart from four or five boxes she'd been able to leave in a neighbour's cellar. L. had no furniture, she explained; she'd sold everything after her husband's death (she emphasised *everything* several times, indicating that no object had escaped this decision). Since then, she'd always preferred to rent furnished apartments. She didn't want to weigh herself down, still less establish roots. On the other hand, L. did own clothes. A lot of them, she freely admitted.

---

I have few memories of the first few weeks L. spent with me.

That's probably because she was very busy with the manuscript she was working on and rarely came out of her room. Through the door I could hear her listening over and over to her interviews, the raw material, hesitant and sometimes confused, from which she worked. She would stop at a phrase, go back and replay it. She could listen to the same passage ten times, as though she was trying to catch something beyond the words that could not be expressed and that she had to guess at. She would fill a teapot with boiling water, and then go four or five hours without leaving her room in a silence that nothing could disturb. I didn't hear her chair slide across the floor. I never heard her pace around to stretch her legs. I never heard her cough or open the window. Her ability to concentrate impressed me.

I'd hoped that living with L. would help me get down to work.

It had often struck me that it was easier to work alongside someone. In relative solitude. I like the idea that not far from me someone else is in a similar situation and is making the same effort. That's why, as a student, I spent so much time in the library.

But L.'s assiduousness at her desk did not stop me pacing the floor.

I couldn't now say what I was doing; the time slipped by, but nothing emerged.

During the morning, I would make a salad or some pasta for L. and me.

Around one, I'd call her and we'd have a quick lunch at the little kitchen table, sitting opposite each other.

Then I'd go for long solitary walks. I'd wrap myself in the huge orange scarf L. had given me the day she moved in, and I would walk. I dreamt about books I was no longer able to write. I trailed around outside until nightfall. I would always finish these wanderings by crossing the square where I used to take Louise and Paul when they were little. At a time when the play area was empty, I would stand in front of the slides and the rocking animals and try to summon up their faces as children. I'd seek their laughter, the sound of coarse sand under their shoes; I'd see the colour of their hats, their wobbly first steps. Something happened here that is impossible to hold on to.

In the evening I'd sometimes hear L. on the phone. Quite long conversations whose tone I could catch but not content. I sometimes also heard her laugh – roar with laughter. As I never heard her mobile ring or vibrate, I remember wondering if L. was talking to herself.

After she'd settled in, L. came to take charge of everything – the mail, statements, subscriptions, in short, everything that required turning the computer on or picking up a pen. Things that seemed insurmountable to me, she dealt with in a few minutes.

When she'd answered correspondence on my behalf, she would give me a quick update on it in the evening: *we* had said no to such and such a thing; *we* had got an extension for another; *we* had postponed writing a short play for *Le Paris des femmes* till next year.

L. compensated for my failure. I was incapable of writing anything or of holding a pen for more than a few minutes, but in the end I wasn't doing so badly.

*We* were coping.

When L. went out on an errand or to a meeting, I couldn't stop myself going into her room. My eyes took it all in within seconds – the clothes on the chair, the shoes lined up under the radiator, the work left out. That was really what interested me most, and was probably my greatest indiscretion: looking at the drafts spread out on the table, corrected in pencil, covered in rubbings-out, which I drew my hand across without reading. And the ochre rings left by her teacup on the paper.

I looked at this space that she had taken possession of, the clear signs of work in progress, notes, Post-its, printed and corrected pages, and all this, far from being familiar to me, seemed to belong to an unknown world, a world that was forbidden to me.

It was at this time that L. began what I soon came to refer to as 'the bookcase ritual'. In the evening, several times a week, L. would devote several minutes to examining the books on the shelves in my living room.

She was not content merely to scan the spines casually, as most people do. She took the time to examine each shelf, sometimes taking a book out to handle it. Sometimes I'd see her face relax in a sign of approval; sometimes she'd frown, visibly displeased. And there would always come the moment, yet again, when she would ask me if I had read them all. Yes, almost all of them, I'd say again, apart from a few. So L. would run her finger from one book to another, reading the titles aloud, as though they were a single sentence, a huge, magnificent sentence whose meaning eluded me. Had I read the declaration, if on a winter's night a traveller, perfect happiness, by the seaside, not one day, the frozen woman, the echo chamber, boy heaven, the life of birds, cliffs, yesterday, after, now, what do you think of me, slow emergencies, Angelina's children, the invention of solitude, what we talk about when we talk about love, oh what a paradise it seems, pray for us, memories, the breakers, I loved her, all I loved, cries, bodies, Friday evening, the kites, the origin of violence, infamy, promenade, scraps, in the photo, in memoriam, sisters, the interval, tiny lives, the night watch, my little boy, other people's skin, any resemblance to the father, those who knew, Joséphine, the sexual night, beginning, the missing part, dead fist, the rain before it falls, between noises, the adversary, dry eyes, the interrogation, the surge, the future, the red notebook, the stand-in, too sensitive, toxic, childhood, play it as it lays, lost memory of skin.

Delphine,
Your lack of response proves how
ashamed you must be feeling. Rightly
so.

You're scary. You can tell just
by looking at how you dress, how
you stand, you only have to look at
your gestures, and see your crafty
look. And that's not new. It's
obvious that something about you's
not right, it's as plain as the nose
on your face, and things haven't
improved. You're not right in the
head, my child.

On the marketing side, no
complaints, you're the tops. As for
the packaging, you scrape by. You
start by selling your mother and
then you go out with a literary

journalist to do your promotion.
Hats off, you had no choice. The
poor man must have serious sexual
problems to be with a woman like
you. And do you believe he loves
you? Do you believe a man like him
could love a woman like you? When
he dumps you, I guess you'll turn
it into a book. One of those nice
crowd-pleasers you know how to churn
out. Give him my number and I'll
tell him a thing or two.
 You've caused a lot of harm around
you. Considerable damage.
 Do you know why?
 Because people believe what they
see in print. They believe it's true.
 And that's disgusting.


I slipped the typewritten sheet back in the envelope and put it away with the others. I told François about it on the phone without going into details. I said I'd received another letter, even more abusive than the previous ones. I reassured him: it wasn't that serious; they'd stop eventually.

At the time, I don't think I told L. about it.

One morning two or three days later, I got up, dressed, made some coffee and then all of a sudden, for no reason, burst into tears. L. was right in front of me and I had time to register her panicked expression before I got up and took refuge in my room. I cried for several minutes. I couldn't stop.

The letters were in my blood: a poison. Since the very first. They'd finally released their poison, a poison designed to be slow-release, capable of breaching all my immunity barriers.

When I re-emerged, L. handed me a packet of paper tissues. She'd made tea. She put her hand on my arm, visibly upset.

I calmed down and she asked to see the letters. She reread them in order, her lips pursed in disgust. She examined the paper as though it could provide an answer, on the lookout for the smallest detail that would betray their author's identity. The address was typed, like the text; the letters had been put in standard envelopes and posted in different districts of Paris. There was nothing more to be deduced from them.

L. found the right words to soothe me, to take the drama out of the situation. To put things back in place. I shouldn't get everything mixed up; take them at face value. L. reminded me of the warm messages I'd received from many people in my family after the book came out. That didn't mean it was straightforward for them, but it meant they'd understood. The book had not put their affection in doubt. In some cases, it may even have strengthened it. Of course, it was obvious that the author was someone close to me. Someone who had borne a grudge for ages, long before the book. Someone who had been nursing their hatred and anger and had now found the opportunity to vent it.

L. didn't think it was sad. Quite the reverse. My book had provoked something, had enabled that aggression to be expressed. An aggression that already existed. That was literature's vocation, a performative vocation, and that was fortunate. It was good news that literature had real-life consequences, that it provoked anger, contempt, jealousy. It meant something was happening. We were at the heart of the matter. And those letters should bring me back to the essential.

L. believed in the violence of domestic and familial relations as a source of literary inspiration. She had outlined this theory to me several times. This violence, whether dormant or expressed, was one of the necessary conditions of creation. Its starting point.

The letters were upsetting me. She could see that and she was sorry. She understood. These letters were eating away at me insidiously, because they were aimed at the child I'd once been but also the woman I'd become. Because they marked me out as guilty. Reminded me of the origin of the violence.

L. reread the last letter in silence before she said: 'Yes, people believe what's written and so much the better. People know that only through literature is it possible to access the truth. People know how much writing about yourself costs. They know how to recognise what's authentic and what isn't. And believe me, they never get that wrong. Yes, *people*, as your friend here says, want truth. They want to know that this existed. People no longer believe in fiction. I'd even go as far as to say they distrust it. They believe in the example, in testimony. Look around. Writers are writing about news stories, or looking inwards, or creating documentary accounts. They're interested in sportsmen, rogues, singers, kings and queens; they're investigating their own families. Why do you think that is? Because that is the only worthwhile material. Why go backwards? You mustn't pick the wrong fight. You're taking flight; you're intending to go back to fiction for one reason: you refuse to write the book that's haunting you. Yes, I'm sorry, I'm going back to that, but you're the one who talked about it, I'm not making it up. Anyway, those are the exact words you used, I reread the article. You can look for yourself – it's easy to find online. Whoever's sending those letters is afraid you'll start again. Those letters should open your eyes, give you the electric shock you need to regain the strength and courage to confront what's ahead of you. Writing is a combat sport. It involves risks; it makes you vulnerable. Otherwise it's worthless. You can put yourself in danger because I'm here. I'm here, Delphine, I won't leave you. I'll stay by your side, trust me, for as long as it takes. And no one will hurt you.'

When she launched into one of her monologues, L. was impervious to any argument. I listened without saying a word. I waited for her to finish before replying. Once again, I couldn't help but feel relieved that she was taking this all so much to heart. I spoke softly, as though to an exhausted child you fear you might anger: 'Yes, it's true, you're right. I remember it. I talked about a hidden book, the book I might write. I didn't rule out going back to it one day in some form or another. But not now. My work has led me somewhere else. I don't want to . . .'

L. interrupted:

'Where? Where has it led you? As far as I can see, right now it's led you precisely nowhere.'

I didn't answer. She was right.

And the fact was, she was here. She was the only person who was really here.

I think it was the same evening, or perhaps the next day, that L. saved me from choking. Subsequently, we often referred to this episode as 'the evening that L. saved my life'. We liked the emphatic sound of this phrase, its dramatic tone, as though it were a piece of third-rate fiction, a pseudo-epic incident in our friendship. But deep down each of us knew that that was exactly what had happened: L. had saved my life.

We were both in the kitchen making dinner, when I swallowed a salted almond, whole and sideways. I've had things go down the wrong way, but never that far. The almond was particularly large and I felt it enter my windpipe. My throat gave a sort of gasp of shock, and I immediately felt short of breath. I tried to cough, and then to speak, but there was no airflow, none at all, as though a tap had been shut off with a single turn. I looked at L. and saw in her eyes the exact moment when, having thought it was a bad joke, she realised what was happening. She hit me on the back three or four times without result, then she grabbed me from behind, put her arms around my body and with her fist gave me a sharp blow in the stomach. At her second attempt, the almond popped out and the air returned. I spent several minutes coughing. My throat was on fire and I had a sudden desire to be sick. Tears of pain and relief streamed from my eyes. I gradually regained my breath, and picked the almond up from the floor.

L. was watching me carefully now, looking for confirmation that everything was back to normal. After a minute, we started to laugh, increasingly loudly. And then, for the first time, L. hugged me. Then I could feel her body shaking and knew she'd been as scared as me.

Later, L. told me that she had a first-aid certificate but had never had occasion to use the Heimlich man-oeuvre, a method of clearing obstructed airways invented in the 1970s by an American doctor, she explained, which was generally taught using dummies. She had greatly enjoyed the experience.

In the days that followed, I had several nightmares. One night, I was woken by my own scream, a scream like the ones that used to rip through the night when, as a teenager, I dreamt that someone was smothering me with a cushion or shooting me in the legs with a rifle.

Since receiving that letter, my nights had been full of torn paper, burned books and ripped pages. Words of anger, indignation, rose up suddenly in my bedroom, an outraged murmur that brutally dragged me from sleep. I also remember a demented laugh of unutterable cruelty, which woke me one night and took several minutes to die away, even after my eyes were wide open.

I would find myself sitting up in bed, sweating, convinced that it was all real. I had to switch on the light and find familiar objects in my room for the beating of my heart to slow down. I then got up without making a noise, my bare feet on the wooden floor and then the tiles, to splash water on my face or make some herbal tea. I sat in the kitchen for an hour or two, long enough for the images to dissipate, before I was able to go back to bed.

I think it was around this time that I reread all the picture books that Louise and Paul had kept. We'd often talked about taking them down to the cellar, but none of us had been able to resolve to do it, and even now that they are twenty, the books are still in their bedrooms. In the middle of the night, I would carefully turn the pages, delightedly rediscovering the pictures that were part of their childhood and the stories I'd read to them a hundred times. The power of these books to bring back memories amazed me. Each of the stories reawakened the precious moment before sleep, the feeling of their little bodies against mine, the velvety softness of their pyjamas. I rediscovered the inflection I'd given to each sentence, the words they loved, which I used to have to repeat ten, twenty times. All of that came back to the surface, intact.

Almost every night, between the hours of four and five, I reread the stories of bears, rabbits, dragons, the blue dog and the musical cow.

I remember one night L. woke up and found me in the kitchen, absorbed in a picture book by Philippe Corentin that Louise loved: the story of a family of mice who live on top of a bookcase and eat the books. Louise was delighted by the thought that you could eat books, and especially the instruction the mother gives to the hero, her son, as he prepares to go off on an expedition with his cousin: 'Bring me back two pages of *Pinocchio*. Your father loves that in a salad!' Louise's childish laughter came back to me. I knew those lines by heart. I may even have been muttering them, smiling, when L. appeared. She filled the kettle, rummaged in the cupboard for a herbal tea and then sat down. She leafed through the book with her fingertips, holding the object at a fair distance (though stylised and colourful, they were mice), and then asked: 'What's the allegory, in your opinion?'

I didn't see what she was getting at. She continued: 'Mice that eat books, as though it were just paper. Isn't that a way of signifying the death of fiction, or at the very least of its normal vocation?'

'That's really got nothing to do with it,' I replied. 'That's not what the book's about at all! If it does have a message, it's nothing to do with that.'

'Really? So what's its message in your view?'

L. had shattered a moment of nostalgia and I was having trouble concealing my irritation. Besides, I had no desire to debate the hidden meaning of *Pipioli the Terror*, a picture book for three- to six-year-olds, at three in the morning.

I made to get up, but L. stopped me: 'You're refusing to see the context. It's the same with everything, Delphine, you refuse to see things as a whole, you make do with focusing on a detail.'

I felt attacked. I riposted in the meanest way possible, mortified with shame even as I asked the question:

'Tell me, if we're talking about context, how are you getting on with your search for an apartment?'

Not only was this unworthy of our friendship, but also I had no desire for her to go.

'If my presence is a burden, you only have to say the word and I'll leave immediately.'

She got up to put her cup in the dishwasher, the sugar in the cupboard. Her movements were brusque and betrayed her anger.

I stayed in my seat, stunned I was capable of saying something so stupid. She was now standing by my chair and she leaned over me: 'Look at me, Delphine. I won't say this again. One word from you and I shall disappear. Even before it's light. One word and that's the last you'll hear of me.'

I almost burst into nervous laughter and asked if she'd been taking lessons from the Actors' Studio, with Pacino or Brando. Her words contained a threat I couldn't ignore. I tried to defuse the situation.

'I'm sorry. That's not what I meant. That's ridiculous. You know you can stay as long as you want.'

L. sat down beside me. She took a deep breath.

'I'll start looking as soon as I've delivered the manuscript. Don't worry.'

We never spoke about this conversation again.

A few days later, when L. had finished the actress's book, we opened a bottle of pink champagne. L. had delivered on time, the publisher congratulated her on her work, and the actress was delighted.

That evening, L. revealed a little writer's quirk that she always adhered to. At the end of every text that she ghosted, she wrote the words 'The End', followed by a star (a sort of asterisk that didn't refer to anything). She insisted in her contract that this sign-off appeared at the end of the book. It was her fingerprint, her maker's mark, a sort of imprint known only to her.

Gently, I teased her. I thought that rather old-fashioned; it was rare to find the words 'The End' in books these days.

'You can tell it's the end,' I said jokingly, 'because there are no more pages!'

'No, I don't think so. I think the reader likes to be told. It's the words "The End" that allow him to emerge from the particular state in which he finds himself, which return him to his life.'


We spent much of the night listening to old records. I showed L. how to dance to ska, because she claimed she'd forgotten.

Sitting on the sofa, L. laughed at me jumping around my living room, then got up and copied me. She shouted over the music: 'Who remembers that ska existed? Who remembers The Specials and The Selecter? What if we're the only people?'

Lots of people remembered. People of our age, or thereabouts. Wasn't that, more than anything, what bound a generation together: shared memories of music videos, jingles, theme tunes? The impression of a poster for a film, an album or a book. But OK, if that was the way she wanted it, for one evening we could believe that we were the only ones who knew how to dance to ska, the only ones who knew the words to 'Missing Words' and 'Too Much Pressure', which we were now singing at the tops of our voices, waving our arms in the air. I caught sight of our reflections in the window and I hadn't laughed so much in ages.

One day when L. was out, I got a call from a radio journalist from France Culture who wanted to interview me about one of my previous novels. She was preparing something on harassment at work and wanted to know how I'd written my book on this and how I'd researched it.

I don't know why I agreed. Perhaps to prove to myself that I could do something by myself. Without L. This time I didn't need her to reply; this time, it was out of her control. I'd noticed that over time, or rather as I grew more distant from them in time, what I said about my books changed. As though something in their fabric – a relief, a motif – was only visible from afar. I was curious to know what design might reveal itself in the pattern of this one and pleased that someone was still interested. And if, until further notice, I was unable to write, I was still capable of talking.

Two days later, the journalist rang the buzzer. She'd told me on the phone that she generally visited people at home to record them in their own environment, with a minimum of equipment, meeting her guests in their world. After the interview, she would produce an edit that would feature in the programme.

We'd just had lunch when the young woman arrived. L. was in a gloomy mood. She disapproved of me still talking about books that weren't worth going back to.

L. disappeared into her room even before I greeted the journalist. The woman decided to sit in the living room; she asked me to half open the window to provide a bit of background ambience and then told me how the interview would work. We had coffee and she turned on her machine. I explained how the idea for my book had come to me one morning when I was feeling exhausted on Line D of the RER, and how I had developed it. Then we spent about an hour talking about various things. The journalist was friendly. I think I remember us talking about my neighbourhood, as she had lived here a few years previously, a couple of films that were on in the cinemas about the connections between violence and workplace relationships, and then the conversation drifted off into inconsequential stuff. At one point, just after we both laughed, I thought I heard L.'s door open. I wondered if she wanted to find out what was going on.

Later, as I went to the door with the young woman, she took out her diary to tell me when exactly the programme would go out. We shook hands, I closed the door and sensed L.'s presence close behind me. When I turned round, L. was blocking my way. For an instant, I thought I must have done something terrible and that access to my own apartment was now forbidden to me. But L. stepped aside to let me pass and followed me to the living room, like a disapproving shadow.

'Made a new friend?'

I laughed.

'You think I didn't hear you?'

I looked for the smile that would confirm she was joking, but her face left no doubt as to the tone of her words. I didn't get time to react.

'If you think that's how you'll get out of this, you're wrong. Yes, you heard, Delphine, and all this play-acting about where you're up to, "And so are you going back to fiction?"' – she made a gesture that put those words in inverted commas – 'what business is that of hers? Do we ask her what kind of journalism she does? With her Nagra recorder that cost two thousand euros? And who she is to have a view on the subject, eh? Did anyone ask her?'

The tiniest of her facial muscles seemed to express anger. L. was resentful because I had given the young woman so much time, had had a laugh with her, had allowed a pleasant afternoon to stretch on. She was accusing me of compromise and complacency. If a man had said these things to me, I would instantly have thought it was an access of jealousy and brought it to a halt without further discussion. As though she had read my thoughts, she softened slightly.

'I'm sorry. It makes me angry to see you wasting time. I'm not getting at you. You know how much I'd love you to find your path with your writing again. To do that, you're going to have to admit some day that you have no connection with the writer that people want you to be. It suits them, all of them, to stick a label on you and for you to conform to it. But I know you. I'm the only one who knows exactly who you are and what you can write.'

I don't know why – perhaps because I'd had a nice time and she'd just spoiled it – I exploded: 'Can't you see that I've no idea what sort of writer I am? Can't you see I can't do anything, that I'm utterly terrified? Can't you see I've reached the end and after that there's nothing? *Absolutely nothing*. You're getting on my nerves going on about the phantom book. There's no such thing. There is no hint of a hidden book, don't you get that? There's nothing up my sleeve, or behind the curtain, no taboo, no treasure, nothing forbidden! There is, however, a void. Take a good look at me. With a bit of luck, you'll see right through me.'

I took my coat and went out. I needed air.

François had been gone too long. I was missing him. I wandered the streets aimlessly. Later, I think I went to the cinema, I'm not entirely sure. Or perhaps I ended up in a café.

---

At about seven in the evening, I went home. The smell of vegetables cooking and chicken stock filled the apartment. I found L. in the kitchen, an apron around her waist. She was making soup. I sat down by her. I watched her for a few minutes without speaking. Her hair was pinned up with a grip; several strands seemed to have escaped from her bun, an unusual disorder in L.'s hair. She suddenly struck me as small, diminished, and then I noticed her bare feet and it occurred to me that this was the first time I'd seen her without heels. She smiled at me; we still hadn't exchanged a word. I smiled back. The oven was on and through the door I could see a dish browning. L. had apparently spent a good deal of time in the kitchen. She'd bought a bottle of wine and opened it. Everything seemed back to normal. I felt better. The afternoon's incident was just a strange, vague memory; I was no longer entirely convinced that the conversation had taken place. Smells mingled in the warmth of the room. I sat down. L. poured me a glass of wine.

When the vegetables were done, I watched L. transfer them into the liquidiser jug. She added some stock and then tried to turn the machine on. Once, twice, without success. I watched her unplug it and plug it back in. With a sigh, she checked that the jug was properly attached to the base. She looked at the blade at the bottom, checked with her fingers that it turned. Then I saw her start again from the beginning: assembling the machine piece by piece, plugging it in, trying to get it to work.

L. appeared calm. Worryingly so.

I was about to offer to take a look when L. raised the blender above her head and smashed it down on the work surface. She did it again, with a fury I had never seen in her before, bringing the blender down again and again with all her strength, until it shattered in several pieces. The blade landed at my feet.

L. suddenly stopped. She leaned on the table, out of breath, contemplating the broken parts of the machine scattered on the floor. I thought her rage had subsided, but in a final access of anger, she seized the rolling pin and, with two blows, smashed what remained of the machine.

And then she looked up at me. I'd never seen such a glint of victory and savagery as flashed in her eyes that evening.

From that day on, there was no further question of her looking for an apartment. I didn't ask about it; I didn't show any sign of impatience. During this time, I don't think L. made any pretence of looking for a new apartment. We no longer went near the subject, as though her long-term presence was a given.

Apart from the blender episode (L. replaced it the next day), L. was calm and even-tempered.

She was attentive, sensitive, didn't leave a mess. She regularly did the shopping, replaced things we ran out of. Our cohabitation jogged along smoothly and we never had the smallest domestic difference.

L. merged into the decor, as though she'd always been there. I cannot deny her presence provided a kind of reassurance. We were close. We were complicit. In all senses of the term. Beyond complicity, I'd made L. privy to a secret that no one else knew. She was the only person who knew that I could no longer write a line or even hold a pen. Not only did she know it, she also *covered* for me. She substituted for me so as not to arouse suspicions. L. responded to official and professional correspondence on my behalf.

*We* turned down meetings and writing commissions.

*We* refused to talk about subjects that authors are often invited to speak about.

*We* were hard at work.

Now I have to admit this: I'm aware that the people I supposedly replied to during this period will realise when they read this that it wasn't me. These people will perhaps find in their inbox or among their correspondence a letter or email, signed by me, not one word of which I wrote.

I hope they'll forgive me for this.

It's clear that living together enabled L. to cement her control and I don't think I put up much resistance. I'd like to be able to write that I fought back, struggled, tried to escape. But all I can say is this: I relied on L. because it seemed as though she was the only person able to get me out of the pit.

Sometimes the rather hackneyed image that comes to mind is of a spider that has patiently spun its web, or an octopus with many tentacles, holding me prisoner. But it wasn't like that. L. was more like a jellyfish, light and translucent, who settled on part of my soul. That contact left a burn, but it wasn't visible to the naked eye. Its imprint left me seemingly free in my movements. But it bound her to me much more than I could have imagined.

To the few people I was in touch with (the children, François, my editor), I gave the impression that I was back at work. I'd got started on *something*. I was right at the beginning, but I was progressing.

I didn't call any of my friends to tell them about the impasse I was in. I was afraid they would, rightly, consider it the whim of a spoilt child. I had no excuse and it seemed impossible to justify my idleness.

I didn't say anything to François either. I was afraid he'd stop loving me. Not only did I not tell him anything, but when he came back, I arranged things so that he never met L. Because I knew that the instant he saw her, he'd understand it all: the lies, the subterfuge, the illicit duo we now formed.

What I must now admit is that I was capable of lying to François and the people who are close to me. I sank into lies with a mixture of fear, disgust and perhaps also a hint of relish.

Some mornings, when I felt anxiety swell in my throat like a ball of silver foil, I clung on to something L. had said to me one day: 'True creative impulses are preceded by a sort of darkness.'

———

In the evenings, when we were both at home, L. would return to the ritual, going over to my bookcase, running her hand along the spines and seemingly stopping at random.

Had I read sack of bones, the little Arab girl, the dog's evening, the dog's night, the knickers, only love, the renunciation, the impossible book, I give up, dark Sunday, purge, the left behind, the unseated, the girls, birth of ghosts, maternity, the art of hunger, scintillation, a feeling of abandonment, no one, the falling man, accidents, the poet, ask the dust, the painted drum, the state of affairs, lone horseman, the summer he didn't die, grace and truth, the life before her eyes, the counter life, the three lights, the falls, the echo chamber, our fictionalised lives, my best friend's daughter, the past, on heroes and graves, everything is illuminated, death with interruptions, a ghost, paradise, the willow tree, the inn at the edge of the world, lighthousekeeping, Sukkwan Island, the isles, Elizabeth is missing, never forget.

When François got back, we spent a few days together in Courseilles. I left L. alone at my place. I didn't bring any work with me (for good reason). I convinced François – who was surprised to see me so free with my time, so far from my construction site – that I was allowing myself a break. And when he asked me about my work, I repeated, as I did every time he'd expressed concern, that it was too soon to talk about it.

When I got home, I found L. in Paul's room, hard at work. She told me that I'd had an email from my publisher about an invitation from a school in Tours, which I'd agreed to months before and which – I forget why – had been postponed several times. The school librarian had called back: a new date had to be set up as soon as possible. One sixth-form and two Year 11 classes had studied several of my novels and were expecting me.

I didn't really feel up to it, but I had agreed. On the face of it, there was no reason why it should go wrong.

I was used to this sort of event. L. and I looked at some dates we could suggest.

L. told me about two or three other requests that she'd replied to in my absence. She thought I was looking the better for my few days in the country. She didn't ask anything about my time there.

That evening she expressed concern about whether it would be a problem for her to stay a while longer. I told her again to take her time.

L. never questioned me about François as she permitted herself to do about my friends. She never asked me to tell her how we met, nor how long we'd been together. When I got back from his place or from Courseilles, she limited herself to asking how I was. She avoided details, anecdotes and any kind of narrative. François was a part of my life, she couldn't ignore that. She considered him, implicitly, as part of the problem. She didn't hide a degree of scepticism about this relationship and sometimes let slip a remark that was enough to convey how much it continued to strike her as against nature. I didn't take offence. In L.'s eyes, François was a permanent feature of my existence with which I had to contend. A complicating factor rather than a positive one. Being in love with a man who spent his time meeting and praising other writers struck her as dangerous. Someone who crossed the Channel or the Atlantic to meet authors whom he judged more interesting than French ones – that was what she thought his endless trips indicated – couldn't help me get my confidence back. One evening when she'd had a bit to drink, L. went so far as to compare me to a primary-school teacher who has chosen to live with a school inspector. That made me smile, so she went on: 'In fact, like a guy who goes home every night and tells her about pilot schemes run by star teachers in outstanding schools, and meanwhile she can't even keep control of her primary class . . .'

I wasn't sure I had grasped the meaning of the metaphor. Or, rather, all of its meanings. With L., the hidden meaning of a conversation sometimes struck me several days later.

And so our life together continued. François's return hadn't altered much. The nights I slept at his, I'd come home early the next morning on the pretext of working. I would find L. in the kitchen, drinking tea.

The only fairly direct question L. asked me about him concerned the possibility of our life together, now that my children had left home.

When I turned the question round on her (did she plan to build a new life?), she laughed at such a naive way of putting it. *Build a new life*, what did that mean, was it simply a matter of building, unbuilding and rebuilding? As though we had only a single strand to knit. She laughed, then added: 'As though we were unequivocal beings, built of a piece, from just one material. As though we had only one life.'

Two or three things come back to me that date, I think, from this period. But I have to say that I am no longer entirely sure of the order in which events took place, since the further I go in this story, the more hazy things become.

First, L. bought a couple of pairs of jeans that were the same brand as mine. At the time, I didn't pay all that much attention to it; these details came back to me much later, when our relationship had really begun to go off the rails. I, too, have sometimes tried to find an item of clothing like one I've seen a friend wear. I've tried them on and even bought them. But what seemed fluid and sensual on another body on me always seems too large, too tight or badly fitting.

I noticed that L. had bought the same jeans as me because she never wore jeans before she met me – as least as far as I could tell from her wardrobe in the early days of our friendship.

In the days that followed, it struck me that L. had changed. I mean that L. was starting to look like me. I'm fully aware that that may seem bizarre (noticing a similarity to yourself in someone else) and probably rather narcissistic. But it's what I felt. Not a true resemblance, of details and features, but a resemblance of contours, or look. I had already noticed that we had the same figure, the same hair colour (though L.'s was tame and well groomed), but there was now an additional aspect: in her gestures, her bearing, something about L. was reminiscent of *me*. At times, her silhouette stood out like a video projection of my own body on a softer, smoother surface. I also noticed that L. was wearing less make-up. For example, she'd stopped using tinted moisturiser, which she'd worn when I met her. Gradually, L. had adopted my gestures, attitudes and little habits. It was troubling, disturbing. But maybe it was only a figment of the imagination, of my imagination.

(People often say that my daughter looks like me, probably mainly through a form of imitation that I can't see. I can perhaps catch our resemblance in some photos of Louise, which remind me of pictures of me at the same age, but when Louise is in front of me, I cannot detect the similarity. I can see the ways that Paul looks like his father: there's the way he sits, what he does with his mouth when he's thinking, the way he uses his hands when he talks. But I don't think his father sees Paul's imitation of him.)

In reality, the imitation of me that L. had developed was not of the same kind. It wasn't natural and unconscious. It was deliberate. That's probably why I picked up on it.

But at that time, I wasn't sure of anything. I think I came to the conclusion I was imagining things.

Very early one morning, after I got back from François's place, I found L. sitting in the kitchen, not yet dressed, her hair not done and her eyes red. She'd just heard that Gérard Depardieu's autobiography, which she had been contacted about a few weeks earlier, had been offered to Lionel Duroy. It wasn't the first time she'd been in competition with this writer. He had clinched it by having dinner with the actor. They hit it off. She understood Depardieu's decision. She knew both men and the decision made sense. But she was disappointed. Anyway, she rarely agreed to write for actors. But Depardieu was different. She would have been able to do it.

Later, seeing her so dejected, I suggested going out for lunch, to take her out of herself. I hadn't had the energy to prepare a meal and the fridge was empty.

She shut herself in the bathroom for half an hour.

When she emerged, I couldn't hold back an exclamation of admiration; the least you could say was that she knew what she was doing. Apart from her slightly puffy eyes, the transformation was dramatic; her cheeks were pink and she looked refreshed and ready to go.

We headed for a local brasserie with a good reputation for its dish of the day where we'd been once or twice before. As we were about to go in, I heard someone call my name. I turned round and saw Nathan, a friend of Louise's she'd known since crèche. They were also in the same class at nursery and primary school, and even later, when their paths diverged, they never lost touch. Over the years, Nathan's mother and I had become friends. A few years back, we went on a trip to the US together with the children.

For a few seconds, with Nathan standing in front of me, the image of him as a little boy (blond hair, round cheeks and the adorable hand-knitted yellow pullover he wore for the nursery photograph) superimposed itself on the tall, handsome young man with dread-locks before me. I hadn't seen him since Louise went to Lyons; we kissed in greeting and began catching up.

If I'd run into one of my friends, I'm sure L. would have stayed. But she didn't feel suspicious, so she motioned that she was going inside to keep warm. 'So I hear that you've shut yourself away for months to work,' Nathan said, teasing me. 'Mum told me you sent an email to all your friends begging them not to contact you!'

I didn't understand immediately. I didn't want to. I think I told myself he was exaggerating; it was just the way young people put things. On the spur of the moment, I may even have nodded. Nathan told me what he was up to and asked about Louise and Paul. We parted after talking about getting together for dinner, with him and Corinne, one weekend when the twins were home.

I thought how nice it was to see other people's children growing up when you'd known them since they were little. The ones you've known in class photos and holiday snaps, that you've comforted, fed, tucked in, told off, sometimes held in your arms. I thought of all those boys and girls who had grown so tall, so different from each other; I thought I'd like to write about the enormously tender bond that links me to my children's friends and my friends' children.

I went into the café and spotted L., sitting at a large table. I sat down. While she was looking at the menu, the waiter came over.

'Are you waiting for the other person before you order?'

L. looked up with a disappointed smile.

'I think we'll start without her. She can catch up with us along the way.'

We had set a date for my visit to Tours in May. And May had come.

As this trip got closer, my anxiety gradually mounted. I tried not to think about it. Late on the day before, I had a panic attack. I suddenly felt completely unable to face four or five secondary-school classes. What I found paralysing was the thought of having to put on a brave face, put on a show, answer questions about my current work when I felt so depleted and at a loss. It's all a matter of being able to visualise it. And I couldn't picture myself in front of eighty teenagers, pretending that I was working hard on my writing. I couldn't see myself answering the inevitable: 'What can you write *after that*?'

These secondary-school students had read several of my books, had prepared questions, some had done supplementary work (collages, short films), which they planned to show me. I couldn't decently pull out. But I was incapable of going.

That evening, seeing me in such a state, L. suggested she could pretend to be me. As though it were the most natural thing in the world; there, it was a solution like any other, the students wouldn't be let down. It would avoid having to postpone the trip again, change train tickets, face the same fear once more.

I was stunned. In my place? How could she imagine that people wouldn't realise? But L. was utterly certain it would work. These people had only ever seen me in a photo. Now, I had to admit that generally speaking most photos were deceptive and bore little relation to reality. In addition, she maintained that the photos of me on the internet didn't look like me. They didn't add up to a coherent portrait; quite the reverse – they contributed to creating a fluctuating, hard-to-read image. The points of reference were blurred. Sometimes I had curly hair, sometimes straight; in some shots I looked like I had just got back from Club Med, and in other as though I'd just come out of prison. I could be thirty-five or fifty-five; middle-class respectable or tousled and grungy. In short, it all left genuine room for manoeuvre to, as she put it, 'reinvent' me. A few well-chosen details would make it possible to pull it off. She was sure it could work. The risk wasn't all that great. What's more, she'd read all my press interviews (right from the very first, she added); she'd heard me several times on the radio; she felt entirely capable of answering the traditional questions about the origins of my books or writing in my stead. And the rest she could improvise.

I can absolutely see that this must seem completely mad, but I agreed.

At dawn the next morning, L. put on my clothes (we selected what I was wearing on the most visible online photos, starting from the assumption that they'd have left some subconscious trace with my hosts), then I spent half an hour curling her hair using tongs that Louise had left in her room. L.'s hair was the same length as mine and just a shade lighter. The result made us laugh, especially when L. really started imitating my gestures and intonation, as though she'd practised this exercise dozens of times, alone in front of the mirror. She had real talent.

At six o'clock, with my train ticket in her pocket, she took a taxi to Montparnasse station.

She sent me a couple of texts from the TGV, and then I didn't hear from her again for the rest of the day. We'd agreed she wouldn't call unless she found herself in a police station for identity theft.

Apart from looking at my phone every ten minutes, there was nothing I could do. I had allowed myself to imagine a few disaster scenarios: L. unmasked by the students, who would throw their books at her; L. coming out with nonsense in response to the questions she was asked; L. insulting a teacher who didn't show her enough respect.

L. hadn't wanted me to pick her up from the station. She thought it better that I made the most of being alone. Around 10 p.m. – by which time I could hardly bear it any more – I heard her coming up the stairs.

From her expression, I recognised the exhaustion I knew well. L. confirmed that everything had gone smoothly without a break: the train, lunch in the canteen, meeting the classes, signing books, tea in the staffroom, the train back. With no time to spare and without the smallest incident. There had only been a little moment of uncertainty at Tours station, when the librarian met her. She'd looked at L. several times before approaching her, and then, once they'd greeted each other, the librarian had continued casting sidelong glances. After a few moments' perplexity, she had apologised for not having recognised her at once; she hadn't imagined me quite like that. By contrast, the two literature teachers at the school had had no doubts. They were delighted to meet me; the students were waiting eagerly. During the session, a boy caused general hilarity by asking L. if she'd had plastic surgery: she looked younger than in her photos. The teacher gave him a lecture. The students asked lots of questions about the autobiographical aspect of my books, especially the most recent. L. was struck by the fact that most of their questions focused on this: Why did I consider my book a novel? Was it all true? What had happened to such and such a character? How had my family reacted to the book? All questions that I was familiar with and had had to answer many times.

Standing before me, L. could not conceal her excitement or pride: she'd pretended to be me and it had worked! Did I realise what that meant? We'd now become interchangeable, or at any rate she could stand in for me. There were probably ways to perfect the representation, because she could improve, she was sure of that, and that would free me from all sorts of obligations, if that was what I wanted.

'You know, I can do it again, Delphine. Any time you need me to. And I'm sure it could work with people who know you. Booksellers, librarians, journalists. Absolutely certain. Believe me, people don't know how to look properly. They're too wrapped up in themselves. We can test it out whenever you like.'

L. was as happy as if she'd just won a major drama award.

Such was her joy that she didn't notice my unease, even though I was having trouble hiding it. I banished the odd sensation that was making me feel slightly numb. This time, she had saved the day.

I thanked her. I think I even added: I don't know what I can do to thank you.

The next day, L. told me we'd received a very grateful email from the teachers. They'd had excellent feedback, the students had loved the session, which they had found lively, exciting and relaxed.

*We* had done well.

I'm a clumsy person. I collide with walls, trip over carpets, knock things over, spill water, wine, tea; I slip, stumble, get involved in uncontrolled mishaps, sometimes all in the same day. It's not necessarily due to the unevenness of the ground or the presence of camouflaged objects. It's more a matter of me being distracted, or a crafty form of misadaptation to the world around. To this may be added other factors: tiredness and being observed by other people. Even today, if I know I'm being watched, I will cross a room or go down a staircase entirely preoccupied with accomplishing it without falling. Even today, if I feel intimated, I can spend a whole meal only half-listening to the conversation, because I'm focusing on not choking or dropping something, and that requires my full attention.

I've learned to conceal this handicap and by now I think I know how to hide what I'm up to quite well. I've developed a number of automatic reflexes, strategies, preventative measures that enable me to go for days on end without banging into anything, making a fool of myself in public or endangering anyone else's life. But I also now know how to spot the moments of exhaustion, unhappiness and confusion that oblige me to redouble my attention.

I have on several occasions distinguished myself, sometimes publicly, with acts of improbable clumsiness. I don't know if other people my age – that is, who have had a certain numbers of hours of practice – find themselves in the same situation.

One day a few years ago, my English publisher invited me to London for the publication of one of my novels in translation. I hadn't been to London for some time and I was preparing, not without some apprehension, for my first interview in English. My publisher came to meet me at St Pancras station and we took a taxi straight to the studio where the programme was going to be recorded. I may have been wearing a skirt or a dress for the occasion. In the cab, we swapped news. My English publisher is a significant figure in the world of publishing. He's in his fifties, extremely English and extremely seductive. To me, he embodies the very essence of British chic. When we reached our destination, he got out of the taxi first and held the door for me, smiling. All I had to do was get out the cab. In the few seconds before I moved, a voice in my head warned me: you're not going to manage it. That made no sense, had no rational basis, but the fear was there, as though, from high up in the big top, I now had to jump from one swinging trapeze to another. I was scared. I wanted to look good. I wanted to show I could be fluid and feminine. I wanted to please him. And suddenly getting out of that car in front of my English publisher seemed an insurmountable challenge.

At that precise moment, I thought: There are some words and some glances you cannot recover from. In spite of the passage of time, in spite of the kindness of other words and glances.

As I got out of the taxi, through some unfathomable tangle of my legs or feet, I pitched forward. I didn't quite go flying, which would at least have been worth the spectacle, but rather, through a sort of pitiful plunge, found myself on the ground with the contents of my bag scattered on the road. My English publisher held out his hand to help me up in a gesture of the greatest delicacy, without showing any surprise, as though this was a phenomenon frequently encountered in French writers.

Through contact with L., in particular during the period when she lived with me, this clumsiness kept increasing, developing, like a reactivated virus that might have mutated into a more harmful, tenacious form. I bumped into things all the time. Objects slipped from my hands and seemed to possess an energy of their own. My movements weren't functioning properly. The bumps, falls and collisions increased.

I lost count of the bruises and breakages. My body's ill-adaptedness to its surroundings, which I'd got used to and had learned to hide, had been reawakened in a sort of permanent rift. I progressed through an accident-strewn terrain full of traps, at every moment on the lookout for the slip, landslide, collapse. Wherever I went, I was scared of my own instability. I felt feverish and inept. Trembling. Being able to keep myself upright was no longer a given, but a precarious thing I had to struggle to do.

François, who had often teased me about my clumsiness (was I the secret daughter of Pierre Richard or Gaston Lagaffe?), began to worry. He started looking at me sideways, as though seeking irrefutable evidence that something was wrong. In his presence, I sometimes fell over or dropped things, just like that, mid-movement, for no reason, exactly as though the infomation 'I'm raising a glass to my lips' or 'I'm holding a saucepan in my right hand' had suddenly disappeared from my brain. Sometimes the connection was brutally inter-rupted. In addition, as I had increasing difficulty in judging the distance between my body and the rest of the world, the question of whether I should go and see a neurologist frequently came up.

When I think back, my clumsiness was one of a variety of symptoms that appeared or reappeared at that time, symptoms that were to some degree incapacitating, whose coexistence, increase, proliferation I accepted without raising the alarm. Now I'm able to link these events together. But back then, it all merged into a state of unhappiness, loneliness, whose cause I was unaware of and about which I refused to consult any kind of doctor. I was unhappy, that was all there was to it; it wasn't the first time and it probably wouldn't be the last.

Sometimes it did occur to me that L. might have something to do with my state, directly or indirectly.

Ostensibly, she was carrying me, supporting me, protecting me. But in reality, she was absorbing my energy. She was tapping in to my pulse, my tension, my appetite for fantasy, which had never before deserted me.

When I was in her presence, I was emptied of all substance; she spent hours working, going in and out, taking the metro, doing the cooking. When I watched her, it sometimes felt like I was watching myself – or rather my double – reinvented: stronger, more powerful, charged with positive energy.

And soon there would be nothing left of me but a dead, dry husk, an empty shell.

As I try to advance through this story, I see how I'm constantly attempting to provide chronological reference points, through a probably clumsy desire to anchor the narrative in a shared, objective time tangible to everyone. I know that will soon explode and there will come a moment when the temporal markers will become meaningless and there will be nothing but a sort of long, empty corridor.

I would describe in more detail the weeks that led us to the summer if I could. But I have no trace or memory of them. I presume my life continued in that halting masquerade that was going nowhere.

I presume L. continued working, looking after my correspondence and papers, and I continued doing nothing. I presume the two of us went out together a few times in the evening for a drink and for a change of scene.

Louise and Paul came home for the weekend twice. The first time, L. took the opportunity to go off and stay with her mother in Brittany. The second time, she said she'd prefer to go to a hotel so as not to get in our way.

One evening when we were at his place, I remember François and I had an argument. I think it was about psychoanalysis (psychoanalysis occupies a significant place among our subjects of disagreement, ahead of Americano coffee, the use of quotations, nostalgia, some authors he doesn't like who I stick up for, and some films he adores but I think are duds, and vice versa). We very rarely argue, and when we do it never lasts more than ten minutes, but that evening I pounced on the first opportunity to contradict him. It's something I'm very good at when a part of me decides to pick a fight (fortunately this doesn't happen often). The pitch rose without me realising. I was tense and tired. There was electricity in the air.

Haven't we all felt the temptation to destroy at least once in our lives? The sudden dizziness of destroying, annihilating, smashing everything, because it would only take a few well-chosen words from who knows where, finely honed and sharpened, words that strike home and wound, irremediably, and cannot be retracted. Haven't we all felt it at least once, that strange, mute, destructive rage, because ultimately it would take so little to lay waste to everything? That is exactly what I felt that evening: I was capable of taking action, sabotaging all I held dear, destroying everything so that I would have nothing left to lose. That's what overwhelmed me, the crazy idea that the moment had come to put an end to all this, this enchanted episode and all the bullshit that I'd ended up believing. I thought I'd found a man capable of loving me, understanding me, following me, supporting me, but in fact, ha, ha, no, that was all just a trap, a clever lure and it was high time I put a stop to it. And I knew the words that would cause the irreparable wound; I knew his weak point, his Achilles heel. All I had to do was aim straight in the right spot, and in less time than it took to utter them, it would be over.

That's what L. had reactivated in me: the insecure person who was capable of destroying everything.

For a minute, I stood on the brink of disaster, and then I pulled back.

Several times during that period, François suggested I come to live with him, at least for a while. He was getting concerned. There was no fooling him. Not with my bravado or my so-called work in progress. He thought that the anonymous letters had got to me much more than I'd admitted. He thought I'd allowed some monster or ghost that had loomed up from the past to catch up with me.

I remember another evening, coming back from Courseilles, we had an odd discussion, as though

François could see around me some abnormal aura without being able to identify it. It had been dark for ages and the road was quiet. In the car, he started asking me questions. Yes, he was worried about me. He could understand that I needed to be alone, that I was protecting my work, that there were things I didn't want to talk to him about. But I was taking it too far, putting myself in danger. I was refusing his help. Perhaps, just once – at least for a short time – I could let someone look after me? He felt that I had again constructed a sort of cordon sanitaire around myself so that no one, not even him, could have access to what was really affecting or worrying me. He understood that I didn't want to share everything, but I didn't have to deploy such a defence system. We weren't at war. He wasn't my enemy. He'd known me calmer.

Then he took his eyes off the road for a moment to look at me.

'You know, sometimes I wonder if someone's taken possession of you.'

I don't know why I didn't tell him that day. Why I didn't mention L. and the impression that, through contact with her, the talons of a bird of prey were crushing my brain.

Anyone who has experienced their mind being controlled, an invisible prison whose rules are incomprehensible; anyone who has experienced the feeling of no longer being able to think for themselves, an ultrasound that you alone can hear and which interferes with every thought, every sensation, every emotion; anyone who has experienced the fear of going mad or of already being mad will probably understand my silence in the presence of the man who loved me.

It was too late.

From the age of twelve until after the birth of the twins, I kept a private diary. I've already mentioned these little school notebooks, which I filled with my writing as a child, then teenager, then young adult. They are numbered and arranged in order in an airtight plastic box that I have several times tried to remove to the cellar, but I always end up bringing it back up. I used these notebooks when I was writing my first and most recent novels. Apart from these two occasions (ten years apart), I haven't reread them. If something happens to me one day, I hope these notebooks will be destroyed. I've told my friends and family and left written instructions: I don't want anyone to open or read them. I know it would be safer to separate myself from them, to burn them, but I can't resolve to do that. The plastic box has found a place in the cupboard by the kitchen where I store all sorts of things: the vacuum cleaner, household linen, my sewing box, a box of stationery, sleeping bags and camping equipment.

One evening, as I was about to take the ironing board out, I noticed that the lid of the plastic box – the box containing my notebooks – was askew. I opened the stepladder and took the box down. At that very moment, perhaps because she'd heard the noise, or because she really did possess a sixth sense, L. came out of her room and joined me in the kitchen.

Having put the box on the floor, I began checking its contents. As I verified that all the notebooks were there, L. whistled in admiration.

'You've got your work cut out, that's for sure.'

I didn't look up. The notebooks were out of sequence, but they were all there.

I almost asked L. if she had opened the box, but it felt too aggressive to do it just like that, without proof or motive; it would amount to accusing her of snooping. Yet there was a probable scenario: L. knew of the notebooks' existence and where they were stored; she could have been interrupted while reading them, which would explain why they had been put back in a muddle.

She didn't take her eyes off me as I closed the box again and put it back in its place. It occurred to me that I needed to find somewhere else to store it in the next few days.

That same evening, L. expressed interest in the use I could make of those diaries. It was, she insisted, an amazing, unbelievable resource. Over fifteen years of memories, anecdotes, sensations, impressions, portraits . . . something about the way she spoke about them confirmed to me that she'd read them, at least in part. It's difficult to explain this: she spoke about them as though she knew in some innate way, through intuition (not indiscretion) what the notebooks contained. So much so that if I'd objected, if I'd accused her, she would immediately have denied it.

She thought it a shame that I refused to extract from the notebooks the precious material for the book that haunted me. Because it was definitely there, she could feel it, she knew it, pages and pages silently waiting for the day when I would consent to recount their contents.

'It's like a mine that you've condemned. You're incredibly lucky to have written all that. Don't you realise?'

Yes, she was right. It was precious. Those notebooks were my memory. They contained all sorts of details, anecdotes and situations that I'd forgotten. They contained my hopes, questions and suffering. My cure. They contained what I'd shed in order to stay afloat. They contained what I thought I'd forgotten but which cannot be erased. What continues to operate, unbeknownst to us.

L. didn't give me time to reply. She spoke more softly, but just as firmly: 'I don't understand why you're still looking for a subject when you have that in your hands.'

I was in a bitter mood.

'First, I'm not looking for a subject, as you put it, and second, that material is only of value to me.'

'I disagree. I think it's what you need to confront, that reality, that truth.'

I was suddenly seized with anger. I hadn't felt it building.

'No one gives a fuck about that truth. Not a flying fuck!'

'Yes, they do. People know. They feel it. I know it when I read a book.'

For once I wanted to argue, to try to understand.

'Don't you think you feel that, as you put it, just because you know it? Because someone has taken the trouble to tell you in some way or another that you're reading a true story, or that it's "inspired by real events" or "highly autobiographical" and that this simple label is enough to arouse a different sort of attention in you, a form of curiosity we all have, not least me, for true stories? But you know, I'm not sure that the real is enough. The real, insofar as it exists at all, for it to be possible to recreate it, the real, as you put it, needs to be incarnated, transformed, interpreted. Without perspective or a viewpoint, at best, it's boring as hell, and at worst it's completely anxiety-producing. And that work, whatever the raw material, is always a form of fiction.'

For once L. didn't respond tit for tat. She thought for a moment, then asked, 'So what are you waiting for to do it?'

'Do what?'

'This work you're talking about.'

That night I had a strange dream, which has stayed sharp in my memory: I'm standing facing the blackboard in a classroom with children's drawings all over the walls. A teacher, whose face I don't recognise, is asking me questions. I get the answer wrong every time and the teacher turns to L. (who is also a child, but a bit older than me) for the correct answer. The other pupils aren't looking at me; they're staring at their notebooks to avoid humiliating me further. Only my friend Mélanie is looking at me and making increasingly desperate signs for me to run away.

I woke up in a sweat.

I turned on the light and waited for my heartbeat to return to normal. I don't think I went back to sleep.

The following day, I spent the morning sorting my correspondence. I keep every letter I receive, the smallest note written by the children, postcards, messages that come with flowers; I keep them all. Every two or three years, I make piles and packets and tidy them into boxes.

That afternoon I went out for a walk.

As I was passing the nursery school, what Nathan (the friend of Louise's I'd bumped into a few weeks earlier) said came back to me with the force of a boomerang: 'Mum told me you sent an email to all your friends begging them not to contact you!'

I'd kept what he said at a distance all that time. It had stayed there, not too far away, suspended, waiting, because I didn't have the courage to try to clarify it, to face up to what it meant, because I'd had neither the strength nor the courage to process this piece of information normally.

I called Corinne, Nathan's mother, from the street. She picked up at once and greeted me warmly. At last, I was coming out of my cave!

Corinne confirmed that I'd sent her a message, as I'd apparently sent to all my contacts – to judge by the length of the recipient list – to warn them that I was getting down to work and I would need to keep myself away from all temptation.

I asked Corinne if I could come round so that she could show me the message. I needed to see it. Corinne is not the sort to take offence at other people's weird behaviour; she told me to come when I liked, she'd be there, she wasn't going anywhere.

When I got to her place, she'd found the message, signed with my name, addressed to all my friends and most of my contacts.

She has since forwarded it to me and I reproduce it here:

*Dear all,*

*As most of you know, I haven't managed to get back to work. Along with this failure, I've also been very distracted in my activities and by a kind of idleness, which I hate and which is eating away at me.*

*So I'm asking you not to get in touch with me for a few months, not to ask me round, or suggest meeting up. Except in case of emergency, of course. For my*

*part, I won't be in touch either while I'm writing
this book.*

*This may seem like a drastic measure. I'm sure now
that it's something I have to go through.*

*Love,*
*Delphine*

The message was dated November, the time when L.
first had access to my computer. Corinne had replied
with a message of encouragement and support and, not
daring to phone me, had written two or three times
since. (As did most of my friends and some members of
my family, as I learned later. L. of course didn't pass any
of these messages on to me.)

I thanked Corinne and promised to come back and
see her or to call her soon so that we could go for a drink.

I set off for home. I felt very tired.

I tried calling François from outside my building –
he'd gone for two days' filming in the provinces – but I
got his voicemail. I was behaving like someone who was
scared. That was ridiculous. Why didn't I wait till I was
home and call him more calmly? Why did I speak in a
low voice when L. was at home?

L. was waiting in the kitchen. She was surprised to see
me back from my walk so late; she'd begun to worry.
She'd made the rooibos tea I liked and bought some
macaroons. She had something important to tell me. I

interrupted her: 'No, I'm the one who's got something important to tell you.'

My voice was shaking.

'I know you sent an email to all my friends telling them not to contact me.'

I waited for her to deny it. Or at least to be taken aback. But L. didn't show the least sign of surprise, or discomfort. She replied without hesitation, as though she were completely sure she was in the right.

'Yes, I did. I wanted to help you. That's my role, you know, to create the best conditions for you to work in. To stop you drifting.'

I was flabbergasted.

'You know, you can't just do that. Don't you get it? You send my friends a ridiculous letter telling them not to contact me. That's serious. It's really serious. You don't have the right to do that without talking to me; I need my friends . . .'

'I'm here. Isn't that enough?'

'No, that's not the issue. I can't get over the fact you did that . . .'

'It was necessary. It still is. Be careful. You need silence and solitude to write that book.'

'Which book?'

'You know very well which book. I don't think you have the choice. You need to respond to the demands of your public.'

It was probably the word 'public' which hit me, which struck me as so jarring. A word she uttered as though I was a variety star on the eve of a tour. Suddenly I could no longer ignore the fact that L. took me for someone else and was projecting a fantasy onto me that had nothing to do with who I was. I protested firmly; I was afraid of my voice becoming shrill. I wanted to stay calm.

'Listen carefully. I'm going to tell you something: I have *never* written to please *anyone* and I have no intention of starting now. When, through some misfortune, that idea comes into my mind – pleasing or giving pleasure, because yes, if you must know, it does come into my mind – I stamp on it with all my strength. Because deep down, writing is much more intimate and much more commanding than that.'

L. stood up and was manifestly making an effort to talk gently to me. 'Exactly. That's what I'm talking about: more intimate. That's what your readers expect of you. Whether you like it or not, you are responsible for the attention, and the love, that you have aroused.'

I think I shouted.

'What the fuck has that got to do with you? Why are you getting involved? Who are you to know what's good or bad, desirable or regrettable? Who are you to know what literature is or is not, and what my readers expect? Who do you think you are?'

She didn't look at me. I saw her get up, pick up the plate on which she had carefully arranged the macaroons. With the tip of her foot, she pressed the bin pedal and, with a movement whose speed surprised me, threw them away.

She walked out of the kitchen without a word. We hadn't touched the tea.

In the night, I heard L. get up several times and thought she must have insomnia. There was a full moon and she'd told me that it disturbed her sleep.

The next morning when I got up I found her ready to leave. Her cases were lined up in the hall. Her face betrayed an unusual degree of tiredness, her eyes had dark rings and it looked to me as though she had no make-up on. She must have spent the night packing. She didn't seem angry (or if she was, she was hiding it successfully); in a very calm voice she told me that she had found a hotel in the 10th arrondissement; the rooms weren't large but she would cope for a while. I tried to protest but she gestured with her hand to stop me.

'This isn't the time to discuss it. I'm aware that my presence is getting you down. I don't want to prevent you writing. You know how much I respect your work. You probably need to be alone for a bit before the children come back for the holidays. I understand. I thought I could help you regain your self-confidence. I thought I could help you avoid wasting time, falling into traps. But perhaps that's something you have to go through. I was wrong and I'm sorry. You're right, only you know how you need to work. What's right for you.

I ask your forgiveness and if I've said anything that has hurt you, that wasn't my intention.'

Suddenly I felt guilty. I was about to throw onto the street the friend who had been helping me for weeks, who'd been lumbered with my dirty work.

L. opened the front door. She hesitated for a moment and came back in.

'You know, Delphine, I'm afraid for you. I hope nothing happens to you. I have a bad feeling. Look after yourself.'

With those words, she left and the door closed behind her. I heard her going down the first steps and then heard nothing. She'd left the keys I'd lent her on the kitchen table.

That afternoon, another boy, as young as the previous one, came to collect her cases.

On the days that followed I didn't hear from L.

I didn't try calling her.

I couldn't stop thinking about her parting words. It wasn't a warning: it was a curse. A dire and inescapable fate that L. had thrust upon me.

# PART THREE

# Betrayal

'Annie, will you tell me one thing?'

'Of course, dear.'

'If I write this story for you—'

'*Novel*! A nice big one like all the others –
maybe even bigger!'

He closed his eyes for a moment, then
opened them. 'Okay – if I write this *novel* for
you, will you let me go when it's done?'

For a moment, unease slipped cloudily
across her face, and then she was looking at him
carefully, studiously. 'You speak as though I were
keeping you prisoner, Paul.'

Stephen King, *Misery*

I have few memories of the summer that followed L.'s departure.

Louise and Paul came back in June to spend two weeks with me, then we all went to Courseilles together, where they stayed with us for a while before they went off with their friends. I remained in the country with François throughout July. I remember the anxiety I felt – a mixture of fascination and revulsion – when I looked at the quantity of books he'd brought with him. It was the same ritual every summer: dozens of books spread around the living room in little piles, on tables or the floor, according to some system only he understood. I remember thinking that L. was right; it was suicide for a novelist to be around someone like him. Someone whose job was reading books, meeting and entertaining novelists, giving his opinion on their work. Hundreds of books would appear every autumn. That's not just a figure quoted in the media. They were all here, arranged in piles or in still-sealed cardboard boxes, which he was about to unpack: five or six hundred novels of various dimensions, which would be published between late August and late September.

I'd met François through his work. At first we'd both stuck to our roles and it took a few weeks before we truly connected.

I loved him. I loved him for a thousand reasons; one of the reasons I loved him was because he loved books. I loved his curiosity. I loved watching him reading. I loved our similarities, the things we disagreed about, our endless discussions. I loved discovering books with him, before him, through him.

But this time, I found all those novels unbearable. Their covers, their belly bands, their blurbs mocked my impotence. Spread out before me, such a quantity of paper suddenly struck me as ostentatious and threatening.

I wanted to grab them from his hands and throw them all out of the window.

I longed to say to François, who sometimes talked about quitting on evenings when he felt dejected or very tired: OK, you're on, I dare you, let's see if you can do it, let's give it all up and go and live somewhere else, let's reinvent ourselves in a new place, in another life.

In August, I went with Louise and Paul to join our friends in the 'holiday house'. As I write this, I realise I have no recollection of the house we rented that summer; the images escape me, they're mixed up with other, older ones; I'm unable to visualise the place, or the little town it was on the edge of.

I only remember the bike track we used to cycle along to get to the sea, the headwind that would get in my mouth, the sensation of speed that I'd seek flying downhill. I was happy to be there, not to miss out on this time with my children and friends; anxiety eventually loosened its grip for a few days.

After two weeks' respite, we took the train back. When Louise, Paul and I took our seats at the family table we'd booked on the train, I found myself projected back a year, almost to the day, behind the grey-green SNCF curtains, in a place that in every respect resembled the one we'd occupied then. All at once, I saw clearly the journey that all three of us had made then, at the same time, returning from the holiday house: the picnic spread out on the table, Paul's new haircut, Louise's red T-shirt, their tanned skin. Suddenly, as though it were yesterday, I remembered the thoughts that had pre-occupied me that day as I looked out of the window at the same landscape flashing by, seeking some impossible point of anchorage. I'd thought about François, whose year was looking very busy; I'd thought about the book I was preparing to write; I'd thought about the documentary on the Armenian genocide that I'd ordered to show the children (they are Armenian on their father's side); I'd thought about winter skies and then I'd knocked over a soft drink and we'd used more than one packet of Kleenex mopping it up. All this came back to me in peculiar detail. I remembered that Paul had wanted to play the Yes-or-No game, like when they were children, but the game had become too noisy for our fellow passengers.

A year had gone by, a whole year since that journey and I'd done nothing. Nothing. I was in the same place. Or not exactly. I was now unable to sit at my computer, open a Word file or answer an email. I was unable to hold a pen for more than a few minutes or look at a white surface, whether lined or squared. In short, I'd lost command of the elementary skills needed to do my job.

In early September, Louise and Paul went back to their studies.

Like many people, I think and calculate in school years, from September to June. The summer seems like a parenthesis, a period of respite from obligations. For a long time I thought this came from being a mother, whose biorhythms eventually fuse with the school calendar, but I think that it's mainly the child within me, within all of us, whose life is chopped in slices for so long: an enduring trace of our perception of time.

It was a new school year. The time for new stationery and good intentions. The time of beginning, or beginning again.

But not a single molecule of air stirred and every-thing seemed frozen.

This time, I didn't promise myself that I'd get back to work. The very notion of writing was a remote one. I no longer had the slightest idea of the form it might take; my body had forgotten the sensations I used to love, of tiredness and excitement, the hours spent sitting in front of a pool of light, fingers on the keyboard, tension in my shoulders, legs stretched out under the desk.

The children left and I once again found myself alone at home. L.'s absence was now added to that of Louise and Paul, an additional loss, the impact of which I was now becoming aware of. All I had to do was look around. Mail was piling up on the table in the living room, my computer screen was covered in a fine layer of dust. I was allowing myself to drift from day to day, continuing to pretend, filling my time with little things, drawing them out as far as possible to make them last, filling the unfathomable void that I'd unwittingly created around me in the course of a lost year.

Maybe this was how old people lived, in a succes-sion of careful, tiny steps, of movements that were slow enough to fill the emptiness. It wasn't so painful.

I imagine that all of us, at some point or another, believe there is no such thing as chance. I imagine all of us have experienced a series of coincidences to which we ascribe special meaning, inevitable meaning, a sense that we alone believe we can work out. How many of us have not thought, at least once in our lives, that some coincidence owed nothing to chance, but was in fact a message amid the hurly-burly of the world, just for us?

That's what happened to me. For two or three weeks, I felt as though L.'s message, the intimate certainties she'd wanted to see me share, no longer required her in order to reach me: they continued to float in the air, to move of their own volition, choosing this or that new vector to convince me.

One evening I got a call from a director I'd worked with a few years before on the screenplay for a feature film that had not come to fruition, despite various grants and the backing of different bodies. The financing hadn't been finalised and the project had fallen through. The director suggested we get together for a drink so he could update me on his projects. We met in a café where we used to go to work. He didn't beat about the bush: he was looking for a true story to adapt. That was the only kind of thing that was working; you only had to look at the posters, at how many of them spelled out in letters almost as big as the title that they were 'inspired by real events'; you just had to read the magazines, watch TV, with its hordes of witnesses and guinea pigs in all genres, or listen to the radio, to understand what people wanted.

'Reality's the only thing that's real enough,' he'd concluded. He knew I'd turned down various offers to adapt my previous book; he understood that, but if I had any ideas, if I heard of anything – an old news item or a recent one, a forgotten character from history – I shouldn't hesitate to call him; he'd be delighted to work with me again.

I was in a gloomy mood when I left the café. So it was true then; that was what people expected: the real, guaranteed by a label stamped on films and books like the red or organic label on food products, a certificate of authenticity. I thought that people only needed stories to interest them, overwhelm them, sweep them along. But I'd got it wrong. People wanted it to have happened somewhere; they wanted it to be verifiable. They wanted lived experience. People wanted to be able to identify, to empathise, and for that to happen, they needed reassurance about the goods; they demanded a basic level of traceability.

In the following weeks, every time I turned on the television, opened a magazine, or new film posters appeared, it seemed as though it always came back to this: the real, the true, the truthful; all shoved in the same bag as though they were the same thing, a promotional offer, a package, to which we could now lay claim, to which we were entitled.

As I write this, I could not say whether these are genuine coincidences or a subjective impression, fabricated by my own preoccupations.

Twenty years earlier, in the months before I became pregnant, which seemed to be taking ages, hadn't I been certain there were pregnant women everywhere? A genuine epidemic, I told myself, as though all the women in my neighbourhood of child-bearing age had spread the word to get pregnant before me, and what's more, the only things I saw were them and their prominent, gorgeous, full bellies.

These signs always pointed in the direction of L.

What if L. were right? What if L. had sensed and understood a profound change in our way of reading, seeing, thinking? As a reader and viewer, I wasn't an exception to the rule. Reality TV fascinated me to an extent that went beyond my literary plans. I pounced on the gossip magazines every time I went to the hairdresser or dentist. I regularly went to see biopics and films based on real events, and afterwards I'd go on the internet to check the facts, look for the real faces, hungry for details, proof, confirmation.

What if L. had understood something I refused to acknowledge? I'd written an autobiographical book in which all the characters were inspired by members of my family. Some readers had become attached to them and had asked me about what had happened to them. They'd confessed to me that they had a particular affection for one character or another. Some readers had quizzed me about the reality of the events. They'd conducted their own investigations. I couldn't ignore it. And the book's success, ultimately, may all have been down to that. A true story, or one that was thought of as true. No matter what I said about it. Whatever precautions I had deployed to assert that reality was ungraspable and claim my subjectivity.

I had poked my finger into the real and the trap had snapped shut.

And now all the characters I might invent, whatever their stature, their history, their wound, would never measure up. From these wholly invented characters nothing would emerge, no emanation, no juice, no smell. No matter what I might be capable of imagining, they would be small, shrivelled, sickly; they would never have sufficient weight. They'd be bloodless, dispensable; they'd lack flesh.

Yes, L. was right. It was necessary to grapple with reality.

The publisher for whom I'd written the Maupassant preface (or rather, for whom L. had written a preface that I'd put my name to) organised regular public events at the Théâtre de l'Odéon. When the reissue of the book came out, the editor rang me to check I hadn't forgotten about my event, which had been arranged when I signed the contract. The event was to take place in the small Roger Blin room, which accommodates a hundred people. It would last about an hour and would begin, if I was happy with this, with me reading an extract from the novel. The interviewer's questions would then focus on my reading of the book, the appeal of the author to me, the idea being to make people want to discover or reread this less well-known Maupassant novel.

When I hung up, my first instinct was to call L. and ask her to go in my stead. I kept going through to voice-mail. As though this phone number was reserved for me and would be unobtainable as long as she remained angry. I didn't leave a message.

Once again, I was committed. The event had been announced on various sites; it was much too late for me to pull out. And when I stopped to think about it, it was completely out of the question to ask L. to impersonate me. I knew several people at the publishing house, and readers I'd already met in bookshops were likely to come. In this environment, L. wouldn't last two minutes before she was unmasked.

The night before, I reread the novel and the preface L. had written. I didn't sleep a wink. On the evening of the event, I arrived early to chat with the theatre's literary adviser, who was preparing to interview me. He tried to reassure me (I must have looked especially tense) and ran through the format with me again. And then it was time for us to take our places on the little stage in front of the audience.

The room was full. I read an extract from the novel that lasted about ten minutes. When I looked up, I saw her.

She was sitting in the third row, dressed like me. I don't mean in the same style of clothing, I mean dressed *exactly* like me: same jeans, same blouse, same black jacket. Only the colour of her ankle boots, which were a shade darker, differed from mine. I wanted to laugh. L. was playing a joke. L. had dressed up and had decided to be my understudy, like in films. L. was signalling to me that in the event of a problem, she was ready to jump on stage and replace me at the drop of a hat. She gave me a discreet wink. No one but me seemed to have noticed her little game.

I have only a vague memory of discussing the book. My answers were mediocre and, as the hour ticked by, I felt as though I was sinking into bland opinions of the utmost vacuousness. I looked at L., who was now in the middle of the audience. In spite of myself, I came back to her attentive, impassive face, which reminded me of the deception I was indulging in. In spite of her smile, in spite of her repeated nods (as though encouraging a child in a school show), I couldn't suppress the thought that her place was here on the platform, and that her answers would have been so much more focused than mine.

After the event, people lingered briefly before drifting off. I signed some books, chatted with a few people. In the distance, I saw L. mingling with a little group, then talking to the editor who had commissioned me to write the preface. I shuddered. No one seemed to have noticed her. No one seemed to have noticed that L. resembled me, or was imitating me. L. blended in to the background, arousing neither surprise nor suspicion. And then it struck me that the whole thing was nothing more than pure projection on my part. A narcissistic fantasy. An interpretative hallucination. L. wasn't dressed like me – she was dressed like most women of our age. Who was I, who did I think I was, imagining that L. had done this to copy me? What I needed to face up to was this: I had developed a disproportionate fear of L. True, L. was a rather intrusive friend, but she'd tried to help me, advise me, and in return all I had shown her was mistrust and suspicion. No one but me thought her strange, and I was the only person casting worried glances in her direction.

Later, when the room had emptied, I went for a drink with the people from the publishers. We sat around a large table in the café nearest the theatre. I was happy to be there, in good company. The atmosphere was simple and warm, I felt good.

After about ten minutes, I saw L. pass the café window and give me a sad wave. And then she disappeared.

The next day, I tried to call L. several times, but her mobile always went to voicemail. Then, one evening she sent me a text to say she was thinking of me, and she'd call me as soon as she could 'see things a bit more clearly'.

We'd lived together for several weeks; we'd shared the same bathroom and dozens of meals; we'd acted in such a way as to make our various moods coincide – and then L. had left. No trace of her remained in my apartment; no item of clothing or object left behind, no little note stuck to the fridge. She'd taken everything, packed it all up and left nothing.

---

A couple of weeks went by without leaving any trace in my memory. I didn't turn on my computer once.

And then François had to go abroad again.

I could have called my friends, got back in touch, let them know I was happy to be contacted and available, but I didn't have the energy. I would have had to tell them about L., explain why she'd come to live with me, why she'd had unrestricted access to my computer. I would have had to admit that I was unable to write, my phobia undiminished. Or else, I would have had to lie, and admit I was the author of that stupid message that had distanced them from me.

So I found myself alone, prisoner of a lie that offered no possibility of turning the clock back.

One morning in October, I found an anonymous letter in my mailbox. The envelope was the same as before. I reproduce the contents here:

Delphine,
Even when you were a child, you already caused fear. You exuded unease. Everyone could see it and talked about it. Everyone. You didn't get over it. In fact, it just got worse. Because now madam is in the literary world.

But no one is taken in any more. Your moment of glory, your little tricks, your contemptible cheap shots: over. No one feels sorry for you any more. Every day I have to listen to unpleasant comments about your publications, everywhere, in shops, in the street,

at dinner parties. Everywhere I hear
mockery, sniggers. You don't take
anyone in any more. And no one could
care less. About your stories and your
jokes that amuse no one but you. I
know your childhood and adolescence
were very disturbed, pathological
even; you've described them very well.
The masses were knocked out by your
book. But it's over.

    Shit-stirrers like you always
end up chewing their own fingers.
Your behaviour is just making your
psychiatric condition worse. You think
all you have to do is withdraw from
the media spotlight and people will
forget why you're sleeping with him?
Your number's up for good. And the
worst thing is you haven't realised.

I put the typewritten sheet back in the envelope and filed the letter with the others. Anxiety seeped into the apartment like a pool of blood.

I could no longer deny that the letters hurt me, made me feel soiled.

I didn't say anything to François, or to anyone.

I didn't talk about my throat feeling permanently constricted, nor the acid invading my stomach from the moment I woke and then spreading throughout my body.

A few days later, in the metro, two teenagers who had just come from the cinema sat down opposite me. One of them was explaining to the other that the film they'd seen, according to what he'd read on AlloCiné, was closely based on reality: it was almost all true. The second one nodded and then said with surprise, 'Have you seen how many films are coming out that're based on true stories? You gotta wonder if those guys've run out of inspiration!'

The first one thought for a moment, then said, 'Nah . . . it's cos reality's got the balls to go much further.'

That phrase really struck me, a phrase from the lips of a kid of fifteen, in Nikes that looked like they'd been designed for walking on another planet; this phrase that was so banal in his words, but expressed in such a particular way: reality's got balls. Reality possesses a will, its own dynamic. Reality is the fruit of a superior force, far more creative, bold, imaginative than anything that we could invent. Reality was a huge plot steered by a demiurge of unequalled power.

Another evening, as I was coming in, I smelled L.'s perfume in the lobby of my building. I put it down to coincidence, or perhaps an olfactory hallucination.

When I opened the door to my apartment, the lights from the street illuminated part of the living room and projected the shadows of the furniture onto the floor. I didn't turn on the lights immediately and I probably sensed someone was watching me, because I went over and looked out the window. In the stairwell of the building opposite, I thought I could discern a human form. As my eyes gradually adjusted to the darkness, and tried to make it out, my impression turned to certainty. Someone was standing there, completely still. The timer on the stair lights had gone off and this person probably thought they could no longer be seen. From this distance, it was impossible to make out their face, or even tell if it was a man or a woman.

I stayed there for a moment, peering into the darkness, trying to make out a sign, a garment, a body shape. And then the figure withdrew and vanished completely.

I closed the curtains and stayed still a moment longer behind the opaque fabric, watching through a tiny gap for the figure to return. But it didn't.

The next morning, when I looked out of the window in daylight, I wondered if I had imagined it. Everything seemed so normal.

A couple of hours later, as I was leaving to go to the market on boulevard Richard-Lenoir, I fell on the stairs. It's hard to describe this fall. I think I simply forgot that I was going downstairs. For just a fraction of a second (a tiny instant of disconnection), I put one foot in front of the other as though I was walking on a level surface. I landed with a dull thud about ten steps down, on the landing below. After a few minutes, I realised I couldn't get up. One of my neighbours called the fire brigade.

They parked their truck outside my building and got me to lie on a trolley. They carried me to their truck. A little crowd of curious bystanders had already gathered around it, held back by one of the firemen. Just as the doors were closing, I saw L. rush forward from the crowd, looking panicked. The firemen told her they were taking me to Saint-Louis hospital and she called to me that she'd get her car and meet me there.

At that moment, I didn't wonder by what chance she had turned up like that, at exactly the right moment. I was happy to see a familiar face, someone I hadn't needed to call for help, who'd shown up at the perfect moment, popping up from nowhere as if by magic.

L. found me in A & E half an hour later. Normally, friends and relatives aren't allowed in the treatment areas, but L. had rapidly persuaded someone to let her through the swing doors to be beside me. Nor did it take her long to find a chair and sit down beside the trolley I was on. I asked her how she'd managed to get in and she said she'd told the junior doctor on duty that I was suffering from severe depression and it would be better if she were there to reassure me. I didn't know if that was a joke or what she actually believed. In any case, I knew her powers of persuasion.

My foot really hurt, but apart from some bruising, everything else seemed to be working. The emergency was relative, and I waited a good while before being taken for X-ray. All this time, L. stayed with me. I hadn't seen her for several weeks and I have to admit that I was pleased to see her. The last conversations we'd had were consigned to the past and I couldn't find it in myself to be annoyed with her. I think that at that moment I'd completely absorbed the fact that L. was odd, neurotic, over the top and unpredictable, but I didn't realise the extent of the danger. I knew a fair number of people who were odd, neurotic, over the top and unpredictable, and I, too, was probably all those things. And anyway, the suspicions I'd had about her may have been groundless. Yes, in the hope of helping me to concentrate, she'd taken it upon herself to send that email to my friends. Perhaps she hadn't realised the significance of what she'd done. But I wasn't sure I wanted to fall out with her definitively over it. Because there was all the other stuff. All that she'd done for me. For weeks, L. had offered me her help, her presence and her encouragement.

And once again, here she was beside me, showing her ability to understand, reassure, say the right thing. Within minutes we had re-established the complicity that bound us.

It was while we were waiting there that L. began to open up to me for the first time.

I couldn't say how the conversation came round to this. We were probably talking about hospitals, hospital life, and L. alluded to the fact that she'd spent several months in a psychiatric clinic. I asked her about it. At first she was vague and then she told me about it. After her husband's funeral, she lost her power of speech. All of a sudden, overnight. Without warning. She woke up one night with aching bones and short of breath. She had a fever. Under the sheets she could feel the heat her own body was giving off. She thought she'd caught a cold or some sort of virus. She stayed in bed and waited for morning. Through the window, she watched the lights come on in nearby buildings and the sky turn from black to grey. When her alarm went off, she got up to make tea. And there, alone in the kitchen, she tried to speak. As though, by intuition, she'd already grasped what was happening to her. No sound came from her mouth. She looked in the bathroom mirror. She brushed her teeth. She examined the back of her throat and felt the glands in her neck. She tried to cough. Nothing, not even a whisper. Her throat wasn't inflamed and her glands weren't swollen. She spent the day at home; she didn't go out. She tried to speak several times, but didn't manage to make a sound.

After a few days, people in her family became worried that they hadn't heard from her. Someone took her to a clinic; she didn't remember who.

She stayed for six months. She was twenty-five. She tried as far as she could to avoid taking the medicines they gave her. She was shut up in silence, as though a wad of cotton had become lodged in her throat, where it grew and enveloped her entirely. A soft, compact material that protected her.

One day she realised she couldn't remain mute for the rest of her life. That she would have to make the journey back and recover her power of speech. That she was going to have to confront this thing. For several days, she practised speaking alone at night, under the covers. She whispered, quietly articulating short words, with her hands over her mouth so as not to be heard.

Hello.

Is anyone there? Yes.

Me.

L.

Alive.

Able to speak.

The warmth of her breath in her hands. Catching the words one by one, gently. Then she knew that she would recover the power of speech and would never again stop talking. She uttered new words.

It was a Tuesday when she spoke for the first time. The nurse came into her room with her breakfast. The sun was projecting the shadow of the window bars onto the wall by her bed. The young woman spoke to her in the cheerful tone you hear in hospitals, clinics and retirement homes, anywhere that healthy people look after the powerless. She put her tray down on the over-bed table.

L. watched her. She wanted to say something. The memory of a poem that she had learned suddenly came into her mind: 'I've dreamed of you so much that my arms, accustomed to being crossed on my breast while hugging your shadow, would perhaps not bend to the shape of your body.'

That made the nurse stop, and she said in the same tone: 'Isn't that marvellous? You've got your voice back.' She wanted to smile at her, but she burst into tears. Not sobs, just silent, involuntary tears that rolled down her cheeks.

Jean was dead, but she was alive.

L. had finished her story. Her emotion was palpable.

She'd spent six months of her life without uttering a word. I could tell how painful this memory still was for her.

I think that it was at this moment that the idea first came to me.

Because of this story, this first confidence.

While injured, damaged, terrified people kept arriving all around us, people who were suffering, whose lives had collapsed, for the first time the idea came to me that I would write about L.

It was a project in itself. An adventure. I would have to do the research and that wouldn't be easy. L. didn't readily give of herself. She knew how to keep her secrets.

But suddenly everything was clear. It all made sense. The strange way we met, the speed with which she'd come to occupy such a place in my life, and even my fall on the stairs. Suddenly things fell into place, found their raison d'être.

Suddenly I could no longer think of anything but this: a novel about L. What I knew about her. Her whims, her phobias. Her life.

It was obvious. Inevitable.

She was right. It was no longer the right time to create entirely invented characters and shake them around in a vacuum, like poor, worn puppets.

The time had come to recount real life.

And hers felt more like a novel than mine.

L. went back to the waiting room while I had my X-rays. They revealed a non-displaced fracture of the fifth metatarsal.

A little later, I left A & E with my foot immobilised by a splint that extended to my knee.

L. fetched her car. We'd turned down an ambulance, which would have meant waiting at least another hour.

She carefully helped me ease into the front seat. We stopped at a chemist's to buy the painkillers and crutches prescribed by the hospital.

According to the doctors, I would need to keep the splint on for at least four weeks before I could put my foot down.

L. remained silent in the car on the way back to my apartment. After a time, she pointed out that with six flights of stairs and no lift, and with François away, my life looked like it would be very complicated. For starters, it wouldn't be easy to haul myself upstairs, with only one foot to put my weight on. And once I'd got up, going back down again would be out of the question. For someone like me, who couldn't bear a day without going out, it was looking tricky.

I can't remember how she brought up the idea of going to Courseilles, but I'm sure that it was her idea, not mine. To me, Courseilles was primarily François's domain. Even though in the preceding years he had always done everything he could to make me feel at home (in fact, an especially nice room on the ground floor had become my office), I continued to think of it as his place, alive with his particular energy. I never went there without him.

That's probably partly why, when I phoned François to tell him about the accident and ask if I could spend some time at Courseilles, once he'd been reassured I was OK, he immediately became enthusiastic. Of course! It was an excellent idea, especially if I wasn't alone. The house was on a level and I had somewhere to work. Unfortunately he wouldn't be able to get home early (he was with a crew of four, there were flights, shooting schedules, appointments with authors that had been made ages ago), but he would be happier knowing that I was there with a friend, rather than on my own at home, a recluse on the sixth floor. Since I had keys, all we had to do was set off. During this conversation, François had returned several times to my fall, concerned about how I had 'actually done it'. I thought that I hadn't *done* anything, nothing at all. But now I had a project. A big one. Because I was still thinking about writing about L. And that being so, going to the country with her, having her right there, was perfect.

At the end of our conversation, François asked me again who I was going with, and when I mentioned L.'s name for the second time, there was a short silence. He told me to be careful. I think he was just thinking about our journey and my immobilised foot.

When I hung up, L. left me in a café on my block so that I could warm up a bit while she organised our departure. She offered to go up to my apartment to get my things together. I agreed. I was exhausted by my fall, the hours I'd spent in A & E and the pain, which was returning in waves. I didn't have the strength to climb six flights.

She said she'd also take the opportunity to water my plants and turn down the heating. Then she'd go and fetch her things from the hotel.

I sat in the café for over an hour, maybe even longer. I felt dazed. I remember looking at the clock several times.

Then I saw L.'s car draw up outside the window again. She gestured to indicate she'd come in and get me.

Everything was ready.

We set off at once.

The roads out of Paris were quite busy. We'd been driving for twenty minutes when, without my having asked about it, L. told me how she'd met her husband, one evening when the city was paralysed by a transport strike. In the middle of the traffic jams, some man had tapped on her car window. Through some rather absurd reflex of distrust, she'd locked the car door and driven on to the traffic lights. When the man had caught up with her, she thought for a moment that he was going to tap again, but she saw him get into another car. He gave an ironic smile and she felt ashamed of how she'd reacted. That's probably why, a little further on, she'd picked up another hitchhiker. The man, who was tall, and older than he first appeared, slipped into the seat beside her, and then he looked at her. She was instantly captivated by this man's scent, a blend of tobacco and leather. They drove on in silence for a while. Then later, they parked in a side street and went into a Parisian hotel, most of whose rooms were empty. L. had wanted Jean. From the second he got into her car, from the second she inhaled his scent. She'd known, from the first hours of the day, that she would stay with him. Because everything that had gone before seemed suddenly never to have existed. She was nineteen and he was twenty-eight.

She broke off from her story. I remember saying it sounded like an encounter from a novel, or a film. I'm certain that at that moment I didn't have anything in particular in mind.

As the car sped along the dual carriageway and I eyed the speedometer in spite of myself, I kept asking questions. For the first time, L. responded. I discovered that she'd lived with Jean for six years. And then he'd died. When she met him, Jean was a dental surgeon. He'd gone into partnership with two fellow practitioners. A few months before their wedding, they'd taken an apartment together. And then after a year or two, Jean had given up his career. He'd spent six or seven years studying, but he was no longer interested in being a dentist. When L. was starting out as a ghostwriter, Jean had worked as a courier, then in a bar. He talked about opening a deli or a second-hand shop in their neighbourhood. And then there was talk of going to live abroad. And then there wasn't talk of anything. Quietly, by her side, Jean sank into a silent sadness whose dangers she had failed to see.

We drove on in silence for ten minutes. Then L. told me how her husband died. I think she chose this moment because it was impossible for us to be face to face. I noticed the same thing with Louise and Paul when they were younger; they'd talk to me when we were walking along the street, or sitting side by side on the metro or a train, or while I was making dinner. During their adolescence, our most intense exchanges had happened like that, while we were involved in doing something else.

That's what it made me think of, as we drove along the N12 and L. began telling me what she had always avoided: It's because we aren't face to face, because I can only see her in profile, that she's finally been able to tell me about her husband's death.

L. loved the mountains. The isolation, the encounter with the elements. She and Jean often went there together. For ages, she'd wanted to spend several weeks in a lodge in the middle of the Alps, away from everything. Shortly after their third wedding anniversary, she suggested to Jean that he come with her. He didn't want to, but she kept on at him. She thought that it might get him out of his torpor, that it would give them a chance to reconnect. In the end he agreed. Jean played along with the preparations and even researched what they should take with them. They acquired everything they needed to live completely independently: clothes, sleeping bags, a camping stove, dried food and all sorts of tins. It was a day's walk to the hut from the nearest village. Jean had wanted to bring a rifle in case they were attacked by a wild animal. A customer in the bar had lent him one.

They made their ascent on a clear, sunny day. The cabin consisted of a large room with a stove and windows, and a small bedroom with no openings to the outside.

There was snow all around. And silence interrupted by noises that in time they learned to identify. They were alone and far away. Time seemed to stretch out and was like nothing they had experienced before.

After a week, Jean wanted to go home. He wasn't feeling well; he felt oppressed. He needed to get back to the city, the sound of cars, horns, voices. But L. didn't want to give up. They had promised each other they'd stay as long as their provisions lasted. She wanted to see the experience through to the end.

Jean wanted to leave. She told him to go back without her; she was testing his loyalty. She said something a bit sharp (when she mentioned this detail, L.'s voice choked); she was no longer sure of the terms she used, but her words had been harsh, and reproached him again for being evasive.

Jean stayed.

Every day they went out walking in their snowshoes. They read a lot. They no longer made love. In the evenings they went straight to sleep, exhausted by the cold. Despite the stove, the cold was a constant struggle. A struggle that made time expand. She eventually forgot that Jean was ill, because Jean no longer seemed so ill.

One evening he even said he was happy.

For a few days, there was a storm so violent that they couldn't go out. They stayed indoors and the frost on the windows got thicker and thicker. For a few days, all they heard was the howl of the wind and the sound of their own voices. Then a terrible idea came into her mind, which she couldn't get rid of. She no longer loved this man whom she had once loved.

On the fourth day, when the storm had at last abated, L. went out for some fresh air. She had left Jean in the chalet, huddled beneath the quilts. She was alone and walking towards the forest when she suddenly heard a shot ring out. The shot resonated in the silence, yet a few seconds later, nothing of it remained. No echo. She wondered if she had in fact imagined it.

When she returned to the cabin, she found Jean's body. It was no longer really Jean, because his head was missing. His head had been blown off and there was blood everywhere. L. looked down and then recoiled because she realised that she had trodden on a piece of her husband's skull. His dark hair was sticky with blood.

She screamed but no one heard her.

L. finished her story and I couldn't speak for several minutes. I would have liked to find words of compassion, consolation worthy of the confidence she had just shared.

Eventually I said, 'You must have suffered such a lot.'
L. smiled.
'It was a long time ago.'

We drove on in silence as darkness fell.

When we reached our destination, I let L. get out of the car to open the gates. In the headlights, I watched her pull open the gates one at a time, with powerful, energetic movements. *She holds the key*, I thought, a phrase that emerged from some corner of my consciousness or a detective novel, whose double meaning wasn't lost on me. When she'd opened them, she turned to me, triumphant. Her hair, as though electrified, formed a shining halo around her face. And then she got back in the car.

L. turned the wheel and parked in front of the house. She pointed out that the garden was a minefield; in several places, in the part adjacent to the street, deep holes had been dug for a sewer pipe installation. The works affected the whole village and there were red and white barriers to mark the presence of works all over.

L. opened the front door and took our bags inside. I showed her round the ground floor but left her to go upstairs alone. I couldn't yet use the crutches well enough to follow her. We'd decided to sleep in the two guest bedrooms downstairs. The stairs that led to the bedroom where I normally slept with François struck me as too dangerous.

In the larder, we found packet soup and pasta.

I went to bed straight after dinner, exhausted.

The next day, I told L. how to get to the nearest Intermarché. Together we made a shopping list that would allow us to last a good week.

After L. drove off, I opened the door to my office, a small room on the ground floor on the far side of the house. I turned the heating up full. I opened the curtains. From the window, I could see the gates, which she'd been careful to close behind her. There was a low, cement-coloured sky, which nothing seemed capable of penetrating.

I felt something beat within my body, my hands, a familiar pulse, a kind of impulse of hope, which the slightest sign of rain could compromise.

I didn't attempt to turn the computer on, or pick up pencil and paper. I sat down gently. I slid the chair towards the table. Then, rather than trying to write, I had the idea of using my phone's dicta-phone app.

I made a recording about L. meeting her husband, then Jean's death, just as she had described them, with all the details I could recall.

I dictated this story as if I were writing it, sentence by sentence.

I redid it several times to capture L.'s words and give them shape.

L.'s story had haunted me during the night. It resonated within me as though I knew it, as though I'd heard it before.

Suicide (and the impotence, guilt and regrets that come with it) remained a sensitive subject for me. L.'s story had reawakened in me the terror I experienced when I'd discovered my mother's body a few years earlier, and the memory of the adrenalin-filled weeks that followed.

But it wasn't that. Not only. Something familiar, which I couldn't explain, was troubling me.

L. had often hinted at pain, wounds, that she'd never spoken about. This time, she'd confided part of the story, which illuminated some things I knew about her: the solitude in which she lived, the friends who drew away from her and no longer came to her birthday, a sort of brutality in her way of being. L. probably concealed other stories, intact fossils, buried in the silt of her memory, stories kept secret, kept away from the light. Something that could be written about. That had to be written about.

I took advantage of L. being out to record other things I remembered, scattered through our conversations. There weren't many of them. A few sparse pieces of a puzzle whose complexity I was getting some sense of.

But I was going to write. By dictating aloud if necessary.

I'd begin by describing the party where she first approached me, and then all that followed.

I would write about my fascination with L., and the strange bond that had formed between us.

I would find the way to get her to talk. To harvest her confidences.

I would try to find out who she was, this woman who once told me: 'I could finish all your sentences,' and, 'I didn't meet you, I recognised you.'

The gate opened as I was making a list of questions I felt I needed to ask her. As L. drove up to the house, I checked that my audio file appeared in the list of recordings. Then I closed the door behind me and went to meet her.

L. was smiling. The boot was full of supplies; I remember thinking that she had thought big, or else was planning to stay for several weeks.

Leaning on my crutches, I watched her bring in packages without being able to help. As she went towards the kitchen again, I took the last bag, which looked light, from the boot. L. came back to the car.

'You can't stay still for two minutes! You didn't need to come out, I'm managing perfectly well by myself! I don't want you under my feet.'

She closed the boot, then handed me the crutch I'd leaned against the car door. With a strange laugh that didn't sound familiar, she added: 'Otherwise, I'll break the other foot!'

I waited for what felt like the right moment to ask L. why she'd been outside my building the day of my fall. She explained what had happened. She was going along the street, when a searing pain in her foot had stopped her in her tracks for a few minutes. And then a thought had come into her mind, as lucid as this: something had happened to me. A presentiment, or rather a certainty, she explained, so much so that she decided to come and find me straight away. At the corner of my street, she encountered the fire truck.

For various reasons, I'm the sort of person who is likely to believe such a tale without seeking a more rational explanation. The day Paul broke his arm, during one Easter holiday (in a square in our neighbourhood, he fell from a piece of play equipment right in front of my eyes), Louise, who was staying with a classmate, asked her friend's mother to phone me. In the middle of the afternoon, hundreds of miles away, sitting in front of a brioche and a jar of Nutella, she told this woman: 'Paul's hurt himself, I have to call mummy.'

Another time, when the twins were still babies and slept in the same room, Paul started crying in the middle of the night. A strange, unfamiliar cry. I turned on the light and went into their room. Paul was crying, but Louise was the one with spots all over her face.

Even today, Louise doesn't have to assign her brother a specific ringtone to know when he's calling.

I can't remember if I told L. either of these anecdotes. The fact remains, I took her at her word.

At lunchtime, I told L. I was starting work on a book project that would explore my intellectual, affective and emotional make-up. Something very personal.

No, I couldn't tell her more, for fear of blocking this unexpected impulse.

Yes, it would be very autobiographical.

I saw L.'s face light up. Her features suddenly relaxed and, since she couldn't suppress a smile of satisfaction, I quickly added that nothing was certain, it was too soon to celebrate.

I admitted to L. that I still couldn't turn on my computer or even take notes on paper. The very idea of doing either of those things made my hands start to shake again. But that would change. I sensed it. I was sure that things would get back on track as soon as I had properly begun a new manuscript; it was just a matter of time. Meanwhile, I was going to try a different tack.

I told her I was going to attempt to write by dictating each day until I could eventually hold a pen again. As it would be a sort of confession, a type of introspection, I would make do initially with recording a first draft, which I could then revise when I felt better.

L. was happy. Beside herself with joy.

She'd won.

In the hours that followed this news, her face became more open, her attitude changed. I'd never seen her so relaxed. Calm. As though her entire life for months had been dependent on this capitulation.

On the second evening we opened a bottle of champagne to celebrate my return to writing. L., who had restrained herself from asking more detailed questions since the day before, could hold back no longer:

'Does the thing you've begun have something to do with the phantom book?'

I hesitated before replying. The phantom book again. What had she imagined? What story of childhood or adolescence would she have me tell? What did we have in common, real or imagined, that interested her so much?

I saw the hope in her eyes, an intermittent light waiting for my assent, and without thinking, I said, Yes. Yes, of course it had something to do with the phantom book. I added that it would be a hard book to write, as she might imagine. But she was right. It was high time I got down to it.

I heard the inflection of my own voice, serious, assured, and I thought that the wind had changed. I was no longer the spent writer that L. had been carrying single-handedly for months; I was the vampire who would soon be nourishing herself on her blood. A shiver of fear and excitement ran up my spine.

'You know, what interests me,' I went on, 'is understanding what we're made of. How we manage to assimilate some events, some memories, which mix with our own saliva, spread through our flesh, while others remain like sharp stones in our shoes. How can we decipher the traces of the child on the skin of the adults we claim to have become? Who can read these invisible tattoos? What language are they written in? Who is capable of understanding the scars we think we've learned to hide?'

'Your scars?' she asked.

There was no hint of suspicion in her voice. I hesitated again, then said yes.

It happened exactly as I'd hoped.

Believing I was in the state of introspection that writing the hidden book required, L. began talking about herself. As a sign of encouragement and solidarity, she started talking about specific events in her childhood and youth that she'd never spoken of before. She probably regarded these confidences as stimuli likely to help me summon my own memories, excavate my own wounds. I'd been right. All I had to do was get her to believe that I was progressing with my work for her to provide me with the things that would, without her realising, gradually feed the text.

From L. I would create a character whose complexity and authenticity would be palpable.

Of course, one day, when the book was sufficiently developed, perhaps finished, I would have to tell her the truth. Then I'd remind her of her rejection of any writing that was detached from life. I'd remind her of the conviction she had so strongly wanted me to share and which I'd eventually yielded to. I'd talk about our meeting, of the months spent close to her, of how it had become obvious to me that she alone could be the subject of the book. I'd talk about the necessity I felt to bring together the fragments she had willingly confided in me, and give them a new order.

I was now dependent on L. in every respect.

First, because I couldn't put my foot on the ground. And then because I needed her words, her memories, to nourish the beginning of a novel she knew nothing about.

But I wasn't afraid of this state of dependence.

It was justified by a higher project, which would develop without her knowing.

L., meanwhile, was working on a manuscript that she'd begun before the summer. One of those books where a lot was at stake which she was contractually bound not to discuss. A book that would bear the name of someone else who would pretend to have written it.

I asked L. who it was. Which actress, singer or female politician had called upon her services this time?

L. was sorry, but she couldn't tell me anything about it. The confidentiality clause was longer than the actual contract and she couldn't take any risks. Once she'd let slip a confidence and the person she'd told had accidentally betrayed her. I hazarded a few guesses: Mireille Mathieu? Ségolène Royal?

L.'s face remained impassive. I didn't press her.

Within a few days, we'd resumed the rituals of our recent time together. L. got up before me. From her room, I heard the sound of the shower, then the coffee maker. I'd get up and we'd have a quick breakfast before she got down to work. From the first day, she settled in a small room by the kitchen. There was no daylight; she liked that atmosphere. On a little table she'd set up her computer, her drafts, her plans, her research.

I would shut myself away in my office on the other side of the house a bit later. I sat in the same position as I would have done to write, my upper body leaning slightly forward. I kept my crutches within reach, propped up on the dressing-table drawer. I wrapped myself in a shawl and began dictating in a hushed voice. Given the distance between us, it would have been impossible for L. to hear me.

Yet I couldn't stop myself checking that the door was properly closed several times a day. And that she wasn't behind it.

Around one, I'd join L. in the kitchen for the soup or pasta that she'd made.

At the start of the afternoon, we'd both go back to work, each on our side. As L. progressed with her manuscript, I continued to record my dictation without her knowledge, the account of our increasingly intimate conversations.

After a few days, I managed to turn on my computer to back up the audio files from my mobile.

At the end of the day, we sometimes went out to take the air.

As my arm muscles grew stronger, the range of our walks expanded.

In the evening, we'd have a glass of wine in the kitchen while L. made dinner. I could help her sitting down: I sliced sausage and mozzarella; I peeled onions and vegetables; I chopped herbs. L. did everything else.

We'd start off talking about nothing in particular and then drift imperceptibly to the subjects that interested me. I would tell L. my own memories. Memories of childhood and adolescence, which might resonate with hers.

After dinner, L. would light a fire and we'd draw closer to the hearth, warming our hands in front of the flames. I knew her well. With time, I'd learned to decipher her answers, her emotions and reactions. I knew how to read the most fleeting signs of pleasure or annoyance on her face. I knew how to tell from her posture when she was about to say something important, and when she was about to reimpose some distance. Over the weeks, I'd become familiar with L.'s language, her way of side-stepping certain subjects and then confronting them in a sudden reversal when I least expected it. I'd never known her so calm. So relaxed.

According to L., I hadn't broken my foot by accident. The fracture was a visible way of signifying the block-age, the entanglement that had consigned me to silence. The *fall* needed to be understood in every sense of the term: beyond the physical loss of balance, I'd fallen in order to put an end to something. To close a chapter. Falling or having a psychosomatic reaction ultimately came down to the same thing. And also, according to L., the main function of our psychosomatic reactions was to reveal an anxiety, a fear, a tension that we refused to acknowledge. They were sending an alarm signal.

L. hadn't expounded one of her theories to me for some time. She adopted a tone that amused me, a learned tone in which a hint of self-mockery was easily discernible. We laughed. L.'s theory seemed quite prob-able: in her view, in order to avoid always stressing the same organs, we change how we manifest psycho-somatic reactions over time, switching from migraines to heartburn, then from heartburn to bloating, and from bloating to rib pain. Had I noticed? When you thought about it, each of us had experienced different periods of psychosomatic reactions and had put different organs to the test so as not to always exhaust the same one. You just had to listen to people talking about their aches and pains. Falls were simply a more spectacular way, at pivotal moments, of triggering a normal alarm system. You had to take the trouble to decipher them.

François called every day. I'd take my crutches and limp to the end of the garden, then haul myself as best I could onto the little mound of earth that enabled me to get a signal. We talked for a few minutes, me precariously balanced on my crutches, and him in a hotel room in the Midwest or Montana. He quickly sensed that I was doing better and asked if I was managing to write. I told him I'd decided to begin a new project, and even better, I was on to something; I couldn't wait to tell him about it. I didn't say more.

In the house at Courseilles, L. had made herself at home with disconcerting ease. She was one of those people who are able to adapt to unfamiliar places in record time. In a matter of hours, she knew where everything was. No drawer or recess had escaped her radar. It was *as though she was at home*, and I must say that to see her moving around without the slightest hesitation in a place that seemed perfectly familiar to her, that expression seemed entirely appropriate.

I found some audio files on the computer at Courseilles that I saved during the early days of our stay. Beyond the feeling of strangeness we all experience when we hear our own voices, I have difficulty recognising mine. I speak softly so that L. can't hear me. I reproduce below the contents of these files.

### AUDIO FILE, 4 NOVEMBER 2013

L.'s mother died when she was seven or eight.

She was the one who found her, on the floor. Her mother was lying in the hall, on the parquet. She raised her hair from her ear so that she could hear her better. She didn't respond. And then she felt something was wrong and lay down beside her, full length. Her mother was wearing the dress with yellow flowers that L. loved. She stayed like that for some time, in that position; she even fell asleep, with her arms draped over her mother's side, her head on her chest (this image really moved me).

Then the phone rang and woke her up. She got up to answer it, her hair still clammy from the sweat of her sleep. When she picked up the receiver, she heard the voice of one of her mother's friends, who wanted to speak to her. She said 'Mummy's asleep' and the friend got worried because her mother never slept during the day. She asked if she was ill. L. said no, but she wouldn't wake up. The friend asked her to wait quietly at home, beside her mummy. She said she'd be there right away.

L. went back and lay down again.

After her mother's death, L. stayed shut up in the apartment. I haven't managed to find out how long. Some time. I don't think she went to school.

Need to dig further: I think L.'s father forbade her to cross the threshold except in an emergency. I think she was so afraid of him that she went for several weeks, or even months, without going out. Alone in the apartment.

She didn't go to school.

Under no circumstances was she to open the door.

Her father summoned her to his office to give her his instructions. She had to stand up straight, raise her chin. Stand to attention.

L. imagined a world full of enemies. She didn't know what she would find outside if she managed to escape. She imagined predatory humans, children with weapons.

Go back over what L. has mentioned without dwelling on it: the moment when she told herself that she wouldn't leave that apartment alive. The idea of suicide.

If possible, go back to L.'s father.
I sense this is slippery territory.
L. baulks at telling it in sequence. I sense she'll give me scattered episodes, and I'll have to do my best to stitch them together.

What L. said last night about her father: everything in me that's uncertain, ill-adapted, broken, comes from him.

## AUDIO FILE, 6 NOVEMBER 2013

I'm trying to find the exact words L. used.
She chooses them carefully and it seems to me that every one of her words is important.
I'm sorry I can't record her with my iPhone without her knowing, but it's too risky.
Someone must have intervened at some point because she went back to school. And then on to secondary school.
She lived with her father in a permanent atmosphere of reproach. Each of her actions, each of her words was likely to be interpreted, dissected, taken out of context. Each of her words turned against her some day, coming back to hit her full in the face.
The way he observed her, his accusing look.

The silent fury that filled the house and sometimes made the air so hard to breathe.

He looked for the flaw, the sign of betrayal, the proof of her guilt. He prowled around in search of reasons to lose his temper.

His suppressed violence weighed on her like a permanent threat.

Then L. tells me about the self-control this demands.

Because any sign of excess on her part (joy, enthusiasm, talkativeness) was seen as pathological.

She often comes back to this: her impossible adolescence.

The destructive force of his eyes, just when she was becoming a woman.

But something in her character was being formed in those years, a sort of way of her ensuring her survival in a hostile environment.

L. just hints at this being who was on the lookout, on the alert, ready to fight, that she became.

When she was at school, her father didn't want her to go out with friends. Or to invite them home.

Strange story about a neighbour (try to return to this), which L. has alluded to twice.

AUDIO FILE, 7 NOVEMBER 2013

For several years, L. had an imaginary friend called Ziggy.

Ziggy spent her days with her. L. slept like a gun dog on one side of the bed, to leave space for her. She let her go through doors, made sure she could sit beside her at the table, spoke to her aloud when they were alone.

L.'s father didn't know about Ziggy.

At night, she dreamt of running away with Ziggy. Hitching, taking trains, going far, far away.


One day, Ziggy asked L. if she still wanted to go. L. said yes, but it seemed impossible because of her father.

Ziggy said she'd work something out.

How?

Ziggy put her fingers to her lips, as if to say: don't ask questions, because you might not like the answer.

A few days later the house burned down. Everything went up in smoke.

Furniture, clothes, all her childhood toys, all the photos.

Everything.

They moved to a new house.


I didn't manage to find out how old L. was when this happened.

I had to get her to go back to the start several times to get some chronological details. As though L. wouldn't let me establish links between certain events, she pretended to doubt the order in which they happened.

I asked L. what became of Ziggy. She hesitated for a moment, then told me that Ziggy got run over. One day when they were both going along the street, Ziggy slipped off the pavement and fell under the wheels of a car.

Even if they sometimes struck me as confused, L.'s confidences confirmed my intuition: L. had been the victim of some invisible brutality that language struggled to describe, a tortuous, insidious brutality that had profoundly shaped her being. But L. had wrenched herself from its grasp. Her ability to construct, reconstruct herself, the exercise of her will: that was what continued to impress me about L. One day, long before I met her, she had become this highly protected, tenacious creature of will, whose armour, I knew, could suddenly crack.

During those first days, L. took the car a couple of times to fetch bread or fresh food. The rest of the time, the gate remained shut.

L. was in a joyful mood and redoubled her attentions towards me. During this time, she never made me feel she was taking care of almost everything. It occurred to me that this solicitude, the constant care she lavished on me, was another form of control.

But which of the two of us had the upper hand I couldn't have said.

One thing is certain: as soon as I heard L.'s foot-steps approaching the office where I was shut away,

I stopped recording and for a few minutes, until her steps retreated, I could feel my increased heart rate all through my body. I was terrified at the idea that she'd realise what I was up to.

Several times, before nightfall (and despite the harsh drop in temperature), I saw L. go to the little pond in front of the house. Leaning over the water, she spent a long time looking at the two goldfish François and his daughter had bought a few months previously in a local pet shop. One evening when she came back into the house after one of these strange observation sessions, L. declared that those fish were carnivores. She maintained that if we didn't give them anything to eat as a consequence, they'd end up eating each other. I took this remark as one of her many whims (they were just regular goldfish, after all).

That night, I dreamt that L. found out what I was doing. She had searched my mobile without me knowing, found the audio files and forced me to sit and listen to my own voice retelling her life story. Then she threw the phone on the ground and stamped on it furiously until all that remained were fragments, which she told me to swallow. As I couldn't do it (the pieces were too big, I was choking and coughing up blood), she ordered me to throw them in the bin. As I got up to do this, she picked up a broom and struck my foot with all her strength. It was this pain that woke me from the dream, a real pain: my splint had got stuck between the wall and the mattress and was twisting my foot. I woke up with a sort of groan, which emerged from the dream and continued into the darkness.

I eventually calmed my breathing and watched for daybreak between the shutters, as though this horrible nightmare would disappear along with the darkness.

Another night, I woke with a start, certain that someone was in my room. I sat up in bed, all my senses alert, peering into the blackness and trying to make out the dark, perfectly still shape in front of me. I could hear my heart beating wildly in my chest. I felt my temples pounding, and a panicked buzzing that prevented me making sense of the silence. The air in the room seemed heavy and saturated, as though someone other than me had consumed all the oxygen. I was sure someone was there, someone who was watching me. It took me several minutes to muster the courage to turn on the light and realise that the shape was just clothes on a hanger that I'd hooked onto a shelf the previous evening. And several more minutes for my blood to resume its normal circulation under my frozen skin.

Yet during those early days, there was no sign that L. might suspect what I was doing. The official version seemed to fully satisfy her: I was recording the fragments that would soon enable me to write the hidden book.

Little by little, after our evening conversations, I began jotting down words on Post-its in an uncertain, feverish hand. I then stuck them inside a notebook so that L. wouldn't discover them if she happened to come into my office when I wasn't there. The following day, these reminders helped me to remember L.'s confidences and dictate them. At the stage I was at, I still had trouble making links between them, finding a direction, a through-line. Each day, hunched over the dictaphone, I tried to order the scattered elements, whose coherence still eluded me, that L. had consented to confide in me, convinced that one day it would eventually become clear to me.

For the first time in ages, I was able to hold a pen, to sit at a desk every day and write a few words: I was making progress. I had regained hope. Soon, the impasse I'd been in for months, the physical inability to write, the nausea in front of the computer, all those things would just be a bad memory.

We were at the start of our third week – and I was just beginning to be able to put some weight on the splint – when one morning I heard L. cry out. A cry of terror. We had both only just started work. For a few seconds, I froze. Today, as I describe this moment, my reaction strikes me as strange. I didn't rush to help L. I didn't automatically go and look for her. I stayed where I was, immobile, entrenched, listening for the slightest sound. And then I heard L.'s hurried footsteps and, before I had time to realise that she was about to come into my office, she was standing in front of me, red-faced and breathless, in a state of extraordinary panic. She'd shut the door behind her and was talking at high speed, something about mice in the cellar, at least two of them, she was certain, and before long they'd find their way into the kitchen, she'd heard them one evening but hadn't wanted to believe it, but now she was in no doubt, there were mice in the house. L. was having trouble getting her breath back. I'd never seen her like that, so vulnerable. I got up to give her my seat. She collapsed into the chair, trying to recover her breath, her hands knotted together with anxiety and her fingers white with the pressure she was exerting on them.

I began speaking gently. The cellar door closed securely, there was no reason why the mice should manage to get into the house, we'd put down traps or poison to kill them, I'd call François for his advice, she needn't worry.

After a few minutes, she eventually calmed down. Then her eyes fell on the yellow Post-it stuck inside the notebook lying open on my desk – Post-it on which I'd written the previous night before going to bed:

Try to find out more about her leaving her father's house.
Go back to the consequences of Jean's death.

I saw L.'s eyes light on the Post-it for a fraction of a second and her body flinched backwards almost imperceptibly, as though she'd felt a point of impact, scarcely visible, at chest height. She looked up at me, incredulous.

She must have seen it. She must have realised what I was doing.

She didn't ask any questions. With a sigh she asked if I'd go and close the cellar door. She'd been in such a panic that she'd left it open and didn't feel able to go back.

I had no option. I picked up my crutches and limped to the kitchen.

I closed the door and called to her in a tone I tried to make light: the area had been secured; there wasn't even a shadow of a mouse to be seen; she could come back.

I can't remember if we managed to go back to work or if we hung around in the kitchen until lunchtime.

In the early afternoon, L. took the car to go for the weekly shop. I settled in the living room to read, near the fireplace, where she'd lit a fire before she left. But I couldn't concentrate. After a few lines, my mind began to wander to hypothetical scenarios and, even if I avoided the worst ones, my mind was far from calm. If she had understood, I would know before long and I knew her well enough to fear the violence of her reaction. If she had some lingering doubt, she'd return to the subject and ask me about it.

Gradually it grew dark and wisps of fog curled around the trees. L. was gone so long that I thought she might have abandoned me there, with no car and no warning.

L. came back around 7 p.m. Through the living-room window, I saw her get out of the car, smiling. She came into the house, her arms full of shopping and asked if I'd been worried. She'd tried to ring my mobile several times without success. Most of the time, my phone only got a signal outside the house, so this wasn't very surprising. As she put the shopping away, she described her adventure: having failed to find everything she wanted at the hypermarket, she stopped by at the chemist's in the town centre, where she got some advice on exterminating mice. Triumphantly, she opened the bag she'd brought back in front of my eyes, full of traps and rat poison, enough to exterminate several colonies of rodents. The salesman had told her where to put the poison and the traps, which she set about doing without further ado, though she asked me to go down in the cellar, as she could no longer set foot in it. I left my crutches at the top of the stone staircase, used my arms to support myself and, pressing against the walls on both sides, made it step by step to the bottom. It took me ages to do this; after several weeks of immobility, my muscles had wasted away.

From the top of the stairs, L. threw down the traps and the cake of poison so that I could leave them where she'd told me.

I came back up slowly. My foot hurt.

When I returned to the kitchen, L. announced she had a surprise. She turned to me; I had never seen her look so challenging.

'There's always something to celebrate, isn't there? Starting a book, the end of a story . . .'

She bent down to pick up a crate with a lid that she'd put on the floor, which I hadn't previously noticed. She opened it carefully and took out two live lobsters, the last two from a special delivery that had come in from Brittany, she told me, which she'd bought at the hypermarket fish counter. I watched their distressed, disorientated movements.

I opened the bottle of wine that L. had brought back, a premier cru of which she'd bought several bottles, as opening the cellar door was now out of the question. Sitting at the kitchen table, I chopped vegetables, as she prepared to cook the two crustaceans.

L. first prepared a court-bouillon, to which she added some onion. When the water came to the boil, she picked up the lobsters one at a time and plunged them alive into the pot without hesitation. I saw the expression on her face and the smile of satisfaction as she used the skimmer to hold their heads under the water. I thought I heard their shells crack.

We dined together, a celebration dinner dreamt up by L.

I allowed myself to slip into suspended animation, one of those states of peace that often precedes a drama and of which I would have been suspicious if I'd been in my normal state. I don't know if the alcohol explains the way my anxiety ebbed away, the calming of my senses, my renewed confidence. L. managed to allay all my worries and make me believe in the possibility of my victory.

Because that evening I continued to believe that I would overcome the fear, doubt, nausea – everything that had stopped me writing for months.

We drank white wine late into the night.

I think L. had bought a dessert from a pâtisserie, some sort of strawberry cake that we had second helpings of. The atmosphere was relaxed and friendly. Everything felt normal.

Later, when we were drinking herbal tea, L. spontaneously told me what had happened one day with the neighbour. She'd alluded to it once or twice on previous days, but until then had held off recounting it.

When I fell exhausted into bed, I felt reassured.

I think I'd managed to convince myself that it was possible that L., given the state of panic in which she burst into my office, hadn't seen the Post-it, or rather that she'd seen it without seeing it.

The next morning, in spite of feeling very tired – more tired than usual – I sat down at my desk to record my recollection of the previous day's conversation.

I found this file on my computer. It was the last one I was able to transfer.


AUDIO FILE, 12 NOVEMBER 2013

L. returned to the story about the neighbour. She returned to it without me asking, as though she owed me these details, as though this supplementary information was my due.

It took place in the second house, the one where she lived after the fire.

The neighbour was the father of the little boy L. sometimes babysat after school. He was nice to her; his eyes were kindly. When he came to fetch his son, he'd talk to L. for a few minutes if her father wasn't there. She used to laugh with him.

One day, he rang the doorbell in the middle of the afternoon when L. was home alone.

Without a word, he stood close to the wall and pressed himself against her back. Then his hand slipped into her trousers, under the elastic of her knickers. Then his fingers – first one, then several – entered her and hurt her.

When the neighbour removed his hand, it was covered in blood.

L. never said anything about it.

I need to remember the details of this story, its brutality.

When I finished this recording, I felt drained. A tiredness like I used to experience *before*, when I was able to spend hours writing without looking up and emerged dizzy, my muscles numb. Yet I had only been in my office for twenty minutes and all I'd done was express some ideas aloud.

The sky was bright. I sat outside on the little stone bench. I needed light. I needed to feel the sun on my face, and needed that heat to slowly warm my skin. I stayed there for several minutes, hoping the sun would eventually banish the inner chill than was making me shiver.

A little later, we had lunch in the kitchen as usual. After that, I felt so weak I went to lie down in my room. I read and dozed.

For dinner, L. had made fish soup. I don't like that, but I didn't want to annoy her, because I'd heard her in the kitchen and knew that she'd spent part of the afternoon preparing it.

During dinner, L. seemed talkative and happy. She talked about Ziggy, her imaginary friend. I think she told me other things I've forgotten.

I have no recollection of going back to my room. Nor of going to bed. When I woke up in the middle of the night, the sheets were soaking and clinging to my body. I was only wearing my knickers. I could feel my veins throbbing under my skin. My hair was damp and felt frozen. Suddenly, I leaned out of bed and threw up.

I wanted to get up to rinse my mouth and wash my face, but I couldn't stand. I lay down again. I thought of the fish soup and threw up again.

L. must have heard me. She came into my room and over to my bed. She helped me out of bed and into the bathroom, where she sat me down on a stool while she put the plug in the bath and turned the water on. My body was being shaken by spasms; all my limbs were trembling. When the bath was full, she helped me up. I saw her sharp gaze pass over my shoulders, breasts and legs. She caught me under the arms to get me into the water, then held my fractured foot up so that it remained resting on the edge. She wrapped the splint in a towel to protect it. When she was sure I was OK, she went to get a glass of fresh water from the kitchen, which she handed to me with two pills. She said I was burning and we needed to get my fever down. I took the pills and stayed in the water while she was busy changing the sheets and coming back every two minutes to check everything was OK.

I felt sleep overcoming me again. A heavy, irresistible sleep. I think I fell asleep in the bath. When I opened my eyes, the water was cold and L. was watching me from the stool. Without a word, she went and fetched a bath towel. She helped me out of the bath and back into bed. I think she must have put pyjamas on me. I was frozen.

Next morning, my phone rang. I recognised François's ringtone. I tried to find my mobile by the bed, but couldn't. L. came into the room. She took the mobile, which was out of my reach on the table. I heard L. repeat, 'Hello, hello?' several times and then she went out into the garden.

Later she told me she'd spoken to François and had told him I was ill, most likely with food poisoning. He'd been worried, but she'd reassured him. She'd promised to send him news while I was unable to do so myself.

From that moment, I lost all sense of time. L. would bring me tea or warm milk, sometimes broth. She held my head up while I drank. I'd stopped vomiting, but still had a metallic taste in my mouth. Between L.'s visits, I slept. Heavy hours that I couldn't fight against. I sank into a thick, dense, almost painful sleep. When I woke,

I would register whether it was day or night; sometimes I'd be sweating, sometimes shivering, and L. was almost always there, still and attentive. I'd get up to go to the bathroom, on the other side of the corridor, holding on to the wall for balance. I didn't know how long I'd been in this state. One night, I didn't have the strength to get up. L. took care of changing the wet sheets.

I asked L. to let Louise and Paul know so that they wouldn't worry about not hearing from me. She said she'd already done it.

Time had become unfathomable.

Even now, I don't know how long it lasted: two days? Four? Six?

One night, I woke up and looked for my phone. I searched all around me, but it wasn't there.

This was when I realised L. was keeping it by her and that she'd had plenty of opportunities to listen to my audio files. I'd backed them up on the computer, but hadn't deleted them from the phone.

A wave of fear washed over me.

Of course L. knew.

Of course she'd understood.

But it was too late. Too late for everything.

I no longer had the strength to explain to her the book I wanted to write, nor the strength to convince her, nor even apologise.

One evening, in my half-conscious state, I heard the doorbell ring. Someone must have managed to get through the gate and reach the house. The bell rang several times. I heard L.'s footsteps in the corridor, just outside my door; she remained there for a few minutes and didn't open the front door.

Maybe François had contacted a friend or neighbour. Someone had started to get worried. Someone had come to check up. Had probably looked through the window. Had seen signs that we were there.

Unless L. had closed all the shutters.

That same evening, I couldn't drink the broth L. brought me. My nausea was so great that I couldn't swallow. As she pressed me, I began to cry. I begged her. I couldn't do it, she had to believe me, I wasn't being awkward. L. allowed herself to be persuaded.

In the night my feeling of stiffness seemed less. When I got up to go to the toilet, I also had a drink. I held my mouth to the stream of water from the tap for several minutes.

I woke early and got up before L. appeared. I could stand up a bit more easily. I practised walking by the bed. Baby steps. I could now put my weight on the splint without it hurting. When I heard L. coming, I got back into bed. I felt a little giddy. She came in with a tray. She put it down in front of me, then sat down on the bed. I only took a few sips of the hot chocolate, claiming it made me feel queasy. I said I had stomach ache. I saw a cross look in L.'s eyes. I asked her to leave the bowl by me and promised to drink it when I could.

A little later, I heard L. on the phone and took the chance to pour the chocolate down the toilet. I managed to stay awake for part of the morning.

It was then that I felt sure that L. was poisoning me.

All day I refused to eat what she brought. I pretended to be too weak to sit up and feigned sleep all afternoon. With my eyes shut, I tried to think of a way out. I remembered that François kept a spare set of keys, including one for the front gate, in a kitchen drawer. I would still need to make it that far. How could I escape without her seeing? Without her catching me?

That evening, L. appeared with another tray. She'd made pumpkin soup. She lifted me and propped me up with pillows. In a mild tone that didn't conceal the threat, she asked me to make an effort. She held the bowl in one hand and with the other tried to feed me.

With a precise, skilful movement, she raised the spoon to my mouth as she would have done for a baby. That was when I noticed she was using her right hand. The pretence was over.

We were no longer two similar beings with many affinities and concordant histories; we were no longer two friends whose actions obeyed the same impulse and blended. No. We were two different people, and one was at the mercy of the other.

As though she could read my thoughts, she whispered: 'I've done everything to help you. You're the one who spoiled it all.'

I swallowed a mouthful or two of soup and then said I couldn't eat any more. I didn't open my mouth again. L. cast her eyes around, as though looking for some implement that would enable her to force my teeth open. I'm sure it crossed her mind to thrust the spoon into my mouth, and also to slap me. She gave an angry sigh, picked up the plate and went out. I thought she'd be back with a dessert or some herbal tea, but I didn't see her again all evening.

L. wouldn't put up with my resistance for long. If I continued like this, she'd find another way to weaken me. When I realised this, I felt a wave of horror.

I couldn't wait.

I had to get out of the house.

I had to reach the gates.

When I got to the road, I'd stop the first car that went by.

It had already been dark for a long time when it began to rain. Heavy, squally rain that beat against the windows. In my room, I could hear the wind gusting and in the distance the sound of tyres going through puddles. I didn't know if I was imagining these cars or could really hear them. I didn't know if I was capable of making it all the way to the village. With my eyes closed, I imagined myself, soaked, lurching into the middle of the road, waving my arms in the headlights. I imagined the moment when a car would brake, its door open and I'd be saved.

In spite of myself, I fell asleep.

When I woke again, all the lights were out. I had no idea what time it was, but I reckoned L. had gone to bed. As on previous nights, she'd left her bedroom door open to listen out for the slightest sound.

The chances of me managing to get up and walk to the kitchen without waking her were tiny. I knew that. The splint would strike against the floor and my crutches had disappeared.

The chances of me finding the key in the drawer, getting out of the house and opening the gate without her waking up were zero. But I had no other option.

I put a pullover on over the T-shirt I was wearing. I had no other clothes to hand. The suitcase used to transport my things had disappeared. L. had removed everything.

I sat down on the bed and stayed there for a few minutes, scarcely breathing. I didn't even dare swallow. And then I mustered all my strength and stood up.

I made it to the kitchen, where I opened a drawer and managed to find the key. I could hear my own breathing, laboured and painful.

I went out. I felt icy rain on my thighs, the splint sank into the gravel with a metallic crunch. Within seconds, my hair was soaked and whipping against my face, and I was having trouble walking against the wind. I tried to run but the pain was too intense.

I reached the gate. It was only then that I noticed that L.'s car had gone. I leaned against the wall to recover my breath. A gust of wind raised the branches of a willow with an intense rushing sound. It was like a cascade of broken glass.

Without looking back at the house, I opened the gate and limped out onto the narrow road, then set off towards the village.

———

L. must surely be waiting somewhere, with her engine off, looking out for me. I was certain that at any moment I'd hear her car start up and see her hurtling towards me.

That must be her plan. To allow me to escape half-naked, catch me in her headlights and knock me down like a skittle.

I kept walking along the road, despite the pain, which grew with every step. I couldn't see anything because of the rain except a lighted window in the distance, which stood out in the darkness.

I was just a few yards from the first house in the village when I fell into a trench dug for the sewer pipes by the edge of the road. I have no image of that moment, just the sensation of the ground giving way and then mud. I passed out.

I have a very confused recollection of being taken in the ambulance. Today, all I can remember is the survival blanket, golden and shimmering in the ambulance's rotating light. The feeling of the trolley in my back. The speed of the vehicle.

I woke up in a hospital room in Chartres. Before long, a nurse came in. She told me what had happened. She said my *husband* was on his way, or rather about to catch a flight; he'd been informed.

It was one of the council road workers who'd found me at daybreak. The doctor said I must have fallen shortly before the man found me, otherwise I wouldn't have made it. I was in an advanced state of hypothermia.

No one asked me about how I'd ended up there, in my underwear and a pullover in the hours before dawn. They told me to take my time, to think it all through. They gave me pills for the pain and others to help me sleep.

The splint on my foot had been replaced with a resin cast. I'd been supplied with new crutches. I slept almost the whole time until François arrived.

He was by my bedside the next morning, looking worried and drawn. He hugged me. I needed to rest. The main thing was that I was here, safe and sound.

I later discovered that they'd found traces of several sleeping pills and rat poison in my toxicology results.

Later, when they thought it was the right time to ask me what had happened, I understood that most of the medics – and probably François too – were convinced I'd taken this cocktail myself. And then panicked and gone out in the middle of the night to get help.

L. had gone before I left the house. L. had left me alone, with the possibility that I would escape, but also the possibility that I'd fall asleep and never wake up.

L. disappeared from my life in the same way she came into it. I'm aware that is the sort of sentence that creates the sense that you've read it before. It creates the impression that the story is tied up, that it's just a memory. That in the act of telling it has found a sort of meaning – perhaps even resolution. The fact is that L. disappeared, leaving no trace.

It was several weeks before I was willing to go back to Courseilles. I waited till I was feeling better and walking normally. And was able to conquer the fear that came flooding in at the very thought of crossing the threshold.

When François went back there for the first time, while I was still in the hospital in Chartres, he found the house in perfect order. The dishwasher had been on; the housework was done. Everything was perfect. Folded, tidied, put back in its place. L. had taken time to turn off the water, empty the bins and turn down the thermostat. She'd organised her departure and made sure she left the place nice. In the room where she'd slept, the bed had been stripped. The sheets had been washed, dried and put back in the cupboard, as had the bathroom towels. The toilets were clean.

The only sign of our stay was to be found in my room: an unmade bed, empty, dirty bowls, a T-shirt tossed on the floor.

François never found my suitcase, or my phone, or any of the things I'd brought with me.

When I asked him to tell me exactly what L. had said the evening she'd answered my phone, I could see he doubted my memory. He adopted an indulgent tone to explain that he'd never spoken to L. on the phone, not that evening and not subsequently. It was the over-cautious tone that people use to try to get the mad to return to reason.

François told me he'd actually spent a whole day trying to contact me, but I hadn't picked up or given any sign of life. Thereafter, he went straight through to voicemail, as my mobile was turned off. This made him worried. We never let a day go by without speaking to each other. In the evening, he eventually rang his friend Charles, who lives at the other end of the village, and asked him to go round. When Charles climbed over the garden wall, there was no car in the garden, no lights on, and all the shutters were closed. François assumed we'd gone back to Paris (which is probably what L. wanted him to think). A little later, it occurred to François that I might have a lover. And then he got the call from the mayor's secretary, the morning they found me, and he caught the next plane.

A few days after this conversation, François asked me to tell him again how I'd met L.

I described, once again, the party after the Book Fair, at a friend of Nathalie's, and the woman who'd approached me.

François thought it odd that he'd never met her. Throughout the whole time I'd been seeing L. in Paris, and even had her living with me, how was it possible that he'd never bumped into her?

The fact is that in normal times, for various reasons, I went to his place much more than he came to mine. And during the time that L. was there, I'd arranged it so that he never came once.

He asked me to explain, once again, why I'd decided to go with her to Courseilles on a whim; why I hadn't asked someone else, a closer, more reliable friend to go with me? What make of car did she have? How did she happen to be on the scene after my fall? How had she been able to go away like that, on the spur of the moment? Why had we been living like that, with the shutters closed? Why would she have switched my mobile off?

Behind his desire not to want to hurt or annoy me, I could sense his suspicion.

Perhaps because he was able to imagine an entirely different sort of betrayal, François is the only person I tried to tell the whole story to. From the start. How I met L., how I became attached to her. What she did for me, and what she did on my behalf. What she knew even before I said it, what she understood so well. What she thought of my books, what she expected of me. I had to admit to the pretence and the lies. The weeks when I pretended to everyone that I was busy writing, when I was spending my time wandering the streets or in Monoprix.

I explained how, in the casualty department of Saint-Louis hospital, the idea had come to me to write about L., to take her life as my inspiration. How obvious and powerful this idea had seemed and, for the first time in ages, worthy of interest. That was why the prospect of a stay behind closed doors with her in Courseilles felt like a gift from the gods. It was an incredible opportunity! So no, I hadn't been afraid. The need to write, the certainty that I at last had a book, had erased any mistrust. But L. had discovered my plan and things had gone downhill.

As he looked at me, François wore a perplexed expression that I knew well. I felt he wasn't taking even half my story seriously.

He asked me several times, apparently jokingly, whether L. was a man. But deep down, I think what he really thought was that I had arranged things so that I could escape to Courseilles on my own, through a wish to isolate myself, cut myself off from everything.

Though he didn't say so, I think he later came to share the doctors' opinion. I'd been through a severe depressive episode. The medicines I'd taken had caused a confused, even hallucinatory state, which would explain most of what happened. In the midst of some sort of nocturnal crisis, which I'd distorted in my memory, I'd left the house half-naked and fallen into a municipal ditch. I had a psychiatric history.

The truth was completely different: L. had tried to poison me. Weaken me. She'd put me in danger.

I could have pressed charges against her, or at least tried to find her.

I didn't do so. I didn't have the energy. In any case, I'd have had to answer all sorts of questions, give a description, tell the story over and over, provide details, evidence. And I wasn't sure I had evidence.

When I got back to Paris, after three days under observation in hospital, I turned my computer on. The intuition I'd had was right: L. had deleted all the messages we'd exchanged in the first months we knew each other. All of them. She hadn't missed a single one.

Given the amount of time she'd spent each day on my machine when she was living with me, she'd had plenty of time to sort through them and empty the trash so as to leave no evidence.

There was nothing there: not the slightest trace. By contrast, she'd left all the emails she'd written for me: they had my name at the bottom and nothing to prove (except my word) that I hadn't written them.

I discovered several messages of encouragement and support, kind thoughts, which my friends had sent me after receiving the email from L. in which I (she) asked them not to get in touch. Of course, L. had made sure she didn't tell me about them.

I went several days without going out. Outside scared me. And alone in my apartment I was scared too.

My friends heard I was unwell and came to visit me. They were pleased to see me after all this time. And I was glad to see them. They spoke gently to me.

One night I had a dream about L. She was crawling across the kitchen floor at Courseilles, her head hanging down, blinded by blood. She was trying to reach the back door and was calling for Ziggy. I watched her, unable to go to her aid.

I woke up bathed in sweat, sitting up in bed. The terror remained with me till morning.

After a week or two, I gradually began to go out again.

As soon as I sensed anyone walking behind me or following me a little too closely, I crossed the road. I sometimes thought I felt a presence behind me (the rubbing of my scarf on my leather jacket, the click of a belt buckle) and turned round to find no one there. I felt spied upon, pursued, soiled. I jumped at the slightest noise; I could feel every muscle tensed to its limit. My whole body was on the alert. I was certain that danger was imminent, without knowing what form it would take, without knowing if the danger lurked inside me or outside.

Whatever the time of day, I opened the door to my apartment with a knot in my stomach, certain the day would come when I would find someone waiting for me, sitting on my sofa or lurking under the bed, come to settle the score.

Louise and Paul came back to see me often. François decided to remain in Paris and I postponed any writing plans.

I went back to Saint-Louis hospital for a check-up X-ray. They removed my resin cast. At first, I didn't dare put my foot down. After two or three physio sessions, I was able to walk without limping again.

For several weeks, I continued to hear creaks and other strange noises at the front door. Several times a day I'd check through the spy-hole that no one was listening behind the door. I still closed the curtains, night and day, when I came home. I got it into my head that L. could have hidden video cameras and microphones in the apartment. I ran my hand everywhere: under tables and cushions, inside lampshades, in every nook and cranny. To make sure.

These various signs could be considered the consequence of a psychological trauma or the deterioration of a pre-existing paranoid tendency. I have no view on this.

Nonetheless, little by little, I re-established what is known as a 'normal life'.

I thought about L., of course. I thought about her like a bad dream or a rather shameful memory you'd rather not dwell on. As time passed, the memory of L. became wrapped in a kind of opaque membrane. I wondered if this was about preserving the memory intact, out of the light, so that it didn't alter, perhaps with a view to writing about it one day or, on the other hand, making it disappear. Today I know the answer.

In April I accepted an invitation from the Chalon-sur-Saône literary festival. The plan was for me to meet, in front of a larger audience, a group of readers who had read all my books over the course of the year. I accepted the invitation because I'd known the festival programmer, himself a writer, for ages.

And I probably also wanted to test myself, prove that I could do it on my own.

When I got off the train, I took my things to the hotel. I lay down for half an hour. It's a moment I love, when I feel like I've been teleported to an unfamiliar room, in a town I've never been to, a moment of respite before the public appearance. Later I walked to the theatre. I chatted briefly with members of the reading group while the audience gradually took their seats. I scanned the large space, my silent radar sweeping the crowd without lingering on their faces. As my eyes returned to the centre, I realised what I was doing. I was looking for L. Or rather, I was checking that L. wasn't in the room. Once reassured, I took a deep breath and the event began.

The group asked questions about all my books, and the connection between them. The atmosphere was warm. Kindly. I was glad to be there. It reminded me that I liked meeting readers, hearing their interpretations, talking about my work. That I liked looking for the image, the emotion, the spark from which my books originated, asking myself about writing and trying to express the answers that I felt came closest to the truth.

And then there were other questions from members of the audience. They were mostly about my latest novel. None of these questions was entirely new. But I hadn't answered them for a long time. And time had changed my relationship with the text. My lines had shifted; I had some perspective. It had been a long time since I first presented the book, and burst into tears in front of two-dozen booksellers. Afterwards, I'd felt ashamed of not having been able to hold back my tears. Of having made a spectacle of myself.

But that evening in Chalon, it felt as though I was at last at the right distance from it.

After a few exchanges, a woman in the front row asked a question on behalf of Léa, a girl who was in the audience but was too shy to ask it herself. The woman stood up, holding the microphone. There was something serious in her tone.

'So, Léa would like to know if you're sincere. Sometimes while she was reading your book, she had some doubts. She wondered if you'd made some of it up. Is what you write the truth? Is it all true?'

For a moment, I felt like saying that Léa had hit the nail on the head. Because of course it wasn't, it was all pure invention, nothing I described had happened, none of it, and what's more, Léa my dear, at this very moment, my mother is rolling in the grass somewhere in Creuse; she isn't dead, not at all; she wears cowboy boots summer and winter, gold satin dresses, lives with an old cowboy who's madly in love with her and looks like Ronald Reagan; she's still as beautiful, funny and annoying; ten illegal immigrants from all over the world live with her, in a big house full of plants and chaos; she reads Baudelaire and watches *The Voice* on TV.

Instead, I tried to explain the extent to which I'd tried to be sincere in the sense she meant; yes, as far as possible, and that had probably harmed the book, because now pointless details jumped out at me, absurd explanations, names that I should have disguised, parasitic faithfulness, the whole tribute in fact that I thought I had to pay to reality and that I should have freed myself from. And then I tried to say, as I had already done many times at this sort of event, how inaccessible the real seemed to me. I tried to explain an idea I kept returning to; whatever you write, you are in the domain of fiction: 'Even if it happened, even if something similar occurred, even if the facts are attested, you're always telling a story. *You're telling yourself a story.* And ultimately, maybe that's what matters. Those little things that don't adhere to reality, that transform it. Those places where the tracing paper comes away, in the margins, in the corners. Because no matter what you do, it crinkles and curls and betrays you. And perhaps that's why the book moved you. We're all voyeurs, I grant you, but deep down, what interests us, fascinates us, is not so much reality, but the way it's transformed by those who try to show it to us or tell us about it. It's the filter on the lens. In any case, if a novel's certified as real, that doesn't make it better. That's my view.'

A man spoke up. He had a strong voice and didn't need the microphone: 'You're wrong. That's not what it is. What we like in your book is the ring of truth. You can feel it; you can recognise it. You can't explain the ring of truth. No matter what you say, that's what gives what you wrote its power.'

The man waited for my approval. What could I say to that? I was the least well-placed person to determine what it was about my book that gave pleasure or displeasure. But I wanted to put an end to this notion of the ring of truth.

'I don't believe in the "ring of truth". I don't believe in it at all. I'm almost certain that you, all of us readers, all as much as we are, can be totally taken in by a book that presents itself as the truth and is pure invention, disguise and imagination. I think that any halfway capable author can do that: ramp up the reality effects to make you think that what he's writing actually happened. And I challenge all of us – you, me, anyone – to disentangle true from false. And in any case, it could be a literary project to write a whole book that presents itself as a true story, a book inspired by so-called real events, but in which everything, or nearly everything, is invented.'

As I spoke, my voice grew less sure; it began to shake. For a moment, I felt certain that L. was about to burst from the back of the hall. But I went on. 'Can one book be less sincere than another? I'm not so sure. In fact, it might be highly sincere.'

A murmur rippled through the hall.

The man spoke again. 'You're talking about a con. And readers don't like to feel conned. What they want is for the rules to be clear. We want to know what we're dealing with. It's true or it's not. End of story. It's an auto-biography or it's pure fiction. It's a contract between you and us. But if you con the reader, he's going to resent it.'

L.'s perfume floated in the air not far from me. The scent got closer, coiled around me. I examined the faces in front of me; I could no longer concentrate on the conversation.

I didn't reply. A disappointed murmur rippled through the hall as I took a drink from my glass.

When I went to bed that night, I reflected on the expression the man had used – *pure fiction* – which I'd also used in the past. In what way was fiction pure? From what was it supposedly exempt? Wasn't there always some part of ourselves in fiction – our memory, our intimate being? People talk about 'pure fiction', never 'pure autobiography'. So they're not completely taken in. But ultimately, maybe neither one nor the other existed.

Then an image came back to me: in the kitchen of the family house at Pierremont, my clumsy child's hands breaking eggs over some receptacle, separating the whites from the yolks. This gentle, precise movement that my grandmother Liane had shown me several times, this movement that consisted of transferring the yolk from one half of the shell to the other, so that the white slips into the bowl without getting contaminated. Because the white needs to be pure so that it can be whisked into peaks. But often a tiny bit of yolk or a minuscule fragment of shell breaks off. Once it falls into the dish, lost in the translucent white, the sliver slips away from your finger, evades the spoon, is impossible to catch.

I closed my eyes and heard my grandmother's voice, her singsong voice – the memory of which I preserve religiously – asking me: 'My little princess, is that lie true?'

I stopped jumping at every little sound, constantly checking I wasn't being followed, feeling I was being watched all the time. I stopped seeing L. everywhere – in the bakery queue, in front of me or behind me at the cinema, at the other end of the metro carriage. I stopped being suspicious of any woman with blonde hair or every grey car that came within sight.

I started calling my friends again; I got back in touch with people I hadn't seen in ages. I began a period of *resocialisation*, as I called it, in order to be able to laugh about it. I agreed to co-author a screenplay.

For a few weeks, I felt as though I was picking up broken pots, repairing furniture, rebuilding foundations. I accepted it as a time of convalescence.

One Friday evening four or five months after L. disappeared, I received a text from my editor:

*Safely received your manuscript. What a surprise! I'll
read it very quickly and call you this weekend. You can
imagine how delighted I am . . .*

At first I thought she'd sent it to the wrong person; I knew
that haste could lead to mis-sending a text. Then I imagined a paranoid version of the incident: it wasn't an error
but a base strategy intended to let me know that other
authors were still writing and even delivering manuscripts.
Then I reverted to the original hypothesis and didn't bother
to respond. My editor would realise her mistake.

But late on Sunday night, I received another text
from her:

*I've just finished it. It's risky but marvellous. Bravo!
Will call in the morning.*

I thought to myself that she was pushing things a bit far.
She ought to be a bit more careful not to send things
willy-nilly.

I contemplated various messages in reply, from the
simplest ('received in error') to the deadliest ('too late, I've
already sold it'), but in the end I didn't reply. One of the
company's authors had written a risky, marvellous manuscript that had bowled my editor over . . . I felt annoyed at
myself for experiencing envy, jealousy; it was pitiful and
childish, but that was how I felt. Other people were writing risky, marvellous stuff and that made me unhappy.

In the morning, my editor rang. Before I could open my mouth, she launched into an enthusiastic, heartfelt spiel: she was quite bowled over, it was an intelligent manuscript, she had read it at a sitting, unable to put it down; it was disturbing and captivating, without doubt the best thing I'd written; it just goes to show that all those doubts and the fear that I had reached the end of the road were way off the mark; she knew, in fact she was sure, that it was the start of a new phase.

Eventually I managed to interrupt her and say, with some exasperation, that I hadn't written the manuscript she was talking about. And so as to be perfectly clear, I added, 'I didn't send you anything, Karina, do you get it? Nothing. It wasn't me.'

She gave her familiar laugh of surprise, which is one of the reasons I'm fond of her.

'Yes, of course I understand. In fact, that's what's disturbing about your manuscript, the implicit reflection on the author and her doubles, these fictional characters to whom you leave the task of confronting one another.'

I was stunned. What in God's name had she got her hands on? I carefully adopted my firmest tone and repeated that I had not written ANYTHING for three years and had not sent her any manuscript.

She laughed again and then said affectionately, 'I'm not sure we can stick to that position when it comes to the media, but we can talk about it, if you want. Anyway, I want you to know how confident I feel about it. I'm going to reread it and we can meet up as soon as you like. It's good, it's really good . . .'

I hung up on her. She called me straight back and left a warm, reassuring message. She realised it wasn't straightforward for me: the text was on the edge, it was playing with fire, but that's what gave it its power.

I don't know how long I sat motionless on the sofa. In a state of shock. Staring into space, unable to flex my legs or stretch my arms, or wrap myself in the blanket that lay beside me. Long enough for me to become aware of my body gradually getting colder. My frozen fingers.

It was the cold that roused me from my torpor. I got up, my back stiff, my legs seized up, and stamped on the floor to get rid of the pins and needles.

And then I suddenly realised.

L. had written the manuscript for me and submitted it. L. had written a marvellous, risky text, which had produced such unprecedented rapture in my editor.

L. had stolen my identity to write a text infinitely better than any I had written.

I wish I could describe François's expression when I tried to explain that my editor had received a manuscript that she hoped to publish in the autumn, of which I was purportedly the author but not one word of which I had written.

A few seconds during which he wondered what he had got himself into (not for the first time). A moment of doubt, and perhaps discouragement, before he asked a question which neatly summed up his state of mind: 'What on earth is this all about?'

I think he bumped into my editor the following week and she managed to convince him that she had in her possession a high-quality manuscript whose authorship, she maintained, was not in doubt. I imagine they debated the reasons why I was claiming not to have written it, citing my fragile state since my last book came out, the anonymous letters I'd received, the way I'd isolated myself, turned inwards, my phobic, even paranoid attitudes, my whims, and the fear I probably felt at finding myself exposed again. After all, that was all true. And it was a small step from that to concluding that I needed time to be able to accept this text, to take responsibility for it.

The day I told François that L. had had access to my computer, my personal diary and everything I'd written up till then, and that it was beyond doubt that she was the author of the novel my editor had received, he made the sympathetic face he uses when he doesn't want to make me cross.

He went through the motions of asking me questions about L. (most of which he'd already asked when I came out of hospital). Doubt lay behind each of his questions.

That was when I had the idea of tracking L. down.

To prove that she'd written the manuscript, to understand why she'd done it in my name. Was it a trap? A gift? A way of saying sorry?

L.'s mobile number was no longer in use.

I went back to the building I'd visited on her birthday, where she'd lived before she moved in with me. The entry code had changed. I waited for about ten minutes before someone went in. I went up to L.'s apartment and rang the bell. A young woman of about twenty opened the door. She'd moved in a few months earlier;

the apartment was rented through an agency; she didn't know anything about the person who used to live there. Through the half-open door I recognised L.'s apartment, except now it seemed genuinely inhabited. The young woman gave me the details of the agency that looked after the rental. As it was in the neighbourhood, I went straight there. The person who dealt with that area wasn't in. When I persisted, his colleague agreed to take a look at the file. The agency had only recently taken the property on; the young woman I'd met was their first tenant. The man wouldn't give me the owner's number. When I rang up the next day to beg them to give me even a name, he put the phone down on me.

I phoned Nathalie to ask her for the details of the friend who hosted the party where I met L. I had to supply quite a few details in order for her to work out which party I meant. Nathalie had no recollection of the woman I described. She thought she'd left quite early and couldn't remember seeing me talking to anyone at all. Then I rang Hélène, a friend of Nathalie's, who vaguely remembered me being at the party, but couldn't think which of the guests could have been L., the sophisticated blonde that I described. I wouldn't let it drop. I provided all kinds of details: L. and I were among the last to leave. We drank vodka sitting at the kitchen table. Hélène couldn't picture it. Not at all. Someone must have brought this woman along, but who?

A few days later, I rang Lionel Duroy to ask if he knew a woman, L., a ghostwriter he'd often been in competition with, especially for Gérard Depardieu's book. Lionel didn't seem very surprised; there were other ghostwriters besides him, but one thing he was sure of: there had never been any question of another writer ghosting Gérard's book. He'd met him for dinner one evening and the following night the actor had rung him to say yes. He didn't know this woman; he'd never heard of her.

Then I wrote a note to Agnès Desarthe, reminding her that we'd been on the same preparatory course and asking if she remembered a girl called L., who was also in our class (but unfortunately not in the photo), and if so, whether she knew what became of her. Just before slipping the note into the envelope, I added a PS in red pen to say that my question was urgent and important. If she was still in touch with anyone from back then, I'd be very grateful if she could ask them too. Agnès replied two days later to say that neither she, nor Claire, nor Nathalie, nor Hadrien, all of whom she was still friends with, could remember L.

One night I remembered the secondary school in Tours where she'd gone in my place. I got up and turned on the computer to look for the emails L. had exchanged with the librarian before and after 'my' visit. But bizarrely, even though they'd been written in my name, none of the messages appeared on my computer. L. must have deleted them all. I couldn't recall the name of the school, but with a bit of luck, I might find a trace of 'my' having been there online, even a photo of L. with the students. Schools like posting that kind of thing on their blogs.

It was while searching for this that I stumbled upon an old interview with me which appeared in the magazine of a school in Reims, in which I mentioned *Normal People are Nothing Exceptional* and *Things People Do*, along with *Grande Petite* by Sophie Fillières, as among the films that were important to me.

So it seemed that the strange, incredible coincidences that connected L. and me were probably not so strange after all.

L. was, above all, very well informed.

I didn't find any trace of L. having visited Tours. The next day I rang a few schools in the city. On my second call, I was put through to the librarian who'd invited me. I sensed from the start that this woman had been reluctant to take my call. Her tone was icy. When I asked whether she remembered 'my' visit a few months back, she gave a dry cough and then asked if I was fucking her about. She didn't say, 'Are you joking?' or, 'Are you making fun of me?' No, in a flat tone whose fury she did not try to hide, she said, 'Are you fucking me about?' Because not only had I not turned up, I hadn't let them know. A hundred students had prepared for the occasion, had read my books, had looked forward to it. She'd sent the train tickets, she'd waited for me on the station platform on a very cold day. And I hadn't come. I hadn't thought it appropriate to apologise or to reply to the furious letter she'd sent me.

I hung up. The ground was shifting beneath my feet; this wasn't just a metaphor: the floor was silently pitching, pulled by vanishing lines at the four corners of the room.

L. had tricked me.

L. had disappeared, evaporated. L. had left no trace.

The days that followed brought only dizziness and confusion.

Every detail, every memory I thought I could hold on to, every piece of evidence I thought I could brandish was real only in my memory.

L. had left no imprint. No tangible proof of her existence.

Throughout the whole time, she'd arranged things so that she never met anyone I knew. And I'd been the perfect accomplice. I'd never introduced her to the children, or François, or my friends. I'd lived with her in an exclusive relationship with no witnesses. I had gone to crowded places with her where there was no reason anyone should remember us. She hadn't committed any crime that required a hunt for clues or DNA. And if the idea had occurred to me to visit a police station six months after the event to explain that the sleeping pills and rat poison found in my blood had been administered without my knowledge, I'd have been taken for a madwoman.

I was a novelist who on several occasions had shown serious signs of disturbance, vulnerability, even depression.

I spent entire nights wide awake, looking for the clue, the flaw.

One evening, as I was trying to tell François about the anxiety that sometimes gripped me, stopping me breathing, as he was listening to me for the twentieth time going all the way back to the start, lavishing details, anecdotes, memories of conversations, he came out with something he probably hoped would enable me to turn the page: 'Maybe you invented her so that you could write about her.'

That was when I realised I was wasting my time, tilting at windmills.

Of course, I wanted to read the manuscript. For several days, I pondered how I could get hold of it, or at least find out what it was about, without arousing more concerns about my mental health. For several days, I thought about giving my editor the go-ahead to put it into production and publish this risky, marvellous novel, even if it meant risking L. denouncing my deception publicly. At least then she might reappear and I could prove I hadn't invented her.

It was tempting. A book already written, on a plate, ready to go. And good, to boot. A darker, more powerful book than all the ones I'd managed to write.

I mulled this idea over for several days, maybe for weeks.

And then one morning, I asked my editor to meet me in a café. She was worried by how tired I looked. I asked her as solemnly as possible to throw away or burn the text that she had. I affirmed in a tone that brooked no appeal that I would never publish it.

In response to her question, I admitted that I had no digital back-up. But if she valued our relationship, if she thought that one day I would be able to write another book, I asked her, begged her, to throw that one away.

Shaken by my determination, and probably also by the purple circles round my eyes, which made me look like I'd been beaten, she promised she'd do it.

I'm no fool. I know that the text will be stored in her office somewhere.

One morning, I found another letter in my mailbox:

```
Delphine,
You probably think you're doing OK.
Can move on to something else. You're
more robust than you seem. But you're
not in the clear. Believe me.
```

This time it was signed.

It had occurred to me that L. might be the author of those letters. But I'd been wrong. It wasn't her. I'd rather it had been.

That was the last one I received.

A few weeks later, Paul came home. One morning we were discussing a book he'd just finished, which had profoundly disturbed him; so this morning I was talking to my son about the way some books can haunt us for days, even weeks, and I mentioned David Vann's first novel, *Sukkwan Island* – which prevented me sleeping for several consecutive nights after I read it – and the hallucinatory shock of page 128, which stayed in readers' memories (the novel then plunges into a drama that the reader has sensed from the start, but in a way that is both terrible and completely unexpected). I got up to get my copy from the bookcase. The book is utterly black and I didn't particularly want Paul to read it, but I wanted to confirm the terrifying memory that page had left me with. As I briefly summarised the story and told him what I'd subsequently discovered about what led David Vann to write the book, I opened my copy at page 113, which had a turned-down corner. I began to scan the lines and fell suddenly silent.

The description was, almost word for word, the same as L.'s of her husband's suicide. As I read on, what at first seemed coincidental was plainly nothing of the sort: L. had taken her inspiration from this book, from these words, in describing Jean's death to me. The isolation, the snow, the little cabin that was their refuge, the shot, the return to the cabin and the horrific sight she had described in the car – none of it was missing.

In a panic, I threw the book on the floor.

The two of us went out for a walk. The shiver of fear I'd felt stayed with me all afternoon.

Later that evening, kept awake by some confused intuition, I stood in front of my bookcase reading aloud, as

L. used to do, the titles of my tightly packed books. All of them. Shelf by shelf.

Lying on my back in bed, unable to get to sleep and listening for the slightest sound, I realised: everything that L. had told me about her life, every anecdote, every story, every detail, came from a book on my shelves.

I put on a pullover and jeans, turned on all the lights in the living room and closed the curtains. Until early next morning, I proceeded methodically: I recalled L.'s confidences one by one.

And then I ran my fingers along the spines of the books, and I found them.


L. had drawn from everywhere, without a preference for particular genres, French novels or foreign ones.

What the texts that had inspired her had in common was that they were all by contemporary writers. Her mother's death scene came without any shadow of doubt from a novel by Véronique Ovaldé. The description of her father's personality was in large measure inspired by a Gillian Flynn novel. I found, almost word for word, the terrible visit from the neighbour in Alicia Erian's first novel. The account of the morning when she woke up with a dry throat, unable to utter a sound, and of the return of her voice, was suspiciously close to the same experiences as described in a novel by Jennifer Johnston. As for meeting her husband on the night of the transport strike, it came straight out of a book by Emmanuèle Bernheim.

In the weeks that followed, I continued to discover the links that connected L.'s various stories to my bookcase.

The story of her imaginary friend Ziggy was an odd mixture of a short story by Salinger and a novel by Xavier Mauméjean that Paul had studied at school and that, for some unknown reason, had been shelved with my books in the bookcase in the living room.

I'd experienced a strange, familiar feeling when I heard L. talk about certain memories. They'd resonated with me, making me think we had something deeply intimate in common. Something inexplicable. An impression that came from another time. Only now did I understand the nature of that resonance.

Even today, I still don't know why she did it. As a result of what challenge, or denial. But I'm a novelist and have entertained various theories in turn.

L. deliberately nourished herself on my reading, my books, to offer me a version of her life made up of memorable scenes, not chosen at random, but with discernment, because she thought they would work on me subconsciously: so many powerful stimuli intended to make me want to write my own story. L. began from the assumption that I'd liked those books (since I'd kept them) and therefore being reminded of them was likely to resonate with my own story, and in particular with the hidden book.

Or else L. enjoyed setting me a challenge. Fully aware of what she was doing, she determined to tell me, sometimes word for word, stories I'd read. She pushed the challenge further and further. At the risk of me discovering what she was doing, and saying: but I've read all this! L. filled her stories with fictional effects to see if I was capable of remembering. Perhaps she wanted to prove that these books had only left me with a diffuse, confused, fading impression. In this case, she was wrong. I remembered these books, some of them very clearly. But I'd accorded her my trust and had never doubted her word.

I also thought L. had set another sort of trap into which, this time, I had fallen with both feet. L. knew that by reviving, without my realising, the profound impression left by books I'd read, she'd make me want to write about her. I thought I'd betrayed her, but it was exactly what she wanted. To become my subject. And to lead me, in spite of myself, to plagiarise the authors I loved.

I adopted each of these theories for a few hours. But in truth none of them genuinely satisfied me.

Perhaps L. had really lived through all those scenes. Perhaps these connections between L.'s life and the books in my bookcase were just a strange coincidence. In which case, not only did reality outstrip fiction, it encompassed it, compacted it . . . In which case, reality truly 'had the balls', in fact, to mess around.

---

One morning when we were in Courseilles, François found a dead fish in the pond. All that remained of Djoba was his head and spine with a few scraps of flesh attached. Pearly scales floated on the surface. Djobi was in fine form. I asked François if Djobi had eaten Djoba and he assured me he hadn't. But a few days later, after doing some research on the internet, he admitted it wasn't impossible.

One day just before the summer, when I was feeling much better and had stopped waking up every night thinking about L., I spotted on a café terrace the handsome young man who had helped her move her things in. I was walking along the other side of the street. I don't remember which detail of his features caught my eye, but I stopped dead.

I crossed the street and went over to him. He was having a drink with a girl of his own age. I interrupted them.

'Hello. Excuse me, you came to my apartment early one morning a few months ago with a woman in her forties to help her with her things. She was moving in with me and had quite a lot of cases. Do you remember?'

The boy looked at me. He had a gentle smile.

'No, I'm sorry, I don't remember, madam. Where was it?'

'In the eleventh, rue de la Folie-Méricourt. On the sixth floor; no lift. I'm sure you must remember the woman. She's called L. Tall and blonde. She said you were the son of one of her friends.'

The boy told me he'd worked for a domestic services company for a while. He did DIY, moved furniture, cleared cellars. He vaguely recalled a job that had been a bit of a nightmare, on the sixth floor with no lift, but nothing else. He was sorry, but he really didn't remember me or L. The company had been set up by a friend of his and had gone under quite quickly.

A few months ago, I watched the cult 1990s film *The Usual Suspects* again with Paul; I'd wanted him to see it for ages. When the closing credits came up, I realised why it was so important. The famous final scene had an odd resonance.

The plot is built around a police interview with Roger 'Verbal' Kint, the sole survivor of a bloody massacre that took place the day before. The simple-minded Kint, played by Kevin Spacey, is a limping invalid with a twisted arm. After several hours of interrogation, it seems that he's just a small-time accomplice, himself the victim of a plot he doesn't understand. As bail has been posted, he's released. He collects his personal effects and leaves the police station. After he goes, Agent Kujan lingers for a while in the office (which is someone else's). His eyes automatically scan the notice-board on the wall where wanted notices, information sheets, photos and newspaper clippings are pinned.

This is when he notices that all the names and details mentioned by Kint during his interview appear on this board, which Kint had been facing. And that the name of the so-called accomplice provided by Kint is the crockery manufacturer written on the bottom of his coffee cup. At the same moment, the identikit portrait of Keyser Söze, a criminal of legendary cruelty whom no one has seen, comes through on the fax . . . He looks like Roger Kint.

Intercut with this, we see Kevin Spacey walking down the street. His arm returns to normal and he stops limping. His pace quickens. He lights a cigarette.

That is exactly what had happened to me the day when, standing by my bookcase, remembering the haunting poetry L. liked to recite, I realised she'd invented it all. I was like Agent Kujan, who realises too late that he's been had.

Now, when I think about L., it is that image above all that comes back to me: Roger Kint's legs filmed in close-up, the transition from limping to walking normally, and then the swift, assured gait that takes him to a waiting car.

I know that L. is out there somewhere, not too far away. She's keeping her distance.

I know that one day she'll be back.

One day, at the back of a café, in the gloom of a cinema, in the middle of a little group of readers who've come to see me, I'll recognise her eyes, I'll see them gleam, like the big black marbles I dreamt of winning in the primary school playground at Yerres. L. will content herself with a little wave, of peace or complicity, but she will have that smile of victory, which will pierce my stomach.

I eventually found the book that inspired each of her confidences. Only one still lacks its model, though she recounted it in detail. Perhaps it comes from a book I haven't read. There are some of those in my bookcase. Ones I bought or was given. I need some in reserve.

One day, perhaps I'll come across this scene when I open one of those books.

L. is fourteen. She's at secondary school in a town in the suburbs of Paris. The day before, her father criticised her long into the night. That won't do, it's all wrong, there's something not right about you. She doesn't stand properly, she's hunched, too timorous, she's not feminine, she's always sulking. He suspects she's up to something, she's not being straight, that's all. Also, everyone can see it (he repeats 'everyone', insists, as though he were in touch with the whole world), the chemist and the guy at the Groupama office told him exactly the same thing: your daughter's weird. She's not like other people. Other people are at least happy, joyful, they're at ease in their own skin. They're pleasant.

In the morning when she gets to school, she hangs back. She knows her eyes are red; there's a risk she'll be asked questions.

Sometimes she dreams of running away. Or of someone coming to take her away. Sometimes she tells herself that in spite of everything, she may become a woman. A woman people look at, find beautiful. Whose wounds don't show.

After French class, the teacher tells her to stay behind. When the other students have left, he asks if she's OK. If she has problems at home. He doesn't want to pry, just to know if she's OK.

The teacher is standing in front of her, staring at her. He's looking for some sign. She lowers her eyes.

He tells her that if she can't speak, then perhaps she should write. For herself. She likes writing, doesn't she? She doesn't say anything. She's thinking, very intently, the words she cannot say, she's thinking as intently as she can so that he will hear: Am I so ugly, so ridiculous, so different, so hunched, with such bad hair, such a bad person? I'm scared of going mad. I'm scared and I don't know if this fear is real, if it has a name.

## THE END *

# SO AVAILABLE BY DELPHINE DE VIGAN

## UNDERGROUND TIME

Shortlisted for the Prix Goncourt

Every day Mathilde takes the Metro to the office of a large multinational, where she works in the marketing department. And every day Thibault, a paramedic, drives to the addresses he receives from his controller. Mathilde is unhappy at work, while Thibault is unhappy in love. They seem to be two anonymous figures in a crowded city, pushed and shoved and pressured continuously by the isolating urban world. But surely these two complementary souls, travelling their separate tracks, must meet?

## NO AND ME

A Richard & Judy Book Club selection

Lou Bertignac has an IQ of 160. At home her father cries in secret, while her mother hardly ever leaves the house. To escape this desolate world, Lou goes often to Gare d'Austerlitz to see the smiles and tears of arrival and departure. There she meets a homeless girl called No. Lou and No become friends and Lou asks her parents whether No can live with them. So she goes down into the underworld of Paris's street people to bring her friend up to the light of a home and family life.

## NOTHING HOLDS BACK THE NIGHT

Winner of the Prix FNAC and the Grand Prix des lectrices de *ELLE*

Lucile raises her two daughters largely alone. A former child model from a large Bohemian family, she is younger and more glamorous than the other mothers: always in lipstick and stylishly dressed, wayward and wonderful. But, as the years pass, her occasional sadness gives way to overwhelming despair and delusion. This is a story of luminous beauty and rambunctious joy, of dark secrets and silences, revelations and, ultimately, the unknowability of even those closest to us.

---

ORDER YOUR COPY:

BY PHONE: +44 (0) 1256 302 699; BY EMAIL: DIRECT@MACMILLAN.CO.UK

DELIVERY IS USUALLY 3–5 WORKING DAYS. FREE POSTAGE AND PACKAGING FOR ORDERS OVER £20.

ONLINE: WWW.BLOOMSBURY.COM/BOOKSHOP

PRICES AND AVAILABILITY SUBJECT TO CHANGE WITHOUT NOTICE.

WWW.BLOOMSBURY.COM/AUTHOR/DELPHINE-DE-VIGAN

BLOOMSBURY